# IRON FIST

Wm. J. Messner

*I want to dedicate this book to my mother, her children, her grand children and great grand children and those that follow.*

To:

Sandra Call

From your loving

Husband

12/19/03

# FORWARD

This story is fictional with bits and pieces put together from conversations with my mother, Mary Susan Fetterholft Messner, about what she remembered of her mother, Mattie Miller and her father's family, John S. Fetterholf. The fables and tales she told me were handed down from generation to generation in only an oral manner. These were lost to some extent with each generation.

I felt the bits and pieces needed to be put in print yet not knowing definite facts, it would not make any sense. This is a fictional story on how things could have happened. The names and places are for the story only and carry no historical facts. Any reference to persons living or dead is purely coincidental.

I hope the direct descendants of my mother will keep their copy for their children and their children, too. They, too, can wonder what this land will be like in 200 years from now......

# Acknowledgment

Darlene Sparks - for her patience and type setting

Gene Toler - for his support in getting this book to press

Tammy Toler - Gene's wife - she did all the work (wouldn't you know)

Jean Brooks - for putting up with me through all of this

# ONE

## *Home*

It's hard to understand girls, especially sisters. They love to tattle and tease so John never got away with anything. He was the oldest and the only boy born to Ursula and Hanns Fetterholft. They had a modest chicken farm; one son and six daughters.

It had been a hard life for Hanns and Ursula eaking out a living in this small valley in Grice-Hesson. They sold eggs, chickens, ducks, and geese. When their only cow gave milk they also sold cheese by peddling in the town of Bot Weiser. Like most small towns in Southern Germany in the mid 1700s, items were sold for money, barter, or labor. Trading took skill and luck; skills John wasn't to find easily.

Small children went to school at the one-room school located at the edge of town. It had only one teacher, Hirm Reignhart. He taught two subjects; numbers and reading. When his students learned enough they were generally old enough to work. John and his sister, Fredrica were excused from school and now worked at home. John was a big boy for his 17 years. He had large hands and long, muscled arms. He had a strong back and broad shoulders. His facial features were a blend of his father and mother. He had his mother's blue eyes, firm mouth, and flaxen hair. He also had his father's large roman nose - the family trait that carried to all the children as far back as could be remembered.

The leaves were just beginning to burst from their buds, this early morning in April, 1773. The smells from the woods were rich and pungent. Fredrica was tying on her cloak as she closed the house door and stepped into the warm sunshine.

John came out of the hen house with a basket of eggs he had collected. "John, did you check all the nests?" Fredrica called.

"Of course," he said.

"Well, you better and put fresh straw in for the hens," his sister replied.

Sisters! Bossy sisters! John thought as he put down the basket of eggs and headed for the straw pile beside the cow shed. As he was returning, arms loaded with straw, he noticed Fredrica walking down toward the school with her sisters in tow. He envied her being excused from the work to be done while she took the children to school. He just knew she really took her time on the way back too. She knew full well he needed her help to clean the eggs for market. Today, he also needed a chicken for old Frau Ginther and another cleaned and picked for Frau Hess. She will need a fat one for her brood.

But first he will need to open the water chutes to the hen houses. John was very proud of this project. His mother and father praised him often about his good work with the iron hinges for the doors and latches to keep the water back. He also made tools and pans for the fireplace to make his mother's cooking easier.

John was about ten years old when excused from school. His mother and father started to send him to town with a basket of eggs for trade. At first, his trading was the subject of much teasing, especially from his sisters. It was about that time he became aware of the village blacksmith, Rudolph Gunderman. He loved to watch the sparks fly as Rudolph pounded the iron into shape  then the swoosh as the hot iron hit the cold tub of  water. John would watch Rudolph through an opening in the wood boards on the side of the blacksmith shop. Rudolph knew when John was there peering through the crack, and if Rudolph would let him, he would spend hours there. He knew his family came to depend on his egg trading for the evening table. Two or three times a week, John would actually enter the blacksmith's shop to trade. He knew his entire basket of eggs would not pay for one iron nail. He also knew it wouldn't make a good supper. John would still go through the motions of haggling. Rudolph knew he was there to watch him work so he would go along with a nod here and there; then finally a 'no' to send him off.

Rudolph thought often; this boy would make a good apprentice. He would have to talk with Hanns soon. But like everything else; too much work and too little time.

As John grew in knowledge of smithing by observation, he started his own fire pit, near the woods behind the hen houses. At first, his mother complained to Hanns. "The boy is playing with fire after dark. He should be in his bed - young people need rest."

Hanns mumbled, "I'll talk to him."

John was 14 years old when he presented his father with the first fruits of his labor. It was at the end of supper on a rainy night. "I have a present for you, father."

"Hmmm," his father said finishing the last of the egg custard in his wooden bowl. Carefully, John lifted out of his sash a small object wrapped in cloth. He pushed it to the head of the table in front of his father. "Vots this?" Hanns looked up.

"A present," John said.

Immediately, the girls started, "Where's my present? This is not a holiday. Let me see, father."

Mother snapped, "Quiet! Or off to do the dishes."

Hanns unwrapped the dirty cloth very slowly. As he laid out its contents, his eyes went wide with disbelief. There were nine square nails with heads on top; a very expensive gift.

"Var did you get these?" asked Hanns.

"I made them," John answered.

"Ha, I don't believe it," his father said.

"I did, I did make them," John said.

The girls started to snicker knowing their father was not pleased with John.

"To the dishes or be quiet," exclaimed Ursula.

Hanns rolled the nails between his fingers. They were very crude but looked very strong.

"Where did you get the iron?" his mother said.

"From the scraps at Rudolph's and a broken kettle from Frau Grouthheft," John said.

"Did they just give the iron to you?" asked Hanns.

"No, I worked for the iron," John said.

"So how do you make the nails?" father asked.

"I'll show you," explained John. Later he and his father walked up to the fire pit after the evening work was done.

"I want to go see too. Me too," the girls said to their mother as they saw Hanns and John go up the path.

"That is man's work," Ursula told the girls. "Come, I'll show you woman's work. Tonight, I'll show you how to make a patch for Father's pants." As she was demonstrating to the girls how to prepare the cloth and the patch to be sewn together, she started thinking. Maybe this iron work is a good thing. Hanns used wooden pegs for most of his carpentry work around the farm. With nails, the wood

4

wouldn't need as much attention. Pegs would break or become loose. Yes, this could be a good thing.

As time went on, John had become quite good at smithing. His father and mother encouraged him, and the results were wonderful. John made iron hinges for the doors on the house and all the hen houses. Hanns made great use of the nails John made. John devised a latch for the doors that could be operated from inside or outside the door. His mother loved this invention. Now people could let themselves in and out the door. Even the water chutes had hinged locks controlling the water to the hen houses. John would enjoy seeing his mother's pleasure when he made her something to make her work easier. He made pots and pans with handles on them riveted with wood so she wouldn't burn her hands.

One day, John came to the house with a iron platform to fit in the fireplace - a marvelous invention.

Mother could put pans on this platform to cook or stay hot. She felt so lucky to have such a smart boy.

John will be 17 years old this spring, his mother thought. It made her a little sad to think her little boy; a big strong man now; might soon be on his own. Hanns and Ursula noticed the young ladies looking his way at church on Sundays. Hilga, the blacksmith's daughter, was looking his way as the Fetterholft family stepped down the steps at the conclusion of services. She was looking directly at John as the family proceeded down the path toward the road that would lead them home. John looked her way. Immediately, she looked down; embarrassed that he saw her looking. The flush on her face gave away her feelings to both her parents and his parents. John's mother was pleased. Hilga was a beautiful girl with blue eyes, pretty long eyelashes, and long blond hair. She was a big girl for 14 years with more than a hint of womanhood. Ursula herself was only 15 when she had taken the handsome Hanns Fetterholft for her husband. It all seemed so long ago.

Hilga's mother also noticed the shy little glances between her daughter and young John; such a strong boy too. Her husband had spoken of him as a bright boy with a lot of promise at smithing. This could be a good thing.

As the Fetterholft family passed the Gunderman family, they bid each other a good day. Herr Gunderman exclaimed, "Herr Fetterholft, may I have a word with you?" As the men began to talk, John's eyes met Hilga's. John was transfixed, his heart began to pound, and he started to sweat. "How is your smithing going?" John was standing there in a world of his own, drinking in the beauty of Hilga.

"John!" his father said. "Herr Gunderman asked you a question."

"Yes sir," John blurted.

"How is your smithing?" Herr Gunderman repeated.

"Good!" replied John who was very embarrassed.

Hanns said, "Very good for a young boy, we are very pleased."

Herr Gunderman asked Hanns, "Would you consider an apprenticeship for young John?"

Hanns looked at Ursula. By the look on her face, she was very flattered they would want her son, but perplexed because he would have to leave home. She said, "We must let you know later."

John almost blurted out, "Yes, I'll do it." Out of respect to his parents, he held his tongue. The thought of all he could learn made his head swim, as well as the expectation of seeing Hilga everyday when she brought her father lunch. Hilga's little smile didn't go unnoticed as she looked at John again. Again, John's heart pounded.

The girls began to snicker and giggle. Mother told them to be quiet as they bid the Gundermans good day and started up the road. As they were moving along, John turned his head back for one more look at Hilga, stepped into a rut in the road and fell flat on his stomach.

"Clumsy ox," retorted Fredrica with a giggle.

"John, don't be so clumsy," he heard his mother say. He was so embarrassed. Hilga had seen him fall. She must think I'm so dumb.

Hanns hadn't said anything to John about the apprenticeship, and three days had gone by. He thought his mother and father would have decided by now.

As John was walking into the village one morning with his eggs and chickens, he heard a commotion. Lots of people were talking. As he came closer, he saw several soldiers way down the street in front of the meeting house. They had red and white coats with matching high hats. They had black britches and wonderful shiny black boots. People were all around and there was much excitement.

As John walked closer, he heard one of the soldiers call out, "Boy, would you like a great adventure?"

John stopped and turned around. Was that soldier talking to me, he thought? The big soldier was pushing his way through the crowd towards John.

"Did you hear me boy?" boomed the soldier.

"Yes I did," John answered.

"Well, are you interested?" said the soldier.

"What is this all about?" questioned John.

"There is a war between the British Colonies in the new land and the British Empire. It seems the Colonies have banded together and would like to be free of English rule. Now the English are in need of some good soldiers to put the colonists in their place. They will pay good gold for each soldier."

"I'm not a soldier," John stated meekly.

"We will make you into a fine soldier," boasted the big soldier.

"I will need to talk to my mother and father about this," stated John.

"We will come to your house this evening. What is your name?"

"Don't give them your name," came a small female voice from behind John within the crowd. He turned around and scanned the crowd of people. Hilga was standing back, eyes wide, cheeks flushed with embarrassment. She stepped up to him with great courage and concern in her face. She looked up to John, with tears welling up in her eyes. She forced out, "Don't, don't give them your name. Don't tell them who you are, please don't go away."

Suddenly, she stepped back and looked down at her shoes in total embarrassment. She could hear some of her neighbors whispering. She knew she spoke out of feelings but a girl does not talk to boys unless the family has agreed.

"Do you hide behind petticoats?" called the big soldier. "Are you not a man? Now, your name!"

"My name is John Fetterholft! I live up the road at the chicken farm."

"Good," grunted the soldier as he spun on his heel and stepped off towards his comrades.

John looked around for Hilga. She was gone. Then he saw her running down the street towards her house, and he could see that she was crying. His mind was in a blur. What did he do wrong? Besides, he had eggs to deliver. His thoughts were coming fast. Being an apprentice to Rudolph Gunderman would be good!

Adventure would be good; maybe he could see the new country. John heard it was a wonderful place, and he would have the possibility of becoming wealthy. But, Hilga was crying, and she was very pretty. He had been thinking about her since last Sunday. Her eyes made him dizzy. As he hurried along, John knew he wanted to be near the

8

blacksmith's shop when Hilga brought old Rudolph's noon meal. Just thinking about seeing her made him excited.

Midday, John was on the street of the blacksmith's shop. Suddenly out of the alley; almost bumping into John, came the blacksmith's Frau, carrying a covered basket. "I'm very sorry, Frau Gunderman," John uttered as he stepped aside.

"Thank you," was her only reply as she hurried off toward her husband's shop.

John could see she was not in a pleasant mood.

Frau Gunderman was just leaving the shop as John finished up with his egg customers and had just a few left over. He stepped to the corner of the street to intercept her as she hurried home. "Frau Gunderman, is Hilga not coming to the blacksmith's shop?"

"No, not today," she replied.

"Is she ill?" asked John.

"No, she came home a little while ago crying her eyes out. Now she will not go out," Frau Gunderman replied.

"Why?" questioned John though he knew it was his fault. How stupid of him, he thought.

"Girl problems; you wouldn't understand," she said as she flashed her eyes at John.

He knew in an instant not to pursue the matter with Frau Gunderman. "Auf Wiedersehen," was his reply as he stepped aside.

Again, his head was crazy with thoughts, and Hilga was always there. Why could he not forget her? Her presence clung to him like a briar bush.

Finally, John sold the last of his eggs and started home. Somehow, his path took him past Hilga's house.

As he passed, he watched each window, hoping to see her. When he saw a curtain move, he was almost afraid to look. He turned his head and again the curtain moved.

Oh Hilga, he thought. If only I could talk with you as he trudged up the path to his house. It was late, the shadows were getting longer and a noticeable chill was in the air.

As John came to the gate, his father was coming around the corner of the house.

"You're late. There is a lot of work to be done before supper," grumbled Hanns. "Vot did you do in your trading today!"

"All coins," replied John.

"Gut," his father replied.

John beamed with pleasure to know he pleased his father as he handed him the coins. As he was walking up to the hen house, he noticed his sisters had collected the eggs. Fredrica was coming out of the cow shed with a bucket. Great! John thought she finished milking the cow. John hated that job.

"Finally, you come after the work is near done," snapped Fredrica. "Come sisters," she called out. "John will do what is left to do."

"You're going to quit now with all the feeding and watering to be done for all the animals," whined John.

"Yes, John. That's your punishment for being late. Come sisters, we'll help mother now."

John had just finished the evening's work and was coming toward the house when he heard the crump, crump, crump of marching boots around the front of the house. As he rounded the corner of the house, he saw six soldiers standing in a row with their red and white coats. They stood stiff as boards!

The fancy-dressed one was standing in front of his father at the door. They were talking while his mother and sisters stood just inside the door.

John stood at the corner, waiting for the soldier and his father to finish their conversation.

Soon, the fancy soldier snapped his heels and bowed to father. What a 'pop' his shiny boots made! As he turned around, he shouted to the other soldiers, "Turn, march".

In the blink of an eye, they all turned and started stepping down the path with a clump, clump, clump. John went to the back of the house to wash before going into the house. His mother was hard on her children. She wanted them to be clean before coming into her house. Even her husband, on the coldest days would strip to the waist and wash with soap before coming in for the day.

As John came to the door of the little house built by his Great, Great, Great grandfather, a familiar pang of presence of his ancestors came to him. They had lived on this land for centuries. The little graveyard down the hill held them all. His father would talk about them on long winter nights as if he knew them personally such wonderful stories; some scary ones too. Sometimes, his mother would say, "That's enough. You're scaring the little ones."

Hanns loved to tell the stories of the family over and over. Soon everyone felt as though they knew the people too.

This is a good, predictable and safe land, John thought. He wondered if Hilga would like his father's home (again he was thinking of Hilga).

As the family gathered around the table, good cooking was in the air. There was chicken, cabbage, onions, and potatoes. Fredrica was putting a hot bowl of steaming dumplings on the table. "Have you washed yet? Let me see your hands," she snapped. "Ugh, go out and wash again - this time with soap."

Mother turned around from the fireplace and said very sternly, "Go," pointing to the door with her spoon.

Girls are so bossy. How does father stand it thought John as he wiped his hands dry on his sash? As he came back in, the family was waiting seated at the table.

"Hurry, sit down, father is ready to give the prayer," barked Fredrica.

Father's prayer was long tonight as though he was seeking an answer.

Finally, the plates were passed, and the family settled down to dinner. John noticed father and mother were very quiet. The silly girls were talking about how handsome the soldiers were in their bright red and black uniforms. Even they noticed the wonderful boots they wore.

"What did the soldiers want?" John asked his father though he was sure he knew.

Hanns snapped, "Not now, ve talk after dinner."

As the girls cleared the table and washed the dishes, Hanns took the old family Bible down from its niche on the wall. As he settled in his chair, John could see he was most troubled. When a problem came up, John knew his father would refer to his Bible. Soon mother would join him, and they would talk in low tones.

Now, the children were getting ready for bed. Lisa, the baby, already four years old, asked, "Papa, a story please."

Father rarely refused Lisa anything. She was clearly his favorite. He reached down and picked her up and sat her on his lap.

"Sweet baby," he said. "Tonight, your father has much to ponder. Tomorrow, I promise a nice story."

Lisa hugged her father and kissed him. She knew when her father made a promise, he would honor it. Lisa jumped down and ran over to her chatty sisters still marveling about the soldiers. "Time for bed girls," mother called from the kitchen.

As the girls filed up the ladder to their loft, a mixture of good nights and sweet dreams went back and forth.

John stood up from his seat by the hearth and started to go to the ladder to his loft. He was about to tell his parents good night when his father said, "John, you stay with your mother and I. Ve must talk."

John sat down on a stool by the fireplace. The soft heat made him drowsy and pleasant. Hanns was still reading from the Bible. Ursula, by his side, was sewing a garment. The only sound was a little rustling and whispers from the lofts, and the sizzle and cracking of the fireplace. Hanns stood up and placed the Bible in its nitch.

"Ve talk," Hanns said. "You are now 18 years old which is old enough to marry or work a trade."

"Or both," spoke Ursula.

"Or both," repeated Hanns.

"You are much help to us now. Your iron work has helped much too. Its time for the younger girls to take over your work at the hen houses and for them to do the trading. Now," Hanns went on. "Ve haff Herr Gunderman who wants you to apprentice. Ve haff the soldiers who want you too. Herr Gunderman would train you to become a fine blacksmith."

John's thoughts brightened. He might see Hilga everyday!

"The blacksmith will get John's labor and pay nothing," spoke up Ursula. The soldiers will pay us one frank in gold a month for twelve months. That's a lot of wealth."

Adventure may not be so bad either, thought John.

Hanns suggested, "Ve giff John to the soldiers for one year and Herr Gunderman will get him then. Das ist gut!"

"Das ist gut," spoke Hilga.

# TWO

## *A Soldier*

In the morning, John was hard at work with his duties when father appeared in a hen house with his sister, Fredrica. "John, Fredrica will now do your work, now come with me!"

As John and his father walked by their little house, John's mother stood solemnly in the doorway. Why is mother looking so sad, John thought? As he and his father were walking down the path, John turned and saw his mother put her apron to her mouth, turn, and go inside the house.

Coming to the street where the meeting house was located, John could see the soldiers talking to people. "Stay here," John's father ordered as Hanns strode up the steps to the meeting house. John watched his father go in and close the door.

John hoped Hilga would come this way when she took her father's lunch to him. He wanted to see her, maybe even talk with her if he could talk! He got so dizzy and tongue-tied when she was around.

Four boys were sitting on the brick wall beside the meeting house. They were not much more than children, John thought. One of the boys could not be more than 13 years old. None of them would shave yet. John shaved each week with his father's sharp blade, and was very proud to show he shaved. The first time he shaved, his father said he looked like a butchered pig.

Soon, his father came out of the building. Hanns said to his son, "Go with them, and be back in one year. They vill teach you to be a good soldier. When you are done, you vill come home and start your apprentice with Herr Gunderman. I vill tell your mother and sisters."

Hanns turned and walked down the street and up the path to his farm. John stood and looked after his father until he disappeared up the pathway.

"You there, up on the wall," shouted the fierce soldier. John looked at him with bewilderment. "Up on the wall, NOW!" again the fierce one shouted.

John was twice his size but his demands made him move very fast to sit on the wall with the other boys.

Soon it was past lunch time. Hilga must have gone another way. Now there were six boys.

The sun was low in the afternoon. There were now seven boys on the wall.

"Down from the wall," ordered the fierce soldier. "Now walk."

As the soldiers with their raggedly dressed bunch of boys walked along the street of Bot Weiser, the people started to stare and whisper back and forth.

John could hear remarks.

"So young."

"Just children."

"What a shame."

Soon they were walking along a country road. The sun was going down. As the stars became visible, the moon also began to rise.

John's thoughts were of the fine supper at home. He was very hungry. He also thought of the warm fireplace,

Hilga, and his loft. John could hear whimpering now from the boys as they walked.

After many kilometers, the soldiers stopped. "Line up along the creek," shouted the fierce soldier. Each boy was given a piece of black bread. "You are to drink from the creek. Now sit down and eat your bread," ordered the soldier.

As John sat down on the bank, he placed his bread in a little nest of grass behind him. Then he turned and washed his hands and face. When he reached for his bread, it was gone! What had he done with it, he thought. Then John looked over to the fierce soldier. He was smacking and finishing a piece of black bread. He had no doubt where his bread had gone.

Not wanting to tangle with that one, John took a long drink from the creek, and then laid on the grass.

The stars were out bright and beautiful. The grass smelled  like home. The children would now be in their lofts after a good supper. Mother and Father would be sitting by the fireplace; cozy and warm. His thoughts turned to Hilga. She was so pretty. John wondered if his heart would stand being away from her for a whole year. He had enough of adventure already.

It was still dark when he heard a soldier kick a boy near him. "Get up and stand by the stream," screamed the soldier. John jumped up before the fierce one could get to him. He was in no mood to get a kick in the ribs by this feisty little soldier. "Line up, Line up NOW!" shouted the soldier as they cuffed and pushed the boys in line.  It was still dark, and again they were marching.  Soon the sky showed light, and then a brilliant sun came up. It looked like it was going to be a nice warm day. It might even be a hot day.

Near noon, the boys and soldiers crested a hill. John could see in the distance other soldiers by a river down in the valley. There were 25 or 30 other boys. John noticed how they were in groups of 16 with 4 across and 4 deep. All wore shiny black boots.

As John's group entered the camp, a group of boys were standing by the river. They were ordered to stand with the other group. What a dirty and unkempt bunch they were!

It was late afternoon when a wagon stopped in front of the boys. "Line up here," shouted a soldier. A long line started to file by the wagon. Each boy received a chunk of black bread and a turnip. John was quick to get in line. He received a big turnip and a nice size chunk of bread. He decided to eat then and there - forget washing his hands and face. He sat down and sank his teeth into the bitter turnip and it was good.

A soldier came with a box that had legs. He selected a rock to sit on and set up his box.

"I will call your names, and when I do you will come to me and answer my questions! Soon he called, "John Fetterholft". John walked up to the soldier. "What town do you come from?"

"Bot Weiser," John said.

"Age?" the soldier asked.

"Eighteen years," said John.

"Read?" said the soldier.

"Yes," replied John.

"Write?" the soldier said.

"Yes," John said.

"Numbers?" asked the soldier.

"Yes," John said.

"Father's name?" the soldier wanted to know.

"Hanns," replied John.

"Mother's name?" the soldier asked.

"Ursula," said John.

With a wave of his hand, the soldier called another name.

John went back to the river and selected another spot to sit down. Soon a smaller, younger boy came over and sat beside him. They sat there a long time before either one spoke.

"What's your name?" asked the boy.

"John. What's your name?"

"Fritz. Are you going to be a soldier?"

"I guess," said John.

"Me too," the boy replied.

The soldier started shouting to the boys to stand and line up. The sun disappeared behind a black cloud. It looked like a thunderstorm was brewing.

Fritz lined up with John as the column marched off.

"Don't these soldiers ever rest at night? It's always march, march, march," said Fritz. "Here we are marching in the dark again."

"I don't mind," said John. "Marching in the sun would be a lot hotter. In the evening seems like a good choice.

John felt a sharp blow on his shoulder.

"Shut up," bellowed the soldier to his left.

As they marched, the thunderstorm grew. Soon they were marching in a driving rain. Everyone was soaked to the skin. Lightning flashes lit up the road in an eerie light. It was a hard rain. The road became muddy but still they marched.

Soon the storm passed, the sky became cool and clear. As they marched in the moonlight, you could see the steam coming off each soldier and boy as they marched along.

When the moon was almost overhead, the marching group came to a stop. The boys were told to sit by the road and rest awhile.

Soon two soldiers came up the road, and stopped at the head of the column. Then they started to move along the column of boys. As they passed, two soldiers passed out bread to the boys.

"Bread again," said Fritz.

"I'll take it, I'm hungry," said a boy.

Not a crumb was left in less than a minute.

One of the soldiers was walking down the column and telling the boys to rest for a few hours. He said we would be in our training camp tomorrow.

John and Fritz laid back on the leaves off the road.

Fritz said, "I wish I was home. At least I had a bed and good food."

"Me too," John said. "I could even put up with my pesky sisters. I would even enjoy doing all the work for just one of mother's good dinners."

"Me too," said Fritz.

Lying there looking up at the stars made John sleepy.

Suddenly down the column was a great commotion. There was shouting, hitting - more shouting and hitting - then quiet. There was a whimper now and then.

Fritz whispered to John," What's going on?"

John whispered back, "Don't know."

The boy next to Fritz relayed the message. "Four boys tried to run away. The soldiers caught them. One is only 12 years old. He is to be 13 next month."

"UP UP UP, ON YOUR FEET!" shouted the soldiers coming down the column.

John and Fritz got up quickly. They both knew the lazy ones would get a kick in the head or the ribs. Both decided they didn't need that!

"March, march, march," shouted a soldier along the line. Now they were marching again.

Fritz said, "Again at night."

John said, "Shush, they will hit us."

As they marched, John noticed the boys around him. Fear was what he saw - almost like a cow would look just before Papa would cut its throat....... Afraid!

Light was beginning to appear in the East. It was getting colder. John's thin jacket was not enough when the early morning breezes came up. He noticed some of the boys were wearing only a shirt and pants. Some did not have shoes. Many were very small and young.

The sun was coming up now. There were pastures with neat little houses along the road. This was a wide and well traveled road. The sign at a crossroad read Frankfurt 22 km's'.

"22 km," Fritz said. "To a big city."

"I was never there," said John.

"Nor was I," said Fritz.

Both boys knew they could confide in each other without criticism. John had found a friend. Fritz thought that John was someone he could trust.

The marching group was coming up a hill and emerged onto a main street of a village. People started to gather as they marched on.

"Soldier boys. Peasant boys. Gun fodder for the English. What a shame. Pretty boy. Stupid young men.

What's your name, boy? These are children not soldiers." These are some of the things the people said from the village.

"Keep moving," shouted a soldier.

The commotion and confusion gave way to a quiet countryside. The land was flatter now, with pastures, fields, and clumps of trees. There were neat hedge rows with pretty little farmhouses here and there. Each farmhouse had a little shed and pens to hold the livestock.

Farmers in the field would stop to gaze at the would-be soldiers marching down the road. Sometimes, children would come to the road and run along side them, until a bell or a yell would order them back to the farm.

"Isn't it time for more moldy black bread?" Fritz said to John.

"I guess, I'm sure hungry," John replied.

"Me, too - even for moldy black bread," said Fritz.

The sun continued to climb higher and higher. On they marched hot and sweaty.

Just after midday, John noticed heavy clouds to the West. "Looks like a storm brewing," John remarked.

"Good," said Fritz. "I could use a cooling off."

Shouts at the front of the column proved to be a left turn off the road into a pasture.

"Maybe we will rest now," Fritz said.

"I hope so," added John.

The column of boys kept on marching across a pasture, across a stream, and up a wooded path that led up a hill. John and Fritz crested the hill, and started down the path into a shaded glen. In the bottom of the little valley, they could see a row of huts along a tumbling stream. They could see a small groups of boys marching up and down with sticks on their shoulders.

As John's group came out into the meadow from the dark wooded path, the sunshine was bright. The soldiers ordered the boys to the bank of the creek. "You will rest here. You may relieve yourselves and drink from the creek," shouted a soldier.

John and Fritz immediately dropped unto the bank of the stream and drank the cold delicious water. The water was very cold, and the boys drank and drank again. The water was of little help to get rid of the hunger pangs they all felt.

Most of the boys stretched out along the bank for a nice rest. John and Fritz took their shoes off, and soaked their feet in the cold water. John's shoes were worn through at the bottom. Fritz had a big hole in his shoes too. It was better to have a hole in their shoes than no shoes at all. Many of the boys had bleeding and bruised feet from the long march. No mercy was given to those without shoes.

There was a group of twelve boys marching with a soldier shouting orders at them. As the soldier shouted, the unit as a group would respond to the orders.

Fritz said, "I see seven groups."

"That's what I counted," responded John.

"Look at this group coming. Look at their shiny boots," noted Fritz.

As the group approached in front of the new boys, the soldier was saying in a low tone, "Hup, Hup, Hup," in time with the crump, crump, crump of the boots.

John said, "I wonder if we will get boots."

"I hope so," Fritz said.

"Return march," shouted the soldier. Every boy soldier turned around together and went marching back the way they came.

"Isn't that wonderful to see," exclaimed John. He had never seen such a sight. By the look of the new boys' faces, they hadn't either.

"Such precision," Fritz said. "No one looked around. All their eyes were straight ahead and every step landed at the very same crump, crump, crump.

John caught a whiff of something cooking in the air. He was so hungry. From the hut where the wonderful smells were coming from, John noticed the soldiers and the boys were lined up. Smoke was coming out of the chimney. They were just too far away to see what was going on over there.

Three soldiers from the camp came over to John's group. They told the soldiers that were with John's group to go up to the hut. John noticed the long line at the hut was almost gone.

"Up, Up," shouted a soldier. "Line up NOW!"

"March - move boy," shouted another soldier.

The column moved up to the long hut. Delicious smells were coming with each breeze.

"I'm so hungry, I could eat a horse."

"Hope it's that good."

"I don't care what it is, I'll eat it."

As the boys moved along, they were handed a wooden bowl and a wooden spoon. John stepped up to the huge pot on the table. A crusty, old cook ladled into John's bowl a scoop of beans. On top of that was a scoop of broth with bits of meat in it. They also received a slice of dark bread.

"Move along," grunted the crusty fellow.

John and Fritz sat together among the trees. "The bread looks and smells fresh baked," John said.

Fritz only nodded as he was gulping down his first meal at the Hesson soldier camp.

"Up, Up. Line up. Take your bowls and spoons and splash them in the first tub, then the second tub, and stack here. Move," shouted the soldier.

These soldiers are worse than my sisters at giving orders, thought John.

# THREE

## *In Camp*

They were standing in a row along the path. A cocky, little soldier was walking up and down along the line. He was selecting a boy here and there. The soldier pointed to John. "Come here. Step up here."

John turned around and noticed Fritz was selected too. Now another soldier started to line up the boys selected - three across and four deep. John was in the center of the first row. Fritz was three rows back on the left. As they stood there, John noticed his group was the tallest among the groups.

"You will listen to me from now on. My name is Otto. I am your leader. Your mother and father are behind you now. They are no more to you. You are my men now. I will teach you to be a proud soldier of the Hesson Army. First you will learn to march as one unit."

John noticed Otto was much smaller than any boy in his group. He thought, why should he be our leader?

"Remember your position in your unit. When I instruct you to line up, you will line up in the same position you are now."

A mumble of low talking came from behind John. Almost like an explosion, the soldier jumped into the group where the talking boys were. "You will not speak when lined up. You will look straight ahead," he said while pointing at the boys. "Only straight ahead," Otto shouted. With a red face, clamped down jaws, and tight fists at his side, Otto strutted back to the front of the column. In a snappy turn around, Otto was facing the group. "You are Frankfurt number 22. This you must remember. At times, I will ask you your unit. Remember it's Frankfurt number 22."

John thought I can remember that. I remember a road sign Frankfurt 22 km's.

Otto pointed to his left leg. "You will step with this leg when I shout, march, march, march. Now are you ready? March, march, march."

John stepped off with his left foot and then his right and left as the soldier timed "Hup, Hup, Hup. Line up, Line up."

John looked around. What a mess. John and one other boy were four steps ahead of the group. The rest were all bunched up and tromping all over each other.

Finally, Otto got all the boys lined up again. You could see the frustration in Otto's face. "We will take only one step forward with this leg," pointing to his left leg. "March, Hup."

John thought that marching is harder than it looks, but the one step went pretty good.

"Now we try again, this time with two steps. March, hup, hup," shouted Otto.

Three boys fell down in the middle. "Line up," Otto shouted all red in the face. Otto strutted to the third row. "Your second step, you use this leg." Otto strutted back to the front of the line. "Dumbkoff," was heard as Otto snapped around. "Again two steps. March, hup, hup." This went better. "This time you will march till I tell you to stop."

John could hear the feet behind him as they marched. All evening they marched. John began to feel proud. This is fun, he thought. Once in awhile, they would stop and Otto would shout in the face of a boy who wasn't doing right. They learned to march two times and stop.

The sun was going down when they lined up at the long hut for more food. John was surprised he was hungry again. This time they had potato soup with a large slice of black bread. Fritz and John settled down by a tree to eat their supper.

"The marching makes me tired and my legs hurt," said Fritz.

"I enjoy it," said John. "It's a lot easier than the work at the chicken farm. He thought of Hilga, and wondered what she was doing now.

"Up, up, with your bowls and stack them," Otto was shouting.

They marched up the path into the woods. Otto ordered 'Stop' to the column. "You will make your bed in this tall grass. Unit Frankfurt number 22 will stay together. No wandering off. You may talk but quietly," Otto said.

It was almost dark, a bit cool, but nice. Fritz and John pulled dead grass together for a softer mat.

"Are we to lay in the open all the time?" asked Fritz. "So far, I'm not that interested to be a soldier."

"It's not so bad, maybe it gets better. Besides, this is an adventure," John said.

"Do you have a lady friend?" asked Fritz.

"Almost," said John.

"What's her name?" asked Fritz.

"Hilga," John replied.

"Is she pretty?" Fritz wondered.

"Beautiful," John uttered as his thoughts were again with Hilga.

"Do you?" asked John.

"No, but I would like to," Fritz replied.

They both lay back in the grass looking at the sky with drowsy thoughts of home and loved ones.

It was not yet sun up when, "Up, up. Line up," Otto shouted. "Frankfurt number 22, Line up."

As the boys were lining up, John noticed groups marching toward them on their way out of camp. How precise they looked in their red tall hats, red coats, black pants, and shiny red boots. There were seven groups in all. As they crumped, crumped, crumped past the boys, John noticed the long line looked like a long bug with many legs all moving together.

"March, hup, hup," down the path John's group marched to the floor of the valley, along the stream, past the little huts. At the last hut, Otto commanded, "Frankfurt number 22, stop. This is Frankfurt number 22's Hut. There is one loft for each man. You will get fresh straw from the front of the hut for your loft. You will now select a loft and clean out the old straw replacing it with fresh straw. This hut will be swept clean before I return." Otto turned and went toward the cook hut.

"Phew," John said."This place stinks." John selected a loft near the door. Fritz picked the one above him. They started to clean out the old straw and packed in new straw.

"Don't smell so bad with fresh straw," Fritz remarked.

"Feels pretty good." John laid down and stretched out to rest. Some boys were sweeping; making the board floor look presentable.

Otto came back and stepped in the door, looked around and grunted "Gut, Frankfurt number 22, line up," said Otto.

"Otto's at it again," said John. He was out and lined up with the first ones since the stragglers got cuffed and kicked along.

After breakfast, the boys were waiting for Otto to return. "This was a good breakfast," said John.

"Good breakfast!" sneered Fritz. "A greasy fat sausage and a boiled egg. Some breakfast!"

"I liked it too," said another boy.

"Egg was fresh," said John.

"How would you know?" said another boy.

"I know about chickens and eggs," spoke up John.

"He sounds like a dumb farmer," was another remark.

John stood up. He looked around at the boys and said, "I'm proud to know what I know about chickens, eggs, farming, and iron working."

"Iron working. What are you doing here?" said another boy.

"Same as you. To help my family," John said.

"Stop picking on John," said Fritz as he stood up beside John. "You pick on John, you pick on me too," glaring at the boys knowing big John was behind him.

Things got pretty quiet as the boys looked around at each other. For the next few minutes, John and Fritz looked around the group for a challenger. It seemed to be agreed. After Otto, John and Fritz were the next leaders in the group.

Today, they marched continuously until the sun was past overhead. After eating, they went to their huts by the creek for a rest.

A wagon came down the road, and ambled up to the huts. Otto organized his group in a line and led them up to the back of the wagon. "Everyone take off your shoes," shouted Otto.

"Step up on this board," said the man at the back of the wagon.

The first boy stepped on the board. It had notches on the board with numbers. "Seven," called the man to inside of the wagon.

"Seven," repeated the man from inside the wagon.

"Step aside," said the man at the back of the wagon. "Next."

Crump, plunk. Out of the wagon flew two boots, hitting the boy that stood aside.

When John stepped on the board, the man shouted, "Thirteen, step aside."

John waited for his boots. He planned to catch them. He didn't want fine boots to get bounced in the dirt. Swoosh, slap, slap. John caught one in each hand. They were beautiful boots. John sat down with the other boys and put on his boots.

"Line up," ordered Otto. He had a bag in front of him. "File past me in one line." After the boys lined up, Otto handed each boy a patch of cloth and a chunk of foul smelling saddle soap. "This is for your boots to make them waterproof as well as to make them shine. Use it very sparingly. This is all you will get. Now sit down, and shine your boots." Otto picked up a burnt stick from the fire pit. "Now watch me," he instructed. First he rubbed his fingers on the charcoal. Then he rubbed his fingers on the soap. Next, he took of his boot and started to rub the boot in a circular manner. "Now, polish, polish, polish," he said. The rest of the afternoon the boys worked on their boots. An hour on each boot and John's boots gleamed.

It was late in the afternoon when Otto asked Frankfurt number 22 to line up. As they marched off, John could hear the crump, crump, crump of the marching soldiers. Everyone marched with pride. John thought, with these boots I could march forever.

The next morning they were ordered to line up into place. They were anxious to march. Today, there was another surprise. Each boy was handed a stick that was in the shape of a musket. Otto showed the boys how to put the sticks on their shoulder and to march with them.

Fritz said that evening, "Our group looks better than the other groups. We look handsome, strong, and fearless."

"Who would be afraid of soldiers with wooden guns?" asked John.

Otto appeared in the door of the hut. "Soon you will have real flint-lock muskets, and I will teach you how to load and shoot them. But first you must master the fine art of soldiering. Tomorrow you will get a real workout so get to sleep. You will need it."

In the next week, they learned return march, single march, double march, right march, and left march - one right after the other. Everyday they were getting better and better. Late one afternoon when they were marching, John noticed a bunch of rag tag boys down by the stream. He could see this sorry lot from the corner of his eye. They were dirty unkempt children. Two or three were about as tall as John but most looked 13 or 14 years old.

"Right turn," Otto ordered. This would take the group toward the boys by the creek. "Left turn," Otto said. Now they were headed in front of the boys. "Return march. Right turn. Return march. Right turn." They looked good as they crumped away.

That night, John was washing his shirt down in the stream. Fritz came up to him and sat beside him. "Ever think about home?" asked Fritz.

"All the time," said John.

"I think I want to go home. I want to see my mother and father and eat some good food too," said Fritz.

"This would be good," said John. He was also thinking of Hilga.

"Why don't we just go?" whispered Fritz. "It would be so easy. Just start walking. In three days, we could be home."

"Don't talk silly," growled John. "You know they would catch us and beat us."

"Who would beat us? You and I could handle four of those soldiers and then four more," said Fritz.

"You think so? Well, Fritz, I wouldn't want to match fists with even little Otto. I have a feeling he knows more about fighting than you and I will ever know. Let's not talk anymore about running away."

John could see Fritz was disappointed with the results of their little talk. Maybe he is right, and we could go home. Mother and father would be angry not to get their gold mark each month. It's only a year. He thought he could stand almost anything for a year.

The next morning, Otto woke the boys up early. "We will be going to the next camp after we eat. There you will learn to load a rifle and shoot it. When you file out this morning, you will lay your rifle sticks outside the long hut. Now line up."

As they were marching out of camp, John noticed the boys from along the creek from the night before. They were standing in the tall grass beside the path. They stood there so dumb with awe. What a poor bunch.

The sun got hot that day. The boys were hotter still with the wool coats on. They kept on marching. As they came to a town, Otto ordered Frankfurt number 22 to stop in front of the tavern. The rest of the soldiers marched on down the street. "We will bed down in the stable behind the tavern. You are number one group so you will eat and drink in the tavern. Follow me in a single line."

Otto turned, clicked his heels and bowed to the tavern owner, his wife, and five children. "I have twelve men and myself. You will feed us and give us beer. After that, we will sleep in your stable. For this, you will receive one gold mark."

"Please come in. You are welcome," responded the tavern owner.

John and Fritz sat down at a round table with four other boys and Otto, the tavern owner, his wife, and the children. They had steins of beer. As they were handing out the beer, Otto was gulping his down. Before John could lift his up, Otto's was empty. "Burp - another please," he said. A girl shoved a full stein in front of him.

John thought she was young and pretty. She was probably 12 or 13 but showing some womanhood. Just then, a boy at the next table cupped her breast with his hand. In a flash, she slapped it away. Laughter arose. She seemed to be able to take care of herself.

Otto stood up. "Behave or I will take you outside. I assure you I will, and what I will give you, will not be a slap. Another beer," he bellowed.

The beer was great. John and Fritz were on their second stein when heaping dishes of chicken and dumpling and big slices of bread were put on the table. When the plates were passed around, the big bowl in the middle was soon empty. Out of the kitchen came another bowl and another platter of bread.

"I'm stuffed," croaked Fritz. Where are you putting all the chicken and dumplings, John?"

"You boys are number one of the Frankfurts," Otto remarked obviously feeling his beer. "You will make great soldiers." He looked over to John and lifted his stein in salute. John acknowledged the salute with his stein. Together they said, "More beer." John and Otto looked at each other in amazement, and then they both burst out laughing.

The next morning, John's head ached - too much beer.

"Line up," said Otto. The night before didn't seem to bother Otto. Last night, he could hardly walk, thought John.

As they marched along through town the other Frankfurt groups filed in behind the column. Again they were on the road through the countryside. The stream was wide and deep when the column stopped for a midday rest. The water was good, and John was hungry again.

"Otto seemed almost human last night," observed Fritz. "He said we were number one Frankfurt group."

"He drank a lot of beer," one of the boys said.

"We all did," spoke up John.

"You ate more than anyone," teased Fritz.

"You were too busy looking at the tavern owner's daughter, and she is still a baby," said John.

"A baby? She has tits and good-looking legs too," said Fritz.

"How do you know?" asked John.

"When she stood on a stool to reach a stein, her skirt came up. Nice legs," said Fritz very satisfied with himself.

By midday, the column was approaching an army camp. John had never seen so many soldiers in one area. There must have been at least two hundred. Groups of soldiers were marching, then resting, and then marching. Sharp popping sounds and smoke was in the air at the other end of the camp.

As they marched up to a tent, Otto ordered them to halt. "This will be our lodging. You may go in and make your pallet. John, you will make a pallet for me at the door. I want your pallet on the other side of the door. I have decided that you are second in command in my absence. See that all the men make a straw pallet around the walls of the tent. No one in the middle! You may go in now. John, you stay!" Otto walked up to John. "I must go to the headquarters tent and report in our unit. While I am gone, I want you to keep the men together. Stay at the tent and make them behave. If they do not listen to you, you report them to me. I will deal with them. I will not be long."

Fritz was first to speak to John as he entered the tent. "You are now leader number two. I hope Otto will make me leader number three."

"It was a surprise to me," confessed John.

Straw was piled in the center of the tent, and the boys were busy making pallets on the sides of the tent. John soon had two fine pallets made at the door. Of course, Fritz made his on the other side of John.

In a little while, Otto came back. He looked around the tent, and then glanced at John. Surveying his men, he asked, "Any trouble?"

"No," said John.

"Gut," replied Otto. "Line up".

Off they marched to the cook's tents. The food sure smelled good. There was cornmeal bread along with chunks of pork, sauerkraut, a bucket of butter and cheese sitting on the tables. Also, there were steins of beer served by local fraus and frauleins.

"This is living good," said Fritz.

"They will feed us good here," spoke up Otto. "When you learn to shoot a rifle, we will go on a long march to the sea. So eat hardy, boys. The march to the sea may be a long one." And so they did. Soon the soldiers were filing out to make up their marching groups.

"How do you eat so much?" a boy asked John as they were leaving the cook's tent.

"I don't eat that much," said John.

"Yes you do," added Fritz. "You filled your bowl four times. I think it was because you liked that fat girl that hung around our table and you wanted to keep her around."

"I noticed she dragged her tits over your shoulder - more than once Fritz," said Otto. "She wouldn't get close to me."

Another boy started to snicker, "She was afraid old Otto would run his hand up her skirt."

Another voice said, "Maybe she would like that."

"Line up," said Otto and off they marched.

The next morning, they marched to the shooting field. Groups of soldiers with an Instructor were sitting along a line at the top of the field. Blue smoke hung in the air as rifles were being shot every few seconds.

Otto said to John, "Keep the men here. Don't let anyone wander away. They could get hurt. I'll be back in a few minutes."

Curiosity was getting the better of the boys as they were watching the activities around them. Two boys started to go over to another group where an Instructor was showing his group how to load his rifle.

"Stay here boys," ordered John.

"We'll be right back," said one boy over his shoulder.

"Back here now!" said John.

The boys stopped and turned around. The bigger boy put his hands on his hips and asked, "Are you going to make me?"

John took five long steps and was next to the boy. "Back to the group," shouted John. In a flash, John saw a fist come up towards his face. Instinctively, John caught the fist in his big hand and squeezed. The boy let out a yell and dropped to his knees. "Back to the group," John shouted to the smaller boy, who took off in a run. "Now," said John to the larger boy still squeezing his fist. "Are you ready to do as I say?"

"All right, all right. Just let go of my hand," said the boy. As John let go of his hand, the boy came up with his other fist catching John in the stomach. John took the blow, shook it off, and grabbed the boy by the shirt and swung a mighty blow into the boy's face. The big boy lost his balance and fell flat on his back. John again grabbed him and stood him upright, turned him around and pushed him back to the group. He didn't want to fight John anymore.

Soon Otto came back. He was carrying a rifle, a powder horn, and a cloth bag. Strips of cloth were over his shoulder. "Any trouble?" asked Otto.

"All is quiet," John said.

Otto looked around. They are very quiet, he thought. Holding up the rifle, Otto shouted. "This is a rifle - a Hesson Army rifle. Its only purpose is to kill our enemies. You will learn to load, aim, and shoot this rifle.

This is black gun powder. You must keep it dry or it will not fire. With that remark, Otto poured a small amount onto the ground. Then he took a small amount of dry grass and put it into a bundle in his hand. Next he took his flint out of his pocket with his metal stick. Striking  the stick with the flint produced sparks that caught the end of the bundle of grass on fire. Otto then picked up the bundle of grass with its end on fire.  Suddenly, he flung the fired grass at the black powder on the ground. 'Poof.' The powder exploded in a cloud of blue smoke. John had never seen such a sight. In an instant, the powder was all gone. Burning grass and twigs were all that were left. After stomping out the little smolderings, Otto held up a lead ball. "This is the ball the powder pushes up the barrel of the gun. It comes out so fast you cannot see it. I will now show you how to load the gun. With much flair, Otto loaded and cocked the gun, turned, and aimed and fired down the hill.  "This you will learn how to do with great efficiency. John step up here, you will be the first."

John loaded and cocked the rifle with very few mistakes but aiming was another matter. When John pulled the trigger, he wasn't ready for the smoke, the noise, or the kick against his shoulder. It almost knocked him off his feet. This was quite a surprise.

In the next week, John became comfortable when it was his turn to fire the rifle. He was still a little slow loading but he was getting better with his aim. In the second week, he was even better. He could load the rifle to fire in less than a minute. He even hit the post in the creek below which was a sign of a real marksman. Most of the boys in his group had a hard time getting water to splash in the creek. Otto just shook his head. "The safest place in a battle with you boys would be where the post is in the creek. Only John and Monfred has hit it so far," said Otto.

"Let's see you hit it," exclaimed Gearhardt with a smug expression.

"You will do my laundry from now on if I hit it. If I miss it I will take you into town for a beer," said Otto.

"He'll probably miss on purpose," mumbled Monfred. "We all know how Otto likes beer."

"I'll hit the post. I don't like doing laundry. So Gearhardt, for your big mouth, you will have a job from now on," said Otto.

Otto took plenty of time to load the musket - slow and easy like a cat ready to jump on its prey. He squeezed very slowly on the trigger. Swak - halfway down to the post to the water - a perfect shot. "If that was an enemy, it would have hit him right in the chest. That enemy would march against you no more."

In the past few weeks, the group had gotten remarkably better at musketry. At last, the splashes in the creek were closer to the post. Only Deitrich (the big dumb one) had not hit the post.

Otto seemed pleased with his group. They were coming along. John, Monfred, Fritz, and Gearhardt were very good. Only time would tell when they had to face the enemy shooting back. Most of his boys would keep their nerve, he hoped.

Otto came back to the tent after a meeting of officers at the headquarters. "We will be leaving this camp day after tomorrow," speaking to the group. "It will take us many days to reach the sea. You will wash and mend your uniform. Polish your boots! Tomorrow you will receive a back holder to carry your provisions as well as a wool blanket. Now get plenty of rest. You will need it."

That evening when everyone was settled in for the night, John noticed Otto sitting on his pallet staring into space. John asked, "Are you feeling well?"

"I'm fine. I am just thinking," uttered Otto in a low tone.

"I think of home, my family, Hilga, and good food," said John. They both chuckled and smiled. "Do you have family?" asked John.

"A long time ago. I came into the army 11 years ago when my mother died. My father died when I was a small boy. This is now my family."

"Do we now go to the colonies to fight the rebels?" asked John. "I suppose so, whispered Otto, but it will take a long time to get there. This is not yet summer so I expect not to be there until near Christmas."

"Why will it take so long?" questioned John.

"We will have a great ocean to cross. It may take two or three months. I don't know. I've never been there."

"What is it like to be in a battle?" asked John.

"I don't know. My group went to Spain a few years ago to help the French. When we marched across the field, the Spanish dropped their muskets and ran in all directions. We didn't even have to shoot at them."

"Were you afraid?" asked John.

"Not afraid so much - just tired and hungry from the long march," mused Otto. "Do you miss your family, John?"

"Yes, but I like the adventure too. I'm anxious to see the new world everyone is talking about. I wonder why the colonists are rebelling against the English?"

Otto thought awhile and then replied. "I don't know - some kind of misunderstanding it must be. We need not concern ourselves with why they are fighting. Our job is to make sure the British win. I hope when we show ourselves to the colonists, they do like the Spanish and run for their lives."

# FOUR

## *The March*

The next morning, the entire camp was lined up for the long march to the sea. They were all smartly dressed in shiny black boots, black trousers, red and white coats, black knapsacks, and a rolled blanket tied over the top of the knapsack. Each soldier wore a tall red and white pointed hat. They looked very impressive as the troops marched off in their columns.

As the days went by and the march continued toward the sea, the days and nights became warmer. The troops were feeling the heat. A few soldiers from the other groups fell by the road; red faced and dizzy. Not one man fell out from Otto's group so far.

It was late in the afternoon when a salt air breeze sprang up. An hour later the first sight of the ocean came into view. The troops marched up the beach and made camp for the night. The sound of the surf soon put the tired troops into a sound sleep.

"Gentlemen, let me introduce you to the ocean," said Otto as he waved his hand to the open sea. "We will rest and wait here for the English ship. Meanwhile, you will repair your gear and bathe in the sea. Don't go too far out, the water can pull you out, and you will drown so be careful."

The soldiers were having a great time; splashing, swimming, and resting along the beach. John and Fritz made a net out of an old hemp rope that washed up on the shore. It took three days for them to string and knot the net. Fritz had done this before back home in the streams.

As they worked on the net, the other soldiers poked fun at them. "Going to catch a mermaid? You won't catch anything with that. This is a waste of time," most thought.

"Are you ready to try it out?" asked Fritz.

"What do we do?"

"You take this end, and I'll take the other. The rocks we tied to the bottom will keep the bottom of the net down. We must make sure we have the top of the net above water. We must tie the rope from the corners at the bottom to our ankle so we can move the net along the water. You are the tallest, John, so you will go out to about your chest high. I will be closer in. Let's take the net down to the water and try it out."

As Fritz and John proceeded into the water, a crowd of soldiers gathered on the beach to see what was going on. As Fritz and John moved slowly in the water, they could feel tugging in the net.

"We need to swing to the beach," Fritz said.

As they came up on the beach, John was very surprised to see three fish in the net jumping and wiggling. Two were about two hands long, and the other was about four hands.

"Not a bad five minutes work," boasted Fritz.

Putting the fish on the bank, the boys headed back into the water.

Otto came down to the beach and walked out to the boys as they were bringing in the net. "There are 10 or 12 fish in this catch," John said.

"Do you think you can catch more?" asked Otto.

"There is a lot of fish in this water," said Fritz. "As long as the net holds up, we can get more."

"Gut," said Otto. "I'll find us a pot and make a fire. Maybe the boys can find some potatoes up in the fields. We will make a nice stew with these fish." With that, Otto splashed up the beach shouting orders to the boys lazing around the beach and in the shade of the trees.

"Otto can get our group organized so quick," said John. "Look, the boys are already getting wood together. The other ones are going to look for vegetables. We should have a very good supper tonight."

In about two hours, they had about 50 fish of all types and sizes up on the beach.

"We must dry the net," Fritz said to John as Otto was coming down to the beach.

"So many," said Otto.

Fritz said, "They need to be gutted and scaled."

Otto turned around and shouted to three boys standing by the trees.  "Show them what to do," Otto said to Fritz.

As Fritz was instructing the three boys how to clean the fish, John took the net up to the trees. Then he tied each end to two trees to dry.

Later, the stew was ready and fish was roasting on the rocks around the fire.

"All we need is some beer," explained Otto as he was eating a fish like corn-on-the-cob.

The next two weeks, John and Fritz caught enough fish to feed the entire legion of soldiers. Those that wanted fish just came down to the fish pile that John and Fritz kept in the afternoons each day.

"I'm tired of eating fish," said John one afternoon. "I would like a nice chicken or a nice pig."

"Me too," said Fritz, "but we have fish or what they bring in the wagon and that's not much more then slop and bread.

Later that day when John and Fritz were netting fish, they noticed the little fish in front of them jumping this way and that. All of a sudden a mighty fish landed into the net and got tangled. John and Fritz pulled together toward the beach as this huge fish yanked and wrapped itself in the net. They almost had this fish up to shallow water when Otto came running with the boys.

"You got a big one," Otto shouted.

"We need help. Get behind this fish and push." The boys, Otto, Fritz, and John sweated, grunted, pushed, and shoved. They finally dragged this big black fish up on the beach. They all set around exhausted. This was real work as this fish weighed 200 pounds or more.

"Look at our net, John. Its torn to pieces. We'll never be able to untangle and repair it," Fritz said.

After the fish was untangled from the net, Fritz and John started to cut steaks from its flanks. The fire was hot and sticks were cut to roast the fish.

"This tastes like meat," exclaimed one of the boys. Soon the entire group had a steak roasting on the fire.

"This is great-eating-fish," John said to Fritz. It was almost worth breaking up the net."

"We have enough fish to last at least two days," said Otto. "Can you repair the net by then?"

"I don't think so but we'll try," responded Fritz.

On the third day about midday, the net was almost finished. John and Fritz were sitting on the beach tying up the last of the hook knots..

"What's that?" said John.

"What do you see," asked Fritz.

"Look over there - looks like three dots on the ocean," John replied.

As they watched, they became aware of three sailing ships moving in their direction. In about an hour, the three ships were anchored opposite the troops on the beach. Boats were over the side and started for shore.

As the boats hit the surf, the sailors threw a rope to the boys waiting on the beach. The sailors were shouting something but no one could understand them. Finally, someone got the idea to pull the boats up on the beach.

"Those sailors are a fierce-looking lot," said John.

Fritz agreed, "They sure are. Look at the knives they have in their sashes."

One of the sailors that got out of the second boat to land must have been an officer the way he was dressed. Our own officer was coming down the beach as the sailor officer stepped from the boat.

Both officers came face to face. Our officer snapped his heels and saluted. The sailor officer returned the salute. They talked awhile and then walked up to the headquarter's tent. By this time the beach was full of boats that had landed.

Soon a runner came by and ordered Otto to the headquarter's tent.

"Fritz, I guess we won't need the net anymore," John remarked.

"Help me take the stones off the bottom. I'm going to roll it tight and put it in my pack," said Fritz.

"What for, why do you want to lug this around?"

Fritz said, "We may have a use for it and its hard work to make a net." When the net was packed on Fritz's pack, the boys were aware of dark clouds coming in from the west. A storm was coming up. White caps could be seen out by the ships.

"That's just nice," remarked John. "A storm to give us a nice wet bed for tonight."

The storm kept coming getting darker by the minute, and the wind was picking up. Otto came running down the beach shouting to his group to come down to the boat in front of them and pull it up the beach.

As the boys pulled and pushed the boat up to higher ground, the waves came up and the rain pelted down. Other boats were being brought up by other groups when the stinging hail hit. Everyone crouched down as the hail came down.

The storm was passing with heavy rain still coming down. Some men were down in the water with a boat that got away from them and were pulled out into the waves. They had the rope now and were pulling it out so slowly. The boat was full of water and was very heavy. Finally, the boat was up on the beach, and the water was being drained from it.

The waves were settling down again. The rain had almost stopped.

"I wonder what's going on down there," asked John.

"Looks like a lot of soldiers gathered around something," said Otto. "I'll go see." A little while later Otto came back. "Some poor bastard got drowned," he said. "A wave must have caught him when they were pushing the boat."

"One less soldier to shoot the Colonists," remarked one of the boys.

"That leaves more for us," croaked another.

"We will go to the ship in the morning," said Otto. "Get lots of rest. You will need it to climb the net ladder to the deck of the boat."

In the morning, the troops were loaded in the boats. The weather was cool, and the sea was choppy. As the sailors rode the boats out toward the ships, the little boats bobbed like a cork in the open sea. John was feeling a little queasy and some boys were downright sick. Otto didn't look so good either.

As they pulled up to the ship, John was surprised to see how big it was. Like a wall the side went up. A rope ladder was dropped down to the heavy boat. Otto grabbed the ladder and started up. He was up about five rungs on the ladder as the ship leaned out. The ship leaned sharply the other way. WHAM! Otto slammed into the side of the ship. A string of curses and a scramble to hold onto the ladder had all the boys looking up.

Next John caught the ladder and started up. As the ship leaned out, John climbed as fast as he could as the ship leaned the other way. John braced himself with his feet against the side of the ship. When the ship leaned back again, John climbed as fast as he could again. Now there were four men on the ladder with Otto going over the rail.

Splash - someone fell off the ladder. John looked over the rail. It was Fritz. The sailors were fishing him out of the sea. Fritz was shouting, cursing, and splashing. They got Fritz back into the boat.

After awhile, all were on deck.

"The sea almost got you," said John.

"Almost, my pack and boots were heavy and I almost went down when the sailor's hook caught my arm. At least, I had one last bath in Germany."

They all had a good laugh.

Otto led the boys down the ladders to the holds of the ship. There were 13 pallets across the back of the ship for Otto's group. The men stowed their gear at one end.

"This sure is tight quarters," said John. "I can hardly breathe because of the stink."

"Yes, the stink is bad," agreed Fritz. "Did you have enough adventure yet?"

"Almost," said John.

"Climb up on your pallets and stay out of the way," blasted Otto. "You will stay on your pallet till its time for our group to go up to eat and relieve yourselves. Now be quiet."

John could see this was going to be a miserable trip. He thought of going up and diving off the ship to go home but he didn't know how to swim so maybe that wasn't a good idea.

After much shouting, squeaky noises, popping sounds, and grinding sounds, the ship was moving.

"We're off to the Colonies," murmured John.

"It sure stinks in here," mumbled Fritz.

"There are eighty-two soldiers on this ship, plus the sailors. That's a lot of people on a small ship as this," said Otto.

"What's the iron rings on the pallets for?" asked John.

"This was a slave ship. They took slaves from the African coast to the Colonies before the English captured this ship. It was a Spanish slaver before."

Fritz said, "You mean slaves were chained in here for the trip across."

"Seems that way," said Otto. I've heard that about one-half died till they got them there."

"Those Spanish are bad people then," said John. They are the ones we should be fighting."

"We already did," spoke up Otto. "They ran like the devil."

As the ship moved out into deeper water, the more the sails came into play. Day went into night and back into day again. The daily routine became predictable. Days went into weeks and most of the passages lost all sense of time. The monotony was broken only by meals and deck time, with a fight breaking out from time to time. The monotony, bad food, and the motion of the ship had most nerves on the edge.

It was about 3 or 4 P.M.. Otto's group were on the deck to relieve themselves over the fan tail and for a bit of exercise and fresh air.

"Notice the sea birds. We must be close to land," exclaimed John.

"I hope so," said Fritz. "I had enough of sea life. Sailors must be crazy to like this kind of life."

Shouting from the crows nest had the boys looking up. The sailor up there was pointing straight ahead. There was more shouting. Sailors were coming out of the holds and going to the rails.

"See anything?" asked Otto.

"No, just sea."

"We must go back to our pallets now. Our time is up," said Otto.

It was dark and raining now. The ship was in choppy water and running slow. Rumble, bump, rumble, bump, bump! There was shouting and scrambling on deck. John could feel a shudder run through the ship.

"What was that?" asked Fritz.

"I don't know," said John.

They dropped the anchor to hold the ship fast. "Listen and you can hear the surf on the beach. We're near some land," said Otto. "We'll probably go ashore in the morning."

"Thank God," said Fritz. "I can't wait to get out of this stink hole."

In the morning, the ship was moving up the coast. The sun was well up when the boat was tied up to a dock. This was a pretty rickety bunch of pilings and planks. Each time the ship bumped the dock, it would shudder and shake.

"Do you think its safe to get off the ship onto that thing?" said Fritz.

"You'll have to unless you want to stay on the ship, and I don't think you want that," said Otto.

In a little while, the soldiers were on dry land.

"It feels so funny not to have the motion under my feet - makes me feel queasy. It will take awhile to walk straight," said John.

"Sea legs," a sailor spoke up. "You have sea legs. That means you would make a good sailor."

"Not for me," said Fritz. "Just give me dry land - mountains, trees, fields, houses, and space - not that endless sea. When I'm done here I'll find a way to walk home."

"Line up. March, hup, hup, hup."

They marched into a village and stopped by a long barn.

"They call this town Amboy. We will get our muskets here. We will wait at the edge of this town until the rest of the regiment can assemble. Now line up, single file and follow me," ordered Otto.

The group followed Otto into the barn. Each boy was given a musket, bayonet, powder horn, shot, and a patch of cloth. Then they marched to the edge of town and camped alongside of a stream. Otto ordered them to clean and polish their muskets.

"Mine sure has a lot of rust on it," said John.

Otto looked over and said, "I've got something for that. Take a little of this black oil in your fingers and then add some fine sand. Then work it into the rust spots. It looks like I will have to get all of you to work on the rust."

They were pitiful muskets left over from the Spanish war. The muskets were badly stored and poorly transported to the Colonies.

"We'll try our muskets out tomorrow," Otto told the boys. "I hope you remember how to load and shoot."

"I hope the musket will shoot with all the rust," said John.

"They will," said Otto. "Just be careful you don't put too much powder in the flash pan. It will blow back in your face and knock an eye out."

"Might be an improvement," muttered one of the boys.

Otto spun around, grabbed the boy and pulled him up face to face. With gritted teeth Otto spat out in his face, "You think so, smart boy?" The boy, even though he was head and shoulders over Otto, turned white with fright. Otto pushed him back with a hardy shove. "Anyone else have a smart remark?" Everyone looked down, and there was silence. Otto stomped off down the stream.

"We'll better watch what we say about Otto," said John.

"You're his pet, and I'll say anything I want to," said the boy. John was on his feet in a minute and so was the boy. "Otto's pet," said the boy.

"I'm nobody's pet," replied John defiantly. "You say that again, and I'll flatten you."

With that, the boy took a swing at John, hitting him on the side of the face. John, knocked off balance for a moment, caught the second blow in his big hand with a solid 'smack'. John squeezed the boy's fist as the second blow came around from his left hand. 'Smack', John caught his left fist, and started to squeeze. The boy dropped to his knees as John squeezed his fists even harder. "Stop, you are breaking the bones in my hand," cried the boy.

"Who's pet am I?" growled John.

"No ones, no ones," was the reply.

"Remember that," John shouted as he pushed the boy onto his backside.

When John turned around, Otto was standing square with his hands on his hips. "Vots this?" asked Otto.

"Nothing important," replied John.

"Gut. Now we go eat," said Otto. "Line up."

The next morning, two other groups had come into the clearing during the night. Otto's group marched to the edge of the field and lined up in a long line and loaded their rifles. When Otto shouted for them to shoot, they all shot their rifles into the stream causing a row of splashes opposite the boys. After four shots, Otto ordered the boys back to their camp. "At least the muskets still shoot. Whether we can hit anything is another story," said Otto to Fritz and John.

"I wondered too," said John, "but my musket seems to do fine. Now I don't know if I can shoot at another man."

"I'm not sure either," said Fritz.

Otto with tight jaws said, "You will when they start shooting at you!"

Three more days and the whole Hesson Company was assembled. They marched to the interior to face the Colonists.

The first day they marched to a town called New Brunswick. The next day they camped along the Millstone River. After a wet crossing, they made it to the outskirts to an area called Hopewell.

It rained a little as they made their way to the Delaware River named after an Indian tribe that lived along this river. That evening, the rain turned to a wet heavy snow. The troops huddled around their fires making shelters along the banks of the river.

"This is miserable and cold," Fritz said to John. "Even the fire isn't burning very well. Such a godforsaken land! I wish I was home."

"Stop your complaining. You're here and you must fight the Colonists as you agreed to do," said John.

Otto told the boys, "We'll be marching about a half day down toward the village of Trenton. Then we will make a permanent camp until the English tell us where we can find the enemy. They are probably hiding since they heard the Hessons have come. Maybe we won't need to shoot anyone."

"I hope so," said John.

"Me too," said Fritz.

The weather during the next week was raw cold with raining and snow flurries. The little lean-tos constructed to shelter the boys were of little comfort. Everything was dirty, wet and cold. No one was in a good mood. Otto was showing his mean streak when one of the boys didn't do an assignment right. He was quick to cuff the boys when he lost his temper.

It started to snow again - another cold wet snow. John and Fritz had a hard time keeping the fire going.

"I hope they soon find the Colonists so we can chase them. I'm tired of sitting along this muddy river freezing and wet," complained Fritz.

That evening the wagon came by with pieces of meat to roast on the fire. John wondered what kind of meat this was. It tasted good, and he ate a big chunk.

As they were roasting their meat, Otto came by. "It's venison and mighty good, too," spoke up Otto.

After John had eaten, he felt drowsy since his belly was full. He pushed his way to the back of the lean-to and nestled down in the loose pine boughs they had cut for bedding. Soon John was asleep; warm and comfortable.

# FIVE

## *The Search*

Boom! Boom! Boom! Splat!

"What's that!" someone shouted.

Otto stepped out in the darkness. Plop! John saw Otto drop to his knees by the fire with blood gushing from a ragged hole in his belly. Otto looked down at the gushing blood with disbelief. Someone was running. Boom! Otto's head snapped back with blood pouring out of his head.

"They're shooting at us!" someone shouted. A boy ran out to Otto. Boom! Boom! Then he fell on Otto in the mud.

Fritz shouted as a flash at the open end of the lean-to, resounded in a horrible explosion. John felt the bullet whizz by his ear and out the back of the lean-to. Fritz was up and trampling over the boys getting out of the lean-to.

Boom! Boom! Boom! Fritz went sprawling in the mud as well as the two boys that followed him.. John could see by the blank, staring eyes by the fire that Fritz was gone. Realizing that going out the front would only bring shooting from who knows who, John pushed his way out the back of the lean-to.

As he lay in the mud, he could hear running, shooting, screaming, and swearing with more confusion

53

that he had ever known. It was snowing hard as John crawled into the woods. The battle was still in the camp although he couldn't see much. It was very dark and late at night. Still he could hear shooting, stabbing, and shouting.

The snow on the ground illuminated the shadows enough to determine where the trees were. John got to his feet and started to run. He ran until he was out of breath and slowed to a walk, stopping once in awhile to listen to see if anyone was following him. What do I do now, thought John. I guess it would be best to get back to the river and go north. All night, John walked through the woods without stopping to rest. At the top of a hill, he could see the river through the falling snow. The ridge he was on, ran along the river for a mile or so upstream. He thought he would keep to the high ground and in the woods as much as he could.

About daybreak, John came upon a rocky area with huge boulders. He selected a nitch between two large boulders facing the river. He needed a fire to get warm, but he knew the Colonists would see the smoke and come and get him so there would be no fire. He thought he should turn the red coat inside out. What a target that would make. The other side was a rust color - not so striking.

John huddled in the rocks wondering what to do. Should he go north to the Colonists? They would shoot him. Should he go south? Should he stay there? There was nothing to eat or to keep him warm.

About midday, the snow stopped and a bit later the sun came out. AHHH, thought John as the warm sun came down on him. He dosed off. When he woke up, the sun was setting in the west. As he surveyed his position on the hill, he noticed up river a house near a creek that ran into the river. This looked like a small farm with another roofed area just beyond the house. It looked like a sturdy log construction with a wisp of smoke coming from the chimney. He thought someone must be living there. He should be careful since the Colonists may not be friendly. Maybe tomorrow he would get near and see if he could find something to eat out of their fields.

The night was crystal clear and very cold. John stayed awake all night since it was too cold to sleep. He wondered what happened at the camp. Terrible things had happened - so much noise and blood. He knew then he wanted to put off soldiering. As far as an adventure, he wished he was home which was so very far away.

The next morning was cold, clear, and windy. John ventured down the hill and up along the river. As he came to the first clearing, he still couldn't see the house. The field had been planted last summer. It looked like corn had been a good crop.

John scratched here and there looking for kernels dropped during harvest. He found a few but not many-not enough to satisfy the hunger in his belly.

He stayed close to the edge of the field as he moved along. He could see the house now so he thought it better to get back into the woods. Stooping down in some high weeds, he could see the house very plainly.

Around the side of the house came a man, a dog, and a boy. They were walking to the roofed stalls. John could see two cows and a horse feeding at the troughs.

All of a sudden, the dog ran a few steps in his direction and started to bark furiously. John got down lower in the weeds.

The man and boy shouted to the dog but the dog kept barking. There was more shouting as the man and boy looked in John's direction.

They must not have seen him so they shouted again to the dog. The dog quit barking soon and went back to the man and boy. They were saddling the horse. They had just finished and were leading the horse out of the stall when a lady appeared from the other side of the house. They stood and talked awhile. John could hear a word now and then but he understood nothing. He thought he had better learn English if he was to survive in this country.

The boy and the man were up on the horse now. They waved goodbye to the lady and went off across the creek. They proceeded up the stream with the dog falling behind. The lady waited in the stalls awhile, putting hay down for the cows. Later she went around towards the front of the house.

John could see the blanket they used on the horse hanging on the side of the stall. Slowly, he made his way along the woods until the stalls were in line with the house. He kept low and came up to the stall. He snatched the blanket off the side of the stall. It didn't smell good but it would keep him warm, he thought. He looked over the stall wall and saw corn and oats in the trough. In an instant, he cleared out the trough, filling his pockets.

"AEEEEE!!," screamed the woman. John turned around startled as the woman grabbed the pitchfork and blocked the stall entrance.

She was shouting something John couldn't understand. He took a step towards her. She lunged forward to stick him. In a flash, John grabbed the fork and yanked her to him, twisting the fork out of her hands. She turned and ran to the house screaming. He took the fork, a piece of rope, the blanket, and a bucket and ran into the woods. He ran around the farm through the woods until he came to the stream. He could hear the woman calling up stream.

The horse and rider could be heard before John saw them in a gallop along the path on the other side of the stream. The dog followed somewhat behind them. As John was watching them disappear down the stream, the dog stopped, sniffed the air, barked once or twice and followed after his owners.

John crossed the stream, staying in the water. He went up a small tributary before he stepped out on dry land. He was thinking he had better stay with the river and go north. He was remembering talk on the boat about Germans settling in Penns Woods, Northwest, wherever that was.

John finally came to the river. Staying in the woods, he kept making his way north. Twice he stopped and watched flat rafts with cargo going down the river. It was getting dark when John found a small, rocky cave-like place, back from the river along a tiny stream. As he was drinking from the stream, he noticed some small minnows in the stream. If he could catch them, he could eat them. He was so hungry.

John tried to catch them but they were too fast. Then he realized he had the bucket. Dashing the bucket in the stream and throwing the water on the bank produced three small fish. Soon he had 20 or more fish.

Could he trust a fire? If he would use real dry wood, it wouldn't make much smoke. He decided to try it. After he had settled in his cave, he started a fire. With his fish strung on a birch branch, roasting, he put his blanket around him. When the fish were done, he gobbled them down too fast. He should have saved them but his stomach was more demanding. After chewing on some corn, he settled back and became drowsy.

John awoke with a start. The fire was almost out. It was cold and a little windy. What woke him? As he was looking around, a pair of eyes reflected in the starlight down the hill. He figured it was some kind of animal. He felt a little uneasy and watched very closely pulling the pitchfork to him getting it ready. It was the only weapon he had other than a knife he was issued with his gear. Now, John noticed three or four pairs of eyes looking his way as they moved along the stream. They were small, and he could hear them splashing in the stream. He put some wood on the fire just in case they decided to come up to him. Dawn broke a gray and threatening day. John could smell snow in the air. Should he stay here or move on? Until he decided, he went down to the stream for a drink. He noticed the remains of crawfish. So that's what the little animals were after, he thought. He wondered if they had left any. He turned over rocks in the stream and sure enough, there was one. John ran up to the rocks for his bucket and soon he had several hand fulls of the little critters. They made a good breakfast roasted on the coals. John spent the day catching crawfish and minnows. It was cold and snow flurries came and went but John was too busy. That evening he ate his fill and kept the rest for later. He wrapped the roasted crawfish and fish in a rag they gave him for ramroding his rifle and put it in his pack. They would taste good when he was traveling.

During the night, it started snowing hard enough to put out the fire and by morning, John woke up stiff and cold. It was still snowing but not as much.

As John left his little camp, he headed again up river. The snow changed to sleet and then a light misty rain. It was cold but moving kept him warm enough.

It was in the afternoon when the woods gave way to an open field and then a wagon road ran along the river with patches of woods growing on the bank. Walking along the road was a lot easier than the woods and John thought he would try it for awhile.

Coming around a bend in the road, John noticed a farm to his right. The house was way back and up a hill. It looked like the farm had been there for a long time. A fence of field stone ran along the road.

When John topped a gentle rise on the road, he could see a cluster of houses in the distance. It looked like a village which should be avoided. He decided to go back to the woods away from the river and just in time too. A wagon was coming up from behind. He came up the road toward the village. Then crouched down and kept still until they passed. He thought if he could circle the village he could get back to the river and continue North.

It was getting dark as he walked near a field. A dog was barking over the hill in front of him. John decided to go deeper in the woods and stay away from the dog. When he got to the top of the hill, he spotted a house and barn in front of him. Light could be seen at the window and smoke was coming from the chimney.

He could see the woods were giving way to open fields further on. Now what should I do, he thought. There would be no fire tonight - too many people. He decided to go back into the woods, and there he found a huge dead oak tree. He scooped out a place big enough for him, wrapped himself in his blanket, and crawled in. He was sound asleep in a minute.

John woke up to voices somewhere below him down the hill. Slowly, he worked his way along the ridge. There were two men walking along the road, both carrying a pack and blanket roll. Travelers! He wondered if he should walk the roads instead of the woods. As he watched them, a man on a horse was coming down the road. As the men passed each other, they touched their open hand to their hat. He heard them say something but he couldn't understand it. He supposed it was some kind of greeting.

He decided it would be better not to wear his coat. It would give him away as a soldier. He decided to take off the coat and stuff it in the bucket. Then he put the horse blanket over his head and around him like a cloak. He took the bit of rope and tied it around his waist, like a belt with the end almost to the ground. He sure was a weird sight as he came down to the road.

At first, he saw no one. As he came to a crossroad, a wagon with logs was coming down the road from his right.

There were two horses and two men. John stopped as the wagon went across his path.

"Morning," the men said as they touched their hat brim.

"Morning," uttered John in return.

Bethlehem Lumber Company was painted on the side of the wagon. John had no idea what that meant.

John kept walking north. He saw many men walking and riding as the day went on. He was very careful not to catch up with anyone or to look too long at anyone. The road went away sharply from the river later that day. John stood by the road deciding which way to go. He made up his mind and started off the road heading up the river.·

"Where are you going, boy?"

John turned and saw the two travelers he had seen in the morning to his left in the weeds by the road.

"Look at that get up, will you?"

"Looks like a holy man or monk or something."

"Sure as hell looks weird."

John was dumb struck. He could not understand a word. They were getting up and coming over to him.

He just stood there.

"What are you?" one said.

"Stupid I'll say," said the other.

John decided to not speak but gesture. Maybe, they would think he couldn't talk. He opened and pointed into his mouth.

"Can't talk.

" Heared tell them monks got their tongue cut out so as they can't talk. He must be one of them."

"Big fella, he is."

"Heared tell you don't mess with those holy fellows or you'll get a bunch of bad luck."

"He looks too big to mess with anyway."

John did not know what they were saying but he was ready for trouble. They talked a little more then turned and headed back to the woods. He decided to get along up the river. He wondered if his signaling made them think he was crazy. It worked, whatever it was.

John followed the path along the river, a quiet pristine river with a slow-moving current. Ice was floating along near the edge. He came to a stream blocking his way. He noticed the patch headed upstream. Evidently others had a hard time crossing here and had to go upstream where the stream narrowed.

As John moved along the path upstream, the gray skies started to drop a light snow. It was cold, but John felt comfortable under his blanket and coat. He came to a place where he could cross the stream on the rocks without getting wet. He was half way across when he heard a shot and then some yelling up on the ridge above him. As he got to the other side and away from the noisy stream, he could hear talking. He couldn't understand it, but talking just the same.

John decided to investigate but to be very careful not to be seen. John soon came to a cluster of rocks on the top of the ridge. From here, he could look down into the broad valley and the river far to his left. He could see at least four farms with land cleared around them.

"Chop the other quarter off and leave the rest." John heard this remark which startled him. He couldn't see them nor understand them. They were somewhere to his left and down the mountain a bit. He crept up to a pair of boulders and looked between them. There they were - right in front of him about 10 yards. One was chopping with a hatchet. Finally, he cut what he was chopping. The two men were talking and then they roped the two hindquarters of a deer by the hooves and dropped it over a sapling they had cut. Next, they hoisted the pole on their shoulders, picked up their muskets, and started down the mountain toward the valley. When they were out of sight and earshot, John ventured down to see what was left of the deer. What a find, John thought. He took out his knife and cut off the head. Then he cleaned out the chest cavity. He was hungry, very hungry, but he knew he had better get what he could carry over the ridge and down the river. He cut a pole, sharpened one of its branches like a hook. Then he did another, lying them about a foot apart on the ground, John picked up the front half. Very pleased, John picked up the ends of the saplings and pulled his meat up over the ridge and down along the ridge.

An hour of pulling and tugging brought John to another outcrop of rocks. The snow was really coming down now. Among the rocks was an overhang, a big boulder that provided natural shelter. Someone had used it before. A fire pit in the back had some unburnt wood as well as a pile of sticks near the front. This shelter had not been used in years, John thought as he started to make a fire. He felt very fortunate to find lots of dry wood and pine needles under the shelter. Someone had planned to stay awhile sometime back.

The fire soon warmed the cozy shelter. John had a piece of meat on a stick roasting on the fire. He could hardly wait for the first piece to be done, and ate it half raw. The next piece got a little more done. The third piece roasted fully, and he ate it slowly.

It was dark now and the wind was blowing from the north. It was getting colder. It was good the wind was from the north, John thought. His little shelter faced south, so the wind passed over and by him. Sitting by the fire with a full belly, tired, and a bit dreamy, John thought of home, his parents, his sisters, and Hilga. Oh yes, Hilga. Would he ever see her again? Would he ever see anyone again back in Hesson? So far away. How do I get around that ocean, he thought as he drifted off.

It was cold - very cold. The stars were out, and a hint of light was coming in the sky. John poked his fire and put more wood on. Soon the flames were dancing warming up his little shelter. John reached over to cut some meat and realized it was starting to freeze. He had watched his father freeze dry the meat from a stag back home. He did not have a drying rack like his father's.

As daylight came he thought, if I cut strips and hang them on bushes till they dry, I'll be able to put the strips in my bucket and have something to eat later. That morning and into the afternoon, John cut strips, ate venison, and freeze dried more strips. By evening, John brought the brown dried venison into the shelter. There he piled them on the saplings he had cut. The bitter cold would do the job.

The next morning was cold and cloudy. John thought, it's not wise to stretch his luck by staying this close to farmland so he packed his gear and his frozen meat. He left only the bones for the animals.

The snow wasn't very deep - maybe four inches. It was enough to make tracks, not only his, but deer, rabbits, squirrels, and others he wasn't sure of.

Following the river path, he noted not one person had been on the path. It was so bitter cold he guessed everyone was by the fire. If he had good sense, he'd be there also. Yet he needed to find the German settlement in Penns Woods. All he knew it was north and west.

It stayed very cold for the next five days - so cold that John didn't find it necessary to go back from the river very far to make his camp. The further upstream he went, the more the river was frozen. By the fifth day, the river was frozen all the way across. John was thinking, maybe one more day and he could start west.

The path gave way to a road along the river, and lots of tracks. He came to a sign that read: Frenchtown - 12 Mi. A town, John thought. Wonder what that sign says. 12K maybe? Maybe I should take the river tonight. The moon will be bright, and it's going to be very cold so I suppose the ice will support me. Than I can go west.

John decided to hide along the bank of the river till dark. Twice he heard horses and wagons along the road. He was glad he hid.

The moon didn't come up for hours after dark, so John thought it would be best if it was late at night. When the moon did come up, he decided to chance it.

Very cautiously, John moved over the ice, near the middle of the river. He stopped as he could hear the ice squelch under his weight. Moving very slowly, he was on solid ice again. As he climbed up the bank, he didn't notice before that he was sweating from the excitement.

Now, is this Penns Woods, he asked himself. How do I find out? I must not ask or they will take me to the Colonists. I don't want that.

John found a little ravine to hunker down in until dawn. It didn't seem as cold since the clouds came in the sky.

By dawn, it was snowing slightly and John set out going west through open country, mostly woods, skirting a farm here and there.

On the third day, he came to a road, followed it awhile, and came to a sign that read: Quaker town- 4 Mi. Oops, too close to people, thought John.

John struck off due west again. He felt safe in the woods, being careful not to get too close to houses and farms.

Following another road along the woods, there was another sign. Allentown- 28 Mi. That's due north, so I missed that one, too, John thought.

Two days later, John came upon a road going northwest. He heard a wagon coming and hid in the brush. As the wagon went by, he thought he could almost read the letters on the side of the wagon. Kutztown Dry Goods. Could it be? I'm coming to Penns Woods Dutch, John thought excitedly.

About midday, John came to a valley along a creek. He thought he would try to talk to someone. It had been a long time since he had talked. He wondered if he remembered how. He must have been a sight walking into Kutztown later that afternoon draped in a horse blanket, a bucket, and a pitchfork. John even had a beard. As he walked along the streets, nothing looked familiar. Maybe this isn't such a good idea. He couldn't read any signs, and people stopped and stared. He could smell people smells as he walked along - cooking, outhouses, horses.

Two men were coming his way. "Evening," they said touching the brim of their hat.

"Evening," repeated John as he went past them. Now that was dumb, he thought. I'm not supposed to speak. Next time, I'll not say anything.

He didn't have long to wait. As he was going out of town, a man and woman came towards him.

"Evening," the man and woman said.

John nodded and kept on walking.

"Hold it there stranger," shouted the man.

John instinctively stopped not knowing what the man shouted.

"We greeted you good evening, don't you have the courtesy to return that greeting?"

Wonder what he said, thought John. He opened his mouth and pointed.

"You hungry?" asked the man.

John dropped his head not knowing what to do next.

"You hungry, boy?" asked the man a little louder.

"Maybe, he's deaf," said the woman.

With that, the man clapped his hand sharply and John jumped. "Taint deaf," the man said.

John was thinking, should I run, stand here, and be like a dummy, or talk?

"Maybe he just can't talk," said the woman.

At that moment, John was about the speak and opened his mouth. Then he thought it best not to speak.

"He can't talk, Horise, he is one of them there mutes. Poor feller, young too," she was going on.

"Now don't get no ideas, Ellie. I know how you are with strays, like dogs, cats, rabbits. Now a mute?"

She reached over to take John's hand. Startled, John pulled back. She again reached over and took his hand. "Now you come along, and we'll get you a nice supper," she said in a kindly voice.

Whatever she said, she said it nice thought John as she kept pulling him along. The man didn't seem too happy about the situation, grumbling to her as they went along. They passed a few houses. Then they went down a path to a small cottage by a stream. There was something almost familiar as they approached the little house.

"Phew, he sure stinks," exclaimed the man.

"Poor fellow, probably hasn't had a good bath in weeks. I'll put water on the fire while you take him out in the shanty. Get his clothes off and get the tub ready. I'll bring water when its hot enough. Here take this chunk of soap along. He'll need it."

This tub of hot water feels good, thought John. Wonder where the lady took my clothing?

The door opened and the man burst into the shanty. "Where did you get the soldier coat?" he exclaimed.

Not knowing what the man said, John hung his head.

The man ran back out and then back in with his army coat. "Where did you get this!?" he shouted.

Now what do I do, thought John. Here I am naked in a tub of water and this man's shouting at me.

"Leave him alone! Can't you see he picked it up somewhere just like the horse blanket, the bucket, and pitchfork. He must have been abandoned by his parents or they died. That's bad enough for someone with all their faculties but for someone who can't talk - leave him alone," said the woman.

They both left. Wonder what that was all about, John asked himself.

The door opened and the man came in with trousers and a homemade shirt. As John got into them, he noticed they were a bit tight. The woman came in and gestured to John to come with her. They went into the big room with the fireplace. She pointed to a chair and said something. John took it to mean sit down. The man sat at the other end. The lady dished out a thick stew from the pot at the fireplace. It smelled so good. When the lady sat down, they bowed their heads and said something. It sounded like the Lord's Prayer in another language. The only word John could make out was 'amen'. The man handed John a bowl of stew and bread, then his wife, and then himself.

The man said, "Eat."

That must mean, "Essen," John thought.

It was a wonderful meal with great bread, and no conversation. After the meal, they made a pallet by the fire for John. He noticed his horse blanket, coat, shirt, and pants hung up in the shanty. The lady said something using the greeting 'morning'.

They were talking while John was lying by the fire on the pallet. The steady drone of their voices, the warm fire, the feeling of clean, and a full belly soon had John asleep.

It was light when John woke. The woman was putting wood on the fire, when he sat up, she said some words to him in a pleasant voice. He felt good and smiled at the woman. She looked as if she was about to cry when she quickly motioned him to the shanty.

She handed him his things and left. John changed into his own clothing. When he went into the big room with the man's clothing on his arm, he wanted to say thank you to the woman. He knew she would not understand his words so he just smiled and nodded his head.

"He must go," said the man.

"I know, I know," agreed the woman.

She started packing and wrapping things in a sack. She packed bread, onion, potato, dried meat, and carrots from the root cellar. She stuffed the food into his knapsack, turned him around, and gave him a big hug. The man came over and shook John's hand. He said something. John smiled and nodded. He knew they were sending him on his way.

It was a cold, bright day. He looked a little more presentable now or at least he felt that way.

Six days later, John passed through Shoemakersville. He was feeling a little more at ease meeting people but still no one spoke Hesson. He was beginning to feel he never would.

The land was more hilly here with pleasant little valleys. Seven more days and he was passing through a little town called "Strausstown". Now that name seemed familiar. From where he could not remember.

The next three weeks were very tough walking. The hills gave way to nice size mountains as he traveled northwest. During a heavy snow, John found a cozy cave on the side of the mountain. This seemed like a very uninhabited area. The only thing missing was food. Living off the land would make you miss many meals.

Then John remembered Fritz making the fish net. He wondered if he could unravel this rope and make a net. The stream down below the cave must have fish.

During the next two days, John finished a net. He was hungry for something good. The water was rushing freely with the first thaw of winter. He strung the net across the creek and then went upstream. When he started downstream, he splashed rocks in the creek. When he got to his net, he saw several fish caught in the net. He got them in his bucket and up to his fire in no time. John enjoyed his meal of fish down to the last morsel.

During the next four weeks, John existed on a mountain to be later called Bethel. As spring approached, he felt he needed to move on to the northeast to Penns Woods and The Dutch. The mountains were slow going up and slow going down. The dense forest in the valleys were beginning to show life.

It was the first week of April when John topped the Southern mountain and saw for the first time Armstrong Valley. This was a broad valley with a mighty river to the west and a rim of noble mountains to the east. This valley was dotted with farms and fields. Hedges and woods separated the fields. From where he was standing, he could see some of the fields were plowed - not many but a few. This valley looks inviting, he thought. Again he must be careful, he remembered. People may not be friendly. John started down the mountain on this beautiful spring day. He came to a small stream of crystal clear water which he decided to follow down the mountain. He stopped to drink its sweet water. There was lots of game, he thought. Even this small stream had tiny fish in abundance. Later, he stopped to watch three deer ahead of him standing belly deep in a pool of cool water.

It was getting warm in the sun, almost hot, as he rolled his coat and packed it around his knapsack. Down the stream, deer drifted off in the woods, peacefully feeding. A game trail along the stream made going down the mountain much easier. The stream grew as he descended with wonderful falls, roaring rapids, and deep cold pools. John was amazed at the richness of wild life and fish in the stream. What a wonderful land, he thought.

He came to a plateau where the stream spread out with deep pools one after another, and was flanked by tall pine trees that blocked out the sun. The floor of the forest was thick with years and years of pine needles. John felt an awe as though he had entered a great cathedral. Surely this was the forest of God's work, he thought. It was cool with a soft breeze; the essence of pine in the air. John couldn't help himself, he had to stay awhile. He found a big tree to rest his back and sat down. In a little while, he felt drowsy with a comfortable good feeling with the stream babbling along. He finally fell into a deep sleep.

# SIX

## *A Place to Hide*

As dawn broke, John was washing his face in the stream. He felt good since he had slept like a log all night. He was ready to move on down into the valley. His stomach was growling. He needed to find something to eat and soon. Chewing on bark from birch trees didn't help much but it helped.

John noticed a field through the woods. It looked like a farmer with a team of horses working the next field beyond the hedgerow in between the fields. John decided to cross the stream and follow the hedgerow to observe the farmer and his work. The farmer was an older man, with a white beard, black hat, homespun shirt and pants. From his vantage point, John noticed he wore black boots not unlike his own. The farmer's team was a magnificent pair of work horses, chestnut brown with lots of muscle. They were pulling a plow in a orderly row back and forth across the field. From where John was hiding, they would come to the edge of the field near him, turn around and plow to the other end of the field. This is hard work, John thought, as he saw the farmer sweating hard trying to control the plow and the horses. Up and back they went, and up again. When they were plowing back again toward John, the horses gave a start as the plow hit a rock and went sideways on the

71

ground. The horses kept going dragging the farmer who was tangled in the reins and the plow.

The shouts from the farmer startled the horses even more as they started to bolt into a run. Without thinking, he dropped his things and ran into the field directly toward the horses. As he caught up to them, he grabbed the horses and yoke between the huge horses and pulled with everything he had. He dragged their heads down until they finally stopped.

"Donnerwetter! Dummkopf horses!"

"Heilig Donnerwetter," swore the farmer.

John could hardly believe his ears. He could understand what he said. When he finally got the horses settled down, the farmer untied himself and came up to John.

In John's own language, the farmer said, "Thanks boy, I thought they would drag me back to the barn."

John said meekly," You're welcome."

"Where did you come from?" asked the farmer.

"Bot Weiser," said John.

"Where is Bot Weiser?" asked the farmer.

"Hesson," said John.

"Deutschland?" said the farmer. "You are from Deutschland? How did you get here? It's all the way across the sea."

"I came with the Hesson army to fight the Colonists for the British."

"What, you are a soldier from Hesson, to fight the Colonists. You are just a boy. Why do you do such a thing? You are not a soldier."

"My parents entered me into the Hesson army for a gold mark a month for 12 months," John exclaimed.

"A gold mark for 12 months," the farmer said with disgust in his voice. "Why are you not with your army?"

"Someplace along a river the Colonists came shooting at my group. Many were shot and killed, and I ran away. I don't know the river's name but the place I heard as Trenton. It was near Christmas time and very bad weather with snow and sleet."

"I heard about that battle at the church this winter. How did you get here?" asked the farmer.

"I walked," said John.

"All winter?!" said the farmer.

"Yes."

"God in Heaven, how did you do this?" exclaimed the farmer.

"I just did it," said John.

Hmpf' was the farmer's only reply.

"Help me get the plow straight and the horses unhitched to let them graze by the hedgerow. They must be settled down before they go back to work."

John and the farmer pulled and yanked until they got the plow upright; unhitched the horses and led them to the edge of the hedgerow in silence. After tethering the horses, the farmer sat down in the shade. John followed and sat down also.

"Your name?" asked the farmer.

"John Fetterholft."

"Your father?" the farmer asked for a measure of politeness.

"Hanns Fetterholft."

"What do your parents do?"

"Raise chickens and eggs to sell."

"Sounds right."

"Casper Messner is my name. My wife is Hanna and we have three children - Rose, Ann, and William. We have run this farm since I left my father's farm up the valley further. What do you think you are going to do now, John?"

"I'm looking for Penns Woods and the Dutch that are supposed to have a settlement there. I would like to find work and live there," expressed John.

"There are many settlements, and this is Penns Woods. You are here, boy. What kind of work can you do?"

"I can take care of livestock, and I work iron."

"Black smithing? You are a blacksmith? the farmer asked with delight.

"No, not really a blacksmith. I can work iron to make nails, hooks, hinges for doors, forks, handles, pans, buckets, tack for horses and other things," said John.

"Sounds like black smithing to me. Do you have any tools with you?"

"No, I couldn't take them into the Army."

"Here comes Rose with my midday meal," said the farmer.

John could see a 12- or 13-year-old girl carrying a basket coming towards them across the field. She had long blond hair in a long braid. She wore a blue and white polka dot dress with a cream apron. John thought she would be a pretty woman as she approached.

"Hello, Papa," Rose said in a utterly delightful female voice as she came near.

"What do you have for me?" asked Casper.

"Pickled pig feet, a crock of beans, bread, and Penna Royal Tea."

"Hope you brought enough to share with my new friend, John."

"I'll fetch more Papa, if you want."

As this smiling girl gave the basket to her father, he said, "This is my daughter, Rose. This is John from Hesson Deutschland."

She looked at John, smiled, and said "Welcome."

John rose, and stood straight, bowed from the waist and spoke  Thank you' in his own tongue and was understood.

A long silence lingered between them as they stood there and looked into each others eyes.

"Want a pig knuckle?" broke in Casper.

With embarrassment, Rose and John blushed. They acted like the moment had not happened.

"Well do you? Here, catch," said Casper as he flipped the pickled pig knuckle to John.

John caught it and began hungrily eating the sweet-sour meat off the bones.

"Bread?" said Casper as he flipped John a piece of bread. That was gone in an instant too and John was back sucking the pig knuckle for anything that was left. "How long since you ate?"

"Three days ago I ate some hickory nuts. I ate birch bark ever since."

"Tell mother we have company for supper. We'll bring the team in early. Finish these beans and give the basket to Rose. Then you can help me get the team to work," barked Casper.

The beans were gone in two spoonfuls. John put the bowl into the basket and handed it to Rose. She took the basket in her hand. She looked longingly up to John. He's so tall, she thought, and pretty!

Casper was working the horses up to the plow as the horses stood solemnly still, waiting to do their work.

"You ever do any plowing, John?"

"No."

"You will learn today and earn your supper."

John smiled and enthusiastically said, "Yes sir."

Casper set the plow and smacked his lips twice. Instantly, the horses moved slowly and surely along the row. Casper explained to John as he walked along how to hold the reins, the plow, and the commands for the horses. After two furrows across the field, Casper said, "Ready to try it?"

"Ready," John said eagerly.

John took the reins and got behind the plow. He smacked his lips twice. The horses' ears went back and forth but they stood still.

"Order them again, and slap the reins on their rumps very gently."

"Smack, Smack," and off they went.

The first furrow was a little crooked. The second was much better. By the fourth furrow, it was almost straight. At the end of the fifth furrow, Casper said, "I'm going to sit under that tree; you keep going."

John's furrows were getting pretty straight, and the horses were responding to his commands very well.

He liked plowing. It was hard work but it was also gratifying.

Casper was watching John from the shade of the tree. This boy caught on to plowing pretty quick. He was a smart and strong boy. He wondered what the boy went through walking all the way from Trenton to these valleys. It really took a lot of courage and determination. He works iron, so he says. I'll have to talk to Hanna, and maybe he'll want to work here for his keep. I could use another strong hand for the heavy lifting and taking care of stock. He's got the furrows nice and even now. Casper was deep in thought when John pulled the team to a stop.

"This field is finished," boasted John.

"So it is, John. You have done well. Let me pull the blade, and we'll go to the next field. That won't take so long. It's a small field."

They went around the hedge row to a smaller field when Casper set the blade into the rich soil ."I'll take the plow for awhile. You rest by the hedge row. I'll let you finish the field," said Casper.

John sat watching the smooth slow turning of the soil and the effortless way Casper handled the plow and team. John noted how he held the reins, the plow, and the way he tilted the plow for the horses to pull the plow around.

Casper stopped the horses and motioned John over to take the plow.

The sun was getting low as they approached the barn. A little boy about five and a girl about seven were feeding the chickens as they came by the barnyard.

"Good evening, Father. Good evening, John," they said.

"Good evening, children," acknowledged Casper.

It was a good barn, John noted as they went in. Stalls were strong with plenty of hay for the stock. There were three cows, one calf, seven sheep, three goats, and three horses. One of the horses was a riding mare; gray with dark spots. This farmer is rich, John thought as they closed the stall behind the horses.

"You can help me feed and water the stock before we wash up for supper," said Casper.

"I will be happy to," responded John.

While they were slopping the hogs, Rose came from the house with two big cloths and a big chunk of soap. She put them on a bench behind the house, with two buckets of water.

"Let's go wash up," said Casper.

John thought he had died and gone to Heaven. He washed up, down, around, and over with a promise of a good supper. He wanted to make a good impression.

"Take your boots off, John. No boots are allowed in the house. Put them here with mine in the shanty," Casper said.

Casper and John walked from the shanty to the kitchen; a beehive of activity, Hanna was buzzing around getting the food and table ready for supper. As John and Casper went to the table, John saw Hanna and the children give a quick shy glance as they passed through the kitchen to the big table.

Casper pointed to the chair next to his left against the wall. "Sit there."

"Thank you," John said.

The children brought bowls and platters of sliced meat, potatoes, pickles, beans, red beets, and cabbage.

They also brought a big plate of butter and a large tray of sliced thick bread. John had to sit on his hands for fear he would lose his head and gobble all the food up. It smelled so good, it made his head swim.

Finally, they were all seated. William was seated to his left. Hanna was at the opposite end of the table from Casper. Ann was opposite William, and Rose was to her Father's left opposite John.

"Family, this is John. He comes from Hesson. This is William, Hanna, my wife, and Ann. You met Rose."

As Casper spoke their names, John nodded to each except when he came to Rose. His mind went blank as he looked into her blue eyes.

"Let us pray." Casper's prayer seemed very long.

Plates were passed, and they began their meal. John didn't notice anything as he devoured what was on his plate. When he looked up, everyone was looking at him. They had just begun, and John's plate was clean.

Hanna broke the silence. "You must have another plate full. Hand it to me." John nodded as he handed his plate to her. "When did you last eat, John?" said Hanna.

"Three days ago until we shared my lunch," spoke up Casper, "and I thought he was going to eat the bones off all the pig knuckles." He chuckled.

John's plate was back in front of him; full again. I must eat slower and be more controlled, he thought.

As they were finishing their meal, Rose went to the pantry and brought back a wonderful walnut cake.

She set it in front of her father.

"A nut cake?" Casper said, "This is not Sunday."

"But were have company," spoke up Rose. "Mama said it was proper."

"You are right, Rose," said Hanna. "But we must be careful not to spoil our guest." They all laughed.

"Fetch me plates and a knife," said Casper.

In a flash, Ann went to the kitchen and was back with six small plates, six forks, and one big knife.

As Casper cut and passed the plates with a generous portion on each, John couldn't help wondering at the wonders of this rich farmer. He must be very smart and worked very hard to have so much. The cake was very good, and John was stuffed. This was the first really good meal since he left home last year. The children started to clean the table, taking the few leftovers to the kitchen.

"We will take a little walk," Casper said to John. Out by the barn, Casper said, "Would you like to sleep in the hayloft tonight? We can talk more tomorrow."

"Yes, I would, thank you," John said sincerely.

"I will be coming at first light to feed and water the stock and also milk the cows."

"May I help then if you please?" asked John.

"Of course. It's getting quite dark now so get a good night's sleep. I'll see you in the morning," said Casper.

As Casper walked to his cozy house and family, John could feel the homesickness deep in his belly. How good he had life then. His own family was much like this one. Adventure was not what he expected. John crawled up into the hay and in nothing flat, he was sound asleep.

After the children had gone to bed, Casper and his wife were sitting beside the fireplace resting from the work of the day. Hanna had some sewing on her lap. Casper was smoking his clay pipe.

"What do you think of our visitor, Hanna?"

"He sure can eat a lot."

"He's been living off the land since Christmas. The last three days, just birch bark," mused Casper.

"Birch bark? Not much nourishment in that."

"He deserted from the Hesson Army when the Colonists caught his group sleeping in Trenton last Christmas. During the attack, John ran up the river; must have been the Delaware. He had heard of the Dutch settlements in Penns Woods and decided to look for them. Poor fellow, all he knew they were somewhere Northwest. He didn't even know he was here."

"How did he come to you, Casper?"

"I was plowing the big field when the plow hit a rock and knocked the plow over. The horses bolted, and I got tangled in the reins and the horses started running. I was being dragged when the team stopped and this boy was between them holding their heads down pulling on their bridles. I thought I was done for until he stopped the team."

"He saved you from being dragged by the team? That was a very brave thing to do," said Hanna.

"I guess it was, now that I think about it. He seems like a smart and strong boy. I got him behind the plow for awhile, and he caught on fast. The first furrows were a little ragged, but when he finished the little field he was going along very good. I wonder, would he like to stay awhile? He says he can work iron. Maybe he could work some iron and help with the summer work for his keep. What do you think, Hanna?"

"Well, you sure have a lot of work, and I can see how tired you are from all this work to keep our farm going. I know you would appreciate the help. He does eat a lot, and where would he sleep? Do you think he would do it?"

"I don't know, maybe we could close up the old sheep shed. We just store hay in there now. We could put a door on it, and close the boards come Fall."

"Come Fall?" exclaimed Hanna. "I don't think he'll stay that long."

"He might, yes, he might," mused Casper. "Maybe you didn't notice our little Rose. She already has a crush on our visitor."

"She's too young. She only became a woman last month. No, no, she's too young."

"You didn't tell me she became a woman," exclaimed Casper. "When were you going to tell me, Hanna?"

"After this month if she had her time again. Sometimes, the first time is too early, and it doesn't happen again for three or four months again. We'll see, but she is too young for a man just now."

"Well, Hanna, do you remember you had just turned 15 when you were with me the first time."

"Shush, not so loud. The children may still be awake," Hanna said as she blushed. It made Casper feel good to know she could still blush as he sat there smiling and remembering.

"Besides," broke in Hanna, "I was 16 and a half when I got pregnant with Rose."

"Yes, I remember, very well my sweet Hanna. Now I think it's time for bed."

John woke up from a sound sleep to the chirping of robins and other birds just before dawn. As he stretched, he could see just a faint light in the sky through the breaks in the boards. It feels like it will be a good day, he thought. He decided to get up and make his way down the ladder. As he got to the last rung of the ladder, he heard the door to the house close. Casper was coming out to the barn. John met him by the barn door.

"Sleep good, John?"

"I really did; didn't wake up until just a few minutes ago," said John.

The light was coming on fast. "It's almost light enough to start the feeding," said Casper. "John, will you go over to the sheep shed, and let the sheep out to the pasture? Then help me feed, water, and put hay in the stalls. I'm going to bring the cows and horses to the pasture."

"Yes, sir," and John was off to the sheep shed.

By the time the sun popped over the mountain, all the morning work was finished.

"Ready for breakfast, John?"

"I sure am," expressed John.

"Let's go; breakfast should be ready by now."

As they entered the kitchen, great smells almost overwhelmed John. He saw ham, eggs, potatoes, and bread on the table.

After prayer, they settled in for breakfast. Hanna passed cups of a black brown brew, steaming hot.

"What's this?" asked John.

"Coffee - we roast acorns and ground them up."

John took a sip. "Ugh, it's bitter."

"You must put sugar in it, silly," quipped Rose. John did feel silly as everyone chuckled.

"It takes awhile to get used to coffee," said Hanna. "We all like it. You'll get used to it too, in time."

After breakfast, John and Casper were walking from the house towards the barn. Hanna was watching them walk together. "I think your father found a son for the time being," Hanna said to Rose.

"I hope Father likes him," added Rose.

82

"Do you like him, Rose?"

"Yes, Mama."

"You know you are too young for a man, Rose. Your time will come before you are ready."

"When would I be ready, Mama?"

"You'll know before I do, Rose."

"I feel I'm ready now, Mama."

"Rose! You have not developed enough! Your breasts are just beginning to grow. Now, that's enough talk. We have work to do."

As John and Casper walked along, John was the first to break the silence. "I guess I'll have to get my gear together and move along before I wear out my welcome."

"Don't be in such a hurry. Stay awhile. You can work with me for your keep. Do you like this idea, John?"

"Well, yes. For how long?"

"Maybe until we plant the crops or even until we finish the harvest. Maybe you'll do some black smithing too. Shoot! You can even show me a little smithing."

John was flattered with the offer. He would have very good food, and warm hay to sleep in. The work wasn't that hard. "Yes sir, I'd be glad to show you some smithing but I do not have an anvil, tongs, and hammer. I could make the tools if I had an iron plate and hammer."

"It's settled then. You'll stay awhile. We'll make a trip to Dauphin on the river and order a hammer, an anvil, and some iron. Now! We have two more fields to plow before supper. John, will you bring the work horses down from the pasture and harness them for the plow?"

"Yes sir," said John.

John was enjoying the plowing about midday when he noticed Casper waved to him. When he got to the end of the row, he stopped the team.

Casper shouted, "Unhitch the team and bring them over to the hedge row to graze." As John was leading the team to the hedge row, he noticed a small figure coming toward them from the far end of the field. "Here comes our midday meal," said Casper. "Let's take the horses down to the creek. Rose will know where we are going. We can wash up, and the horses need watering."

Rose caught up to them by the stream, hot and sweaty from the long walk from the house. "Here's your lunch, Papa. Yours too, John," she said as she set the basket down. John watched her turn and go to the stream. She kneeled down and splashed water on her face and arms to cool off. She turned and gave John a pretty smile.

Casper poked John in the ribs. "Time to eat, not look at girls." John blushed and dug into the basket.

Rose came up from the stream wet and refreshed. The men were busy eating lunch. Rose said to John,

"Mama says you'll be staying awhile. I'm glad. Papa needs help with the farm."

"Is that all you are interested in? Having help with the summer work?" teased Casper. "I'll bet there are a couple of other good reasons you would want John to stay."

"Mama said it would be good if John would show you how to work iron. She needs lots of things for the house."

"Mother always needs lots of things," mumbled Casper.

"What kind of things does your mother need?" asked John.

"We have a kettle with one handle off, and it's hard to move it when its hot and our flat pan is cracked so we can't fill it full or food runs out into the fire. We don't have a big spoon except a wooden one and a big fork too and hooks to hold meat and the rods in our butcher block are loose and meat falls down between the wood and ..."

"That's enough. You'll go on all day with what you don't have. We'll get to it when we get the iron. She's just like her mother - always needing something."

"Oh, Papa!" Rose said as she was gathering up the baskets.

"When we get the fire pit set up, I'll ask you to bring me things to fix," said John.

"Oh, John, you make me so happy. I'll hurry and tell Mama." She turned and started across the field.

John watched her every step as she walked away.

"She's not a woman yet, John," said Casper. "Do I have your word you will be a gentleman during this difficult time in Rose's life?"

"I don't know exactly what you mean," said John.

"John, I can see you looking at Rose, and Rose being thrilled with you. I don't want you taking advantage of her."

"I still don't understand," said John.

"Fadumpt!" Casper expressed. Still this bright boy didn't understand. How can I tell him? "You will not be with my daughter like man and wife until she is a woman and the proper arrangements have been made!" shouted Casper.

John sat there stunned. All he could say was "Yes sir." Why did he think I would do such a thing, John thought.

Casper, still red in the face, was looking down at the creek at the horses grazing.

John stood up straight and said, "Sir, I have not or will not be with your daughter as man and wife. I have not done so to this time, and I do not expect I will until it is time and proper. I'm sorry if I caused you concern but you have my word. I will be a gentleman. Should any condition change in this matter, you will be the first to know!"

Casper, slowly getting to his feet, stuck out his hand to John and solemnly they shook hands.

"Thank you, John," muttered Casper.

It was Tuesday morning. The fields were plowed and planted. May was a changeable month. A light drizzle was promising a foul day - all day.

"Today, we hitch the wagon and go down to Dauphin," spoke up Casper after breakfast.

"Don't forget my peppermint stick," spoke up William.

Casper held up his hand. "I know, I know. I have the whole list of wants in my head. I'll get what I can. Where's John and Rose?"

"They went out to hitch up the horse, and I'm a little worried, Casper," Hanna said with a frown.

"What about, Hanna?" Casper replied.

"John," Hanna answered.

"Don't worry sweet, John promised as a gentlemen he will be proper," Casper said.

"He did?" questioned Hanna.

"Yes, and we shook hands on it - a gentlemen's agreement," Casper added.

"Well, Rose didn't, and she's got the biggest crush on that boy you'll never see again!" Hanna said.

"I trust him, Hanna. He must have come from a very fine family. He has honor you know, I don't think he's ever had a woman."

"That's a blessing. Are you sure, Casper?" Hanna asked.

"I'm sure! We'll be back by supper, Hanna. If we are late, we'll be along soon."

Casper kissed his wife and went out the door. What he saw next was not what he expected. John was standing up against the wagon standing full upright. Rose was pressed against him trying to pull John's head down to her.

86

"Rose!" Casper bellowed. "Get in the house."

Rose broke away and ran past her father and into the house. "Sir, sir, I'm sorry. I didn't, I didn't, sir. I'm sorry but I didn't, sir?" John said.

"I know, John, and thank you for honoring our agreement," Casper replied.

John was so relieved. Whatever made Rose do this and want him to touch her, he thought. "I'm sorry, sir," John said after he had composed himself.

"John, it wasn't your fault. I'll have to talk to Rose. Now, we must get going if we want to get back by supper," Casper answered.

John was not about to miss one of Hanna's suppers so they were off down the road to Dauphin. Dauphintown was a sleepy village on the banks of the mighty Susquehanna River named after the Indian tribes that had made their homes along it and its tributaries.

"They were called Susquehannocks. Many still live in the valleys and mountains. Some have married into whites but most folks don't like it. Most folks don't like the Indians in general even though they were here first. Their part of a trading nation called Alquinquin and it goes all the way up North to the French settlement. For thousands of years, they traded along this river," Casper answered.

"Did you ever see any of these Susquehannock Indians?" asked John.

"Oh yes, they travel though for the most part they hunt through the land. They are mostly peaceful but a dirty lot if you hear Hanna tell it," Casper admitted.

"Do they talk Deutsch?" asked John.

"No, that's the problem. They talk their own ancient language and only a few people have been able to understand it so we use sign language," Casper told John.

Bing, bing, bing, bing.' John's head came up. He heard a hammer on an anvil. He smelled stinky hot iron. He thought of home and blacksmith sounds - great sounds. He was hearing his calling.

"This is John from Hesson Deutschland," said Casper introducing John to the blacksmith. "And this is Tom Muller." Tom stuck out his hand to John, and they shook. "John works iron, and will need a few things," said Casper.

"What will you need?" questioned Tom.

"A hammer, anvil, and iron to work," said John.

"Is that all?" asked Tom.

"Yes, I can make the rest," said John in a meek manner.

"He must be a good blacksmith for so young," expressed Tom.

"I'm not so good. I'm still learning. I did make some nice things for my parents in Hesson. They liked what I made," said John.

"I have a nice anvil over here. What size hammer do you want?" Tom questioned.

"This is good," John said picking one up from the bunch where a dozen or more hammers were.

"That's a heavy one!" exclaimed Tom. "Can you handle it?"

"I think so," said John.

"How much iron do you want?" asked Tom.

"That's up to Casper," said John.

"How much is this pile?" asked Casper.

"Fifty cents," Tom replied.

"How much is the hammer and anvil?" Casper questioned.

"Two dollars," Tom said.

"I'll give you one dollar and 25 cents!" Casper said.

"Make it two dollars, and we have a deal," Tom answered.

"One dollar and fifty cents. That's final and you reshoe the horse," said Casper.

"Aw, heck! You always get me, Casper. Dollar and 50 cents it is, and I'll reshoe the horse," Tom replied.

"Done," said Casper as he reached into his shirt and pulled out a pocketbook.

After he paid Tom, Casper and John went over to the General Store. On the porch of the store, there were four funny-looking fellows just sitting on the porch.

"Who are those fellows?" asked John.

"Susquehannock Indians. No use talking to them. They don't understand you and don't want to. All they want to do is hunt, fish, and make the women pregnant. They steal too. If you didn't see them take it, they consider you lost it, and they found it. Sometime back, two mountains to the North near a town called Loylton, a Farmer and his family had a run-in with the local Indians. One morning, they burned him and his family out and then killed them all. So don't cross them. They can be vicious," said Casper.

The store was well stocked with goods, John could see. One man seemed to run it. Two ladies were helping other ladies with cloth. "John, this is Fred Bender. Fred, this is John. He'll be staying with us for a while," said Casper.

"Welcome to the valley, John. Where did you come from?" asked Fred.

"Hesson," John answered.

"Where?" Fred wanted to know.

"Hesson, Deutschland. It's a long story, Fred," said Casper. "I'll tell you sometime when we have more time. John, go back to the blacksmith's shop and make sure Tom shoes my horse right. Might as well load the iron and bring the wagon over to the store."

"Why did you snap Fred off when Hesson came up?" asked John when they were about a mile out of town on their way home.

"He's English. Didn't you notice his accent?" Casper replied.

"He did sound funny," remarked John.

"You can't trust the English. They would turn you over to the English, the Hesson Army or the Colonists, whoever would pay the most money," Casper said.

"He seemed so friendly," said John.

"Sheep in wolf's clothing," mumbled Casper

It was dark and the moon came up, giving them just enough light to make it home nicely. As they pulled up to the barn, Hanna and Rose came to meet them.

"Everything go all right?" asked Hanna.

"Everything is all right," answered Casper. "Everything all right with the homestead?"

"Yes, Papa," answered Rose. "Did you remember William's peppermint?" asked Rose.

"Honey, we got it all," said Casper as he got down from the wagon. "Unhitch the horse, John. She'll go into her stall by herself, and we'll put the wagon away tomorrow. All we'll take off the wagon are the things that go into the house."

"How much flour did you bring?" asked Hanna.

"Two bags - 200 pounds," said Casper.

"How much sugar?"

"One hundred pounds," Casper answered.

"Salt?"

"One hundred pounds."

"Casper, we are going to need at least 100 pounds more salt to butcher this fall," exclaimed Hanna.

"I know. We can get it when we go to town again. It was enough to pull for the horse. Remember, John was also with me," replied Casper.

"Oh yes, I forgot," said Hanna.

"Hand this bag down to Rose, John. She can take that into the house. Here, Hanna take these. John and I will bring the rest."

Hanna and Rose liked the clothes Casper brought. They were very surprised when they opened a little wooden box. It was full of handmade mother-of-pearl buttons.

"Tomorrow, we'll pull the wagon around to the old sheep shed to unload the iron. Hanna, we got John an anvil, hammer, and iron to work. This boy's first job will be to do the repairs to your kitchen."

"I have a long list for John," popped up Rose.

"I bet you do," quipped Hanna.

"Oh, Mama."

John looked over to Rose and smiled. She is beginning to show womanhood, he thought. I gave my word to Casper. I'm determined to honor it. It's been a hard time since I left Hesson so this is not so difficult. I can wait until the right time. I know I can do this, John thought.

"Time for bed, Rose," spoke up Casper.

"Good night, Mama. Good night, Papa and good night, John."

There was no mistaking her last good night to John, and they all knew it.

"Don't worry," John said to Hanna when Rose was out of earshot. "I'll honor our agreement."

"I hope you can," breathed Hanna.

"See you in the morning, boy," said Casper as John went out the door to his hay pile.

When Casper went out to the barn at daybreak, John was busy stacking rocks to make a fire pit.

"You're up early, John," said Casper.

"The stock is watered and fed," grunted John as he placed a large flat rock on top of the neatly piled rocks. John's fire pit would consist of flat shale stones piled in a neat circle. Then John just placed a flat and thick rock on top, forming sort of a table. Now he placed stones around the rim, leaving a hole here and there at the base for draft.

"Looks like a pretty nice fire pit. Different from the blacksmiths down in Dauphin," said Casper.

"This is the way we made them in Hesson. They seem to work well." John's voice trailed off as Rose came out of the house to come to the barn to do the milking.

Casper turned around to see what had gotten John's attention. He didn't have to look at them twice to know John would have to try real hard to keep his word and wait until Rose was old enough.

After breakfast, Casper and John finished the fire pit.

"We need a timber to mount the anvil," spoke up John.

"I know just the timber," said Casper. "It's down in the hedge row by the stream. We'll hitch the wagon up to go down to cut off what you will need. I'll get the buck saw, and you get the wagon ready."

Soon they were bouncing  along the edge of the field, toward the hedge row. They turned along the creek and stopped to water the horse.

"Wheat is coming up nice," muttered Casper. "Need rain soon."

"What's that," exclaimed John.

"Looks like Indians. Three or four. One's a woman. Wonder what they want?"

"Can you talk to them?" asked John.

"Sometimes they will talk. Sometimes they just steal something and run. Well, we'll soon find out. Here they come."

John and Casper pulled the wagon out of the stream and sat in the wagon watching the slow progress of the Indians as they plodded up on the bank along the stream.

John began to feel uneasy as they came closer. The oldest Indian looked grim and fierce. The next one looked fierce too. He was about John's age, he thought. The other was just a boy 10 or 12 years old. The girl was fully a woman - 19 or 20 with black eyes and long black hair. She looked sad as she followed the men. They stopped across the stream opposite the wagon.

"Good day," said Casper as he raised his hand in peace.

"Good day, Casper," spoke the Indian.

"Tongo? Tongo, is that you?" asked Casper.

"Yes, my friend," said Tongo as he started across the creek.

Casper jumped down from the wagon and met Tongo halfway across the stream. "How are you, Casper?" asked Tongo after a big bear hug.

"Fine, fine, and you, Tongo?"

"Many troubles as many children," replied Tongo.

They both had a good laugh and agreed.

As the two men came to the wagon, Casper said to John. "This is Tongo, my friend. We were children together up the valley further when I lived with my father and mother. We hunted, fished, and fought together, and I always won."

"No you didn't!" said Tongo. "Only when I let you. What happened to you, Casper? You got so old."

"So did you. What brings you down the valley this far, Tongo. I know you never liked settlements and white people."

Tongo half turned toward the woman. "My daughter married a Carlile, and she gave him this son. Then she could give no more sons, and he would beat her and go to another woman. I came across the Susquahanna to bring her home. Now she will live with our people."

"Will you stay with us for the night, Tongo?"

"No, my friend. We will try to make it home by nightfall. My wife will be waiting now five days, and I am anxious to be in my own lodge."

"I understand," said Casper. "Let's hunt together sometime, Tongo."

"The morning of the first frost, we will meet by the fork in this stream by your father's farm," said Tongo.

"Yes," replied Casper. "We will meet then."

When the Indians were out of sight up the stream, Casper said, "He and I will always be blood brothers."

"What's a blood brother?" asked John.

"We each cut our thumb and mixed our blood when we were about eight or nine. Now we honor that time. We will always honor that time," said Casper.

"Where is that timber?" broke in John.

"Up here on the left. We'll need to cut if off the height you will want it."

After they found the ancient oak which had fallen from a storm a year or two ago, they picked out a section along the trunk and began sawing. After much sweating, sawing, and lifting, they finally got a 4 1/2 foot section into the wagon. That was hard work, thought John. I'm glad Casper is a strong man. John couldn't help but admire Casper.

It was well past noon when John and Casper pulled up by the sheep shed. Hanna, Rose, and the children came out to meet them.

"You were gone a long time, Casper," scolded Hanna. "You didn't tell us where you were going. We didn't know where to take your lunch. Are you two hungry, now?"

"We sure are, Hanna," said Casper. "We'll wash up and eat here. We ran into an old friend of mine, Tongo. He was passing through to his lodge up the valley."

"I knew something held you up. I told Mama everything was all right," said Rose with relief in her voice. I'll get your dinner, Papa."

As Rose ran to the house, John could not help watching her effortless strides as her hair trailed out behind her. She seems to be growing up in front of my eyes, John thought.

After John and Casper finished their meal, they were back again wrestling the huge cut of wood off the wagon. After much grunting, sweating, and just a little swearing, the cut was firmly planted before the fire pit. Another heft on the anvil, and it was in place.

"I believe you're ready, John," beamed Casper. "What will you make first?"

"Nails, I need your heavy nails to secure the anvil. Then I imagine you could use a dozen or so."

"Those and a lot more, John."

John made a hot hardwood fire and went to the well for a bucket of water. In less than an hour, John had his anvil secure. He had taken his shirt off and hung it on a peg. Toward the end of the day, John had made twenty nails, repaired a barn hinge, fused a tine on a pitch-fork, replaced a handle on a pot and made four hooks for the kitchen. He was tired but he felt good.

"May I go down to the stream to splash off this sweat?" asked John.

"Of course, be back in time to feed and supper just before dark," said Casper.

Evening was coming on when John walked out of the cool pool of the stream. Taking his cloth off the bush it was drying on, he felt eyes watching. He had a funny feeling he wasn't alone. He looked around and saw nothing. Still he had that feeling. Walking along the field, he kept looking around but saw nothing out of place. Finally, he came to the barn. Casper was already pitching hay down from the loft.

"Good swim, John?" Casper called down.

"Fine," John answered as he put grain in the trough for the cows.

Rose looked up from her milking. "Swimming?" she asked.

"Yes, down in the big pool in the stream," said John.

"Oh, I'd love to go with you sometime. I've never been to the stream to swim," Rose said.

"You'll have to ask your Mama," said John.

Rose finished milking, gathered the buckets and started for the kitchens. Over her shoulder she said to John as she passed him, "I will, John. I surely will."

"Done feeding, John?" asked Casper.

"Yes, all are fed," said John.

"Let's go wash up," Casper said.

As they were walking to the washing bowls behind the house, John asked Casper, "Did you ever feel eyes on you when you were alone down by the stream or in the fields?"

"Yes, I have, not often but sometimes I can feel someone is watching."

"Did you ever find out who?" asked John.

"No, not really. One time I seen an Indian on the ridge so I figured it was just a passing Indian that gave me this feeling. Did that happen to you, John?"

"I felt this when I was down at the stream and again when I was walking back. I kept looking around but seen nothing unusual," said John.

During supper, Rose asked her mother, "May I go swimming with John when he goes down to the stream?"

Hanna looked stunned, not knowing how to answer. "You'll have to ask John before I can answer your question, Rose."

"Well," said Rose looking directly at John.

"If it is all right with your parents," said John.

"Your mother and I will consider it," said Casper. "We'll let you know what we decide."

"Why can't you tell me now?" whined Rose.

"Enough! We'll let you know," said Hanna.

Anna and William piped up, "We wanna go, too. We wanna go swimming, too."

"Enough I said! I told you we will let you know. Now its time to clear the dishes. Now get at it," exclaimed Hanna.

"I'm sorry," said John. "I didn't want to cause a problem."

"We could make it an outing," said Casper. "I hadn't thought to go to the creek in the hot days, and it might be fun for the whole family."

"Casper, what will the girls wear to go in the creek? Not their birthday suit like John!"

"Honey, we'll all wear something. I'll leave it up to you and Rose to work out. John, you'll have to have something on as not to embarrass the ladies."

After about a week of toiling in the fields, the blacksmith work, cleaning, cooking, and sweating on the hot days in late June, Hanna and Rose had swimming cloth made for the whole family. It was late in the afternoon when Hanna came to the barn and said, "We'll go swimming this evening. All is ready. We'll have our supper down by the creek if you and John can make a fire?"

"We can, Hanna. We can make a wonderful fire. Let's go," said Casper.

"You will have to wear this, John," said Rose. "I made it myself. I hope you like it."

"I will I'm sure." John was not so sure as he looked at the shirt and pants she had stitched together. I'll probably sink to the bottom with all this on, he thought.

"Are we ready?" asked Hanna.

As if by magic, Anna and William trooped out of the house with big baskets of food for the evening meal. John and Casper picked up the heavy baskets from the children. Hanna had a basket of swimming cloth for all but John, and down the lane toward the stream they went. It didn't take long until all were sitting, slipping, and splashing in the cool water.

Rose was being very coy moving into the deeper water when she let out a scream. Before you could blink, John was at her side lifting her out of the water. "I saw a snake, Father, or at least I think I did," Rose said as John put her down in shallow water.

Hanna and Casper looked at each other and nodded. "Um hum," they both said, together.

The summer progressed along. The wheat and oats ripened. The garden vegetables flourished and canning began. Anything with glass or crock that you could seal with beeswax was used and stored in the root cellar for the hard Penns Woods winter that was sure to come.

During the summer, the neighbors further up and down the valley brought broken items of iron for John to repair or make over. Casper delighted in being not only able to help his friends but also learning the art of iron working.

Rose was beginning to show promise of a handsome woman. By late summer, her bust was noticeable as well as the 25 pounds she put on and the three inches in height. The boys at church were asking permission to visit and to court. Casper and Hanna still thought it too soon and denied all requests. Hanna felt she needed one or two more years. Casper wasn't so sure.

Late one afternoon in August, Casper and John were making a new plow shear with two blades. Casper thought of the idea and was sure it could work well with his two stocky horses when two men came riding up to the blacksmith's pit.

"We're looking for Hesson soldiers that escaped from New Amsterdam and Trenton. Have you seen any such person?"

Casper caught on quickly. "No, my son and family have seen no such soldier in this area. If I do, do I report it to Dauphin Courthouse?"

"That's right. You do just that!" said the man as he wheeled his horse around and trotted off down the lane.

"Head hunters," growled Casper.

"What's that?" asked John.

"People that look for other people for profit," said Casper.

"Like me," said John.

"Like you, and you better be careful from now on. You can be my son for that purpose if necessary," Casper answered.

"I really appreciate the offer," expressed John, "and I will be careful."

September turned into October and the harvest was all in but not without many days of hot sweaty labor. The corn crop was the best Casper had seen in years. Only the turnips, rutabagas, parsnips, and carrots needed to be brought into the root cellar. The few pumpkins were ready though Hanna wasn't too sure what to do with this Indian fruit. Casper had gotten a few seeds from an Indian when at the Dauphin market in the spring. Now every time she split one, thousands of seeds would spill out much like the yellow squash they had gotten seeds from an Indian and the green ones too. Hanna now knew how to save the seeds and make the squash. She knew she could cook, fry, or boil the yellow meat from those big orange things. Finally, she solved the problem. She mashed it and added egg and sugar. She poured this into a flour basket, and called it pumpkin pie. This was a big hit and there was lots of it.

"Casper, when we have Harvest Home at church I'll bring the pumpkin pies and seeds for the ladies to plant for next summer," said Hanna. Casper couldn't see why she was so excited. The pie was good but why all the fuss? So he said what any man would say, "Yes, honey. If that's what you want to do."

As summer started to show signs of Fall, and the crops were full and ripe, the work of putting up the harvest had begun. John and Casper were beginning to have a problem keeping up with the black smithing. Almost every day, a neighbor or beyond would come up with any number of items to be made or repaired. Casper caught on to black smithing and was now almost as good as John. Hanna noticed they became like father and son; teasing, talking, and planning together. John even treated Rose, Anna, and William as an older brother might have. Rose didn't appreciate the sisterly image John had of her. She kept trying to change that image by doing what young ladies do to receive attention. Hanna was thankful John was a gentleman and ignored Rose's attempts or laughed them off. John didn't treat Hanna as a mother though more as a lady and always with respect. She had to admire him for that.

# SEVEN

## *Over the Mountain*

The leaves on the mountain were beginning to turn different colors; fall was upon them. It was a cool late afternoon when two riders rode up to Casper and John as they worked the corn in the little field. Casper didn't recognize either of them.

"Good afternoon," they greeted as they rode up.

"Good afternoon," repeated John and Casper.

"We are looking for a man and his son who are blacksmiths in this valley. The farmer next to you said you would know where we could find them."

Immediately, Casper was suspicious. Could these be Colonists still looking for Hesson boys after all this time?

"What do you want of them?" asked Casper.

"We have a proposition for the son if we can find him," said the man as he got down from his horse. He stepped up to Casper, thrust out his hand, and introduced himself.

"I'm Neal Nye, and this is Fred Boner," nodding towards the fellow still sitting on his horse.

As the men shook hands, Casper said, "I'm Casper Messner, and this is John."

"Looks like we found our blacksmiths," Neal said to Fred as he shook John's hand.

Casper looked puzzled. How did he know? Casper had to ask.

"How would you think we are blacksmiths?" asked Casper.

"Ha ha, that's obvious. The grip of your hands, the heavy calluses, the burn scars especially on the boy. How could you not be blacksmiths?"

"Well, you got us there," said Casper. "What kind of proposition is offered to John?"

"We're from the settlement over the mountain called Benderstettle (now Elizabethville, Pennsylvania). We lost our blacksmith this Spring. A horse he was shoeing kicked him in the head and he died. He left a widow and three children."

"Did he not have an apprentice?" asked John.

"He did for about a year. Then he left and went across the river to a village called Liverpool."

"So, what is the offer?" asked Casper.

"Well, we want to talk to you about it. We need a blacksmith that's for sure. Fred and I have been going down to Dauphin with repairs and orders, as well as others. It takes four to six weeks sometimes and still the items are not ready. Can we go to your house and discuss it?"

Casper saw a way to get some free labor as he proposed, "Help us clear this field, and we'll go in and have a nice supper. John, go tell Mama we'll have two guests for supper. Then get back here, and we'll finish the field.

John thought that crafty old fox; four more hours labor free for a supper that Hanna always made full and plenty.

After a good supper, the men went into the front parlor. John had not been in the parlor before. He knew the family would go in there on Sunday afternoons for more prayers after church and to have family talks. John had to marvel at the pretty furniture, rug on the floor, and a picture on the wall of a fierce looking family. John took a seat next to Casper. The two men sat on the settee.

"It's time to talk," began Casper.

"Yes, it's time," returned Neal.

"You can see the boy is very important to our family, and we would be disappointed to lose him," said Casper laying the ground work for a hard bargain.

"We can see that," expressed Fred looking at Neal and acknowledging they would need a good bargain to get John to Binderstettel.

Neal began, "As we said before, we lost our blacksmith. He has left a family; a handsome woman and three wonderful children. His shop is fully stocked with everything a blacksmith needs. The house is a salt box with a barn, pig shed, two cows, three horses, and a very nice hen house. It is agreed all this will be John's plus a commitment by people to bring the blacksmithing to John rather than go to Liverpool or Dauphin. He will have a wonderful house, family, and business already started. We think it is a wonderful opportunity."

"What about my family?" asked Casper.

"What are you asking?" questioned Neal.

"Cooperation," said Casper with a firm jaw.

Neal looked at Fred. Fred shrugged and looked rather stunned. A long silence followed. You could see Casper was not going to give up so easily. John was thinking, I'll take it, I'll take it and still Casper sat silent.

Finally, Neal said, "We could probably raise some kind of payment - let's say a cow and a horse."

"Make it three cows, a mare, and six pigs - five sows and one boar."

Well, Neal looked at Fred. Fred spoke up, "Two cows, a mare, three pregnant sows will be delivered next week."

Casper looked at John. John nodded. "We'll give you our answer before you leave in the morning. You can sleep in the hayloft. John will show you out."

After the men left for the barn, and the children were asleep, Casper told Hanna of the offer.

"It will break Rose's heart. She sees John as her man when she's ready. Now that he is going away, we're going to have a sad little girl," mused Hanna.

"She'll get over it," growled Casper. "Two cows, a mare, and three pregnant sows is good payment for John."

"Good payment!" exclaimed Hanna. "I'm surprised at you, Casper. It is like you own him! Would you sell me and the children if you got the chance?"

"Now, Hanna. We have an opportunity for John to be on his own and for us to profit by it too. That's good business."

The next morning, Casper agreed they had a deal providing the livestock would be delivered next week. As the men rode off Casper turned to John. "We made a good trade, John. You'll be all set up and soon a rich man. I'll have some new blood for my livestock."

"Have you ever been to Benderstettle?" asked John.

"No, my brother up the valley has. He said it's not very big as far as the town goes but many farms spread out across the valley. Two groups of Indians live further up the two valleys where the mountains form at the east end. My brother said they were friendly, though. Most of the people there talk Deutsch and English so I guess you'll learn English, too."

"I'm not anxious to leave here. You have been good to me, Casper. I feel I owe you something for your kindness and hospitality," said John.

Casper held up his hand. "Don't you ever feel you owe me or this family anything. You more than earned your keep, and I cherish your friendship. Besides, you taught me black smithing, and we started a little business too. Now I can carry it on and maybe someday, I'll have an apprentice too. I don't want to lose you too John, but it's time you make a family for yourself. I know Rose has her heart set on you but she's a good two years away from having a man and you're ready for a good woman now. It's better this way, and if you don't have a family and want Rose, you can come back for her two years from now."

"Casper, I don't know what to say. I'm off on another adventure, and don't know where it will lead me. The last adventure was a disaster. I was supposed to be back in Bot Weiser by now so I guess my family will think I was killed in the battle with the Colonists."

Casper was quiet for a bit, thinking. "Why don't you write them a letter?"

"How will they get it?" asked John.

"We'll send it with the address in German and in English. I know a woman in Dauphin that can write English."

"Do you think it will get there?" asked John.

"In six to twelve months as I've heard. The man who runs the ferry across the river wrote two letters and received one from his family in Heidelberg. So, why don't you try? I have paper, and we can have it sealed in Dauphin."

John labored on his letter for three days until he felt he had it right. He wrote it and made changes on slate until he was ready to commit it to paper. He simply explained how he got to the Colonies and was in a battle. He then left the Army, and was now living with a family in Penns Woods. He said he missed them but had very little hope of ever making it back across the big sea.

Casper read and approved the letter. "I'll have it sealed and the address made into English as well when I get to Dauphin."

As the week went by, John was busy getting his things in order. He didn't have much except the things

Hanna and Rose had made for him - three shirts, two pairs of pants, a nice coat made out of his old horse blanket, two pairs of socks, and his boots now mended with leather. He decided to leave his uniform coat which Casper gladly accepted.

The sixth day was Sunday so the work was only the chores and church. After the midday meal, Casper asked John to go with him to the barn. As they entered the barn, Casper turned to John and said, "I've got something for you to take along to remember us by." He reached under his shirt and pulled out a broad and sharp knife in a leather sheath.

John drew the knife after Casper handed it to him. "This is a magnificent knife, Casper. Thank you."

"I hope you like it, John. I made it myself."

"Great," exclaimed John. "Where did you get the idea of an upper cutting edge and so wide and strong?"

"I've been trying to get a blade that could be used for many things like chopping wood and bone, cutting up and down, and strong enough to pry. The rise to a small peak on top of the knife will allow you to withdraw the knife easily after you penetrate."

"Sure is a handsome knife. I'll bet money that anyone heading for the frontier would want one," said John.

Hanna was calling from the house. She called to John to come to the kitchen. As John came into the kitchen Hanna said, "I've got something for you to remember our family by," and she handed a cloth-wrapped package to John. When he pulled the string holding the package out rolled two round doilies. He looked surprised, "What are these?"

They are table doilies."

"What do you use them for?" asked John.

"To make a table, a server, or a lamp stand look good, John. My heaven, come with me to the parlor to see how ladies use them." Hanna took John's hand and marched him into the parlor.

"See, John. I thought these could make a nice wedding gift for your bride and something to remember our family by."

"Thank you Hanna. I hope someday to have a bride as well as a parlor. So far it doesn't look too good for either."

"Oh, John. You have your whole life ahead of you, and you'll have both and very nicely I'm sure."

John was at the blacksmith shop when little Ann and William came up to John.

"We have a going-away present for you, John," the children chorused.

John sat down on a wood stump.

"Open mine first," said William.

"No mine," said Ann.

"William, ladies before gentlemen. We men must always remember that," said John.

"Yes, us men must stick together," boasted William. "Go ahead, Ann, give John your present."

"No, you go ahead," said Ann.

"No, you go ahead," said William.

John interrupted, "All right! I'll open Ann's present first."

John slowly opened Ann's present. "I will sure be able to use this," exclaimed John. It was a bright red cloth with neat stitches around the edges. It was a sweat cloth like Casper used around his forehead when it was hot.

"Thank you, Ann," John said as he gathered her up in his arms and gave her a kiss on the cheek. When he released her, she was blushing - embarrassed and smiling. She liked John before but now she really liked him.

"Me next," said William as he handed John a folded paper.

Slowly John unfolded it. It was a drawing of the whole family with the house behind them and the barn to the right. Everyone was there including John.

"William, this is very nice. I will hang it on my wall and that way I can always be with the family," John said.

"I drew it all by myself," boasted William.

"You draw very good  William. Thank you very much." John reached out and shook William's hand.

"Us men must stick together," said John.

William stood a full inch taller as he turned to go back to the house with Ann.

After supper, John decided to take a walk. He went around the barn and down through the vegetable patch. He was walking along the meadow near the woods when he thought he heard his name called. He looked around and saw no one. He continued on in a slow walk. Again, he heard someone call. John stopped and looked around - still nothing. He turned around and started back along the meadow toward the barn. Out of the corn patch in the garden came Rose heading straight towards John.

As Rose and John walked toward each other, John noticed Rose was walking with her hands behind her back. "Good evening, John."

"Good evening, Rose," said John.

They stood about an arm's length apart in the long shadow of the trees at the edge of the meadow. They were each waiting for the other to say something, looking into each others eyes.

In a very sad voice, Rose said, "I have a gift for you, John - something to remember me by, and I hope you do remember me," Rose said as she handed John a rolled-up bundle.

John unrolled a beautiful hand-knitted scarf of wool. "This is wonderful," he muttered looking at the scarf.

John looked down to Rose as she stood there with tears streaming down her cheeks.

"Oh, John," she sobbed as she sprang forward throwing her arms around his neck. Her wet cheeks were against his cheek and neck. She kept sobbing and sobbing. After a bit, she released her arms from around John's neck and stepped back wiping her eyes with her apron.

"I'm sorry, John," she snuffled.

"That's all right, Rose. I'm sad to leave you and the family, too, but I think its better that I do," John answered.

"When I'm old enough, I am going to Benderstettle for you. John, I'm going to come to you," said Rose.

"When you're old enough, Rose, you'll have long forgotten me and have so many  beaus, you won't have time for me," John said.

"Oh, John, don't say that," she said half turning away. Rose didn't want to show her unhappiness.

"Come on, Rose! I'll race you to the tomato patch." Hanna smiled as she looked through the kitchen window at the two of them racing from the meadow toward the vegetable garden. She saw John shorten his stride, and with a few stumbles allowed Rose to get ahead of him as they came to the edge of the tomato patch.  They stopped and laughed and pushed each other. They leisurely walked along the rows of tomatoes toward the house catching their breath. Rose will make a pretty woman. It was too bad John is too old for her but she will find another.

About midday, the next day the two men from Benderstettle came up the lane with the promised livestock in tow. Behind their wagon was an extra gray stallion with full saddle and saddle bags.

The whole family came out to meet them at the watering trough by the barn.

"We brought along one of your horses, John. We are in hopes you will be going back with us," said Neal.

"I'm packed and ready to go," said John.

"Gentlemen," Hanna spoke up, "We have your midday meal ready. When you have your bellies full, you can make your trip over the mountain. Besides, John needs his last meal on our farm. Heaven knows if he ever will be back again."

Rose turned and ran into the house. Everyone knew tears had come. John felt a little sad he made Rose feel so bad. He made up his mind to say something nice before he left.

After a great meal, the family gathered once again to see John off. As John swung up on his horse, he tipped his hat and said, "I hope you will come and visit sometime. I do thank you for your kindness and understanding." John leaned forward and shook Casper's hand. Then he turned to face Rose. "I won't forget you, Rose."

They took a long look at each other, then Rose said, "Neither will I." She turned and ran into the house.

About 3 P.M., the three men were at the foot of the mountain that separated the valleys. John wondered if the horses could pull up the short but steep mountain. The wagon path wasn't much of a road but up they went anyway. It took over an hour to make it to the top. There they stopped to give the horses a rest. This is a beautiful valley, John thought. Directly below, there was Benderstettle. To the left, not too far was another small village. The road continued on to another small village by the river. John could see another mountain way across the valley to the north. Straight across from Benderstettle at the foot of the mountain was another small settlement. To the east, a U-shaped mountain came down part of the way in the valley forming two valleys. Another village was nestled in the little valley to the east. It looked like Benderstettle was at the crossroads.

After a drink from an ice-cold spring, they started down the steep and curvy wagon trail. It didn't take nearly as long to go down as it did to go up. The sun was well to the west as they entered the little settlement of Benderstettle; a pleasant, well laid out little village.

"This town was named after John Bender. He laid out the lots and streets. Some of his children still live here," mused Neal. "You'll meet them all for we have a small and friendly town here."

"I'm glad to hear that," expressed John.

The three men rode up to the blacksmith's shop which was all dark and empty.

"This your shop, John. Do you want to look it over before we introduce you to the widow?"

"Yes, I think so," said John as he swung off his horse. It is a big shop, he thought, with lots of iron and tools, three big anvils, and two fire pits. It was the biggest and best equipped shop John had ever seen. He knew he could make the anvils ring. He swung up on his horse. "I'm now anxious to get to work," said John.

"Not until we introduce you to the widow. I'll bet she has a good supper waiting too," said Neal as he started down the street.

As they approached the house of the widow, John noticed how pleasant the little house looked. It was made of log and field stone with two large windows facing the road. Two large oaks were on either side of the wagon path leading to the barn in the rear. As the men rounded the house, John could see livestock on the sloping meadow that had a sizable stream running down the center before the meadow rose to a gentle rounded ridge. This is a very pleasant place, John thought. Flowers in flower boxes and along the path to the rear door of the house gave an orderly, lived-in appearance.

They hitched the horses to the barnyard fence and proceeded to the house. The back door opened. Three children filed out; a boy and two girls. They were followed by a short, round and almost homely woman dressed in a long black dress. They all stopped halfway to the house. After a long silence and looking at each other, John stuttered, "I'm John, John ah John Fetterholft," feeling foolish and probably looking that way.

The widow had a stern look as well as the children. John tried to smile and then there was another silence. The three men felt awkward; just standing there. They were waiting for the widow to say something.

Finally, she said, "Thought he was older. He's just a boy," she spat.

"I thought we told you he was young. He is a good blacksmith, and a bachelor," said Neal.

"You didn't tell me he was that young, and he can't be much of a blacksmith. He's got no experience. No, he just won't do. He'll never be able to support me and my children. You'll have to look for a better man than this boy."

"I wouldn't know where to look, Mary. This boy is all we could find, and he is a good blacksmith. I've seen his work," said Neal.

"Well," Mary said, looking John up and down. He is nice looking, she thought except for the big nose. Mary stepped up to John. "I'm Mary Bender," reaching out her right hand.

"I'm John Fetterholft," as they shook hands.

"John, I'll give you a chance to show me if you can do the job. Thank you, gentlemen," Mary said as she nodded to the other two men.

"This is Susan, Elizabeth, and Luke," Mary said as they turned to go into the house. "I have a nice supper for you, John. The wash basin is on the bench and the pump is on the side of the house. After you have washed up, come in the back door."

She must be a good cook. It sure smells good, John thought as he was washing up. Luke came out of the back door with a drying cloth and handed it to John.

"Supper sure smells good," said John.

"Mom's cooking beans with ham," volunteered Luke. "Do you like beans and ham? I hate beans but I love ham especially with honey on it. Mom says come on. We're waiting."

"I'm ready," said John as they headed for the kitchen door.

"Sit there, John," instructed Mary, "to the head of the table." The children were seated, and the children sat at the opposite end of the table. After prayers and beans, ham, and bread were passed around, the meal began.

"Are you going to be our new papa?" asked Luke.

"Shush!" barked Mary. "These are not questions that should be asked by you, children. We'll let you know in good time."

After supper, Mary asked John to help her with the livestock, feeding, and watering. When they were finished, she came to John and said, "Our house is small, and we only have two bedrooms - one for the children and one for me. You can bed down out here in the barn or the kitchen floor. It may not always be this way but for now it has to be. I would prefer you stay in the barn while it's still warm enough this Fall."

"I understand, ma'am. I'll do my best to support you and your children. I'm very grateful for your offer."

"Where did you come from, John?"

"Hesson Bot Weiser."

"From Deutschland? How did you get here?"

"I came as a Hesson soldier, and I stayed."

Mary looked at him with a hard look. "Stayed or ran away? Ran away I'd say."

John was humiliated because he was not being all together truthful. "I ran because I was scared. The Colonists were shooting everyone, so I ran. I'm not proud of it but I did it."

"John," Mary said with compassion. "We'll not mention it again, and I don't think you need to tell anyone. As far as folks around here, you're from Armstrong Valley. Now, if you think you can be comfortable here, I'll bid you good evening. I'll call from the kitchen when breakfast is ready. That will be at daybreak."

The next few days were very busy. John was getting acquainted with the shop, the folks in town, and his new family. He realized that he and Mary would not ever be like man and wife. She must be at least 30 years old, he thought. She was not a handsome woman either and was too bossy. She did make the children walk a straight line. John was just as happy to stay in the barn for the time being.

As days went into weeks, John fell into the routine of everyday black smithing. He was surprised to find so many customers from all over the valley coming to buy and repair items. When he saw the price list for items and repairs, he had serious doubts whether anyone would pay these prices. That doubt was put aside. Not only would folks pay the prices asked but would pay extra to get the repair done right away. It took no time for John to realize that if a man came in with a horse to be shoed, he would pay a gold coin to have his horse finished while he got his supplies at the general store.

It was late October when John began to realize he may not be able to take the cold nights much longer. He was going to have to find better lodging soon. He knew he didn't want to stay in the house with Mary and the children. Not knowing what to do about it, he decided to talk with Mary.

"Mary, with winter coming on I won't be able to stay in that drafty old barn for long."

"I was expecting that," snapped Mary.

"I think I'll look around town for a room or something. Maybe there's a little house for rent. Do you know of any?" asked John.

With a softer tone, Mary said, "I was thinking you were making a hint to come in the house. I'm glad you want your own place. I'll help you get settled if I can."

"I would appreciate anything you can do for me," said John.

"Now let me think," mused Mary. "I think old Mrs. Stutzman might have a room, or even the Meinharts' might have a room. I know! There is an old abandoned farm near Wiconisco Creek on the back road. The barn isn't much, and the fields haven't been worked for many years, but I'll bet the house is sound. That could be a very nice place for you, John. The children and I will help you make it liveable."

"Good," said John in an excited voice. "Let's go over and take a look at it."

"After you close the shop tomorrow," said Mary, "the children and I will pick you up in the buckboard. We'll eat a picnic supper on the way."

"Wonderful! Wonderful! I'll call it a night. See you at breakfast."

"Good night, John."

John had a hard time sleeping. Finally letting Mary know he was not moving in took pressure off of both of them. The fact that Mary and the children would help him get settled in his own place was also good. He was a little concerned as to how he could keep two homes going. He needed to talk to Mary about it, but lets see what this abandoned farm looked like. He wondered if the well was good.... and finally sleep came.

"We'll need to talk about how we divide the funds to keep both homes going," said John at breakfast.

"John! We'll talk about this later."

"Yes, ma'am."

When the sun was about three-quarters down, Mary and the children pulled up to the blacksmith shop.

"Ready, John," Luke called.

"Not just yet! I've got one horse to shoe. It will take me a few minutes," said John.

"Stay in the wagon, children. John will come when he is finished. John, I'll pull the wagon on the side.

Come when you are ready!"

It didn't take long. John was anxious to get going. Soon they were making their way down the back road along Wiconisco Creek.

The house did look sturdy as they pulled up the lane from the main road. It was an old log cabin with a log and mortar fireplace. As Mary had said, the barn wasn't much. It was hard to tell there were ever any fields from where John was sitting.

"Whoa," Mary called to the horse.

"You just stay in the wagon, children. John and I will see if snakes are inside," chirped Mary.

With shrieks of terror, the children were only too happy to stay in the wagon.

"Looks like the roof is sound," said John as they stepped up on the porch.

"The brush sure grew up around the house. It's even under the porch, John. We're going to have a lot to do to make this liveable.

They opened the front door and went inside. It was darker, and it took a few moments for their eyes to become adjusted. John crossed the room to the back door and opened it. What they saw was a nice surprise.

"Look, John, they left a stove, table, and three chairs. There are even dishes on the shelf. Look at the two oil lamps. This dry sink looks in good shape, too. Come on, let's look into the other rooms."

John lit a lamp, and they went into the room opposite the kitchen. They found a rope bed frame and a wash stand.

"You'll have to rerope that bed frame, John," said Mary. "The wash stand needs some attention too."

From the bedroom, they went into the front room. "Well," remarked Mary. "That's pretty, a nice tapestry love seat with two chairs to match. Ugh, that moldy dear-skin rug on the floor will have to go. That's a real nice oil lamp on that candle table, John. It has a nice big chimney on it. I could use that."

"Look at this, Mary; a spinning wheel. I wonder why they didn't take these things when the left."

"Can't take everything, John. They took what they could, I guess."

"Nice big fireplace in here. I'll have to check the chimneys here and in the kitchen," said John.

"It will soon be dark, John. We'd better get on home. We'll come over tomorrow, and clean up this place."

The next week, they made great improvements on the little house. Mary and the children cleaned, scrubbed, hung curtains, cut and burned brush, and even made the stable liveable for John's horse. He spent the evening there fixing things. Finally, he was in and settled. He felt

117

comfortable and cozy on cool nights with the fireplace aglow and cracking. The business at the shop was better than John ever expected. He was always three to five days behind getting to repairs. He even started folks making appointments to have their horses and mules shod. John was very pleased.

One dreary afternoon, Mary came to the shop and asked John to come by for supper. They needed to talk. He agreed he would be there after he closed the shop.

After a very pleasant supper, Mary and John went into the parlor. Mary poured a little glass of fox grape wine for her and John. He was wondering what she was up to.

Mary began, holding up her glass to John. "To a nice partnership."They clicked glasses and took a sip. "We need to talk about our financial situation, John, as well as our social situation. I realize you agreed to come to Benderstettle to move in, run the shop, and support my family - a ready-made family. When Neal introduced you I was not fully aware of what they promised you or your age. So it took me awhile to find out what they really told you, and get used to your age."

"I'm sorry you didn't know," said John.

"Well, it seems to be working out in spite of the misunderstandings. So now! We need to discuss the financial situation. I know you won't stay long with all the money coming to me and you having your own place to keep up. One day, some young thing will take your heart, and we'll have another problem."

"What do you propose?" asked John.

"After giving it much thought, I've decided to sell you the blacksmith's shop."

"I have no money to buy anything," said John.

"I know, I know... I will sell you the shop for 200 gold sovereigns. You can pay me off as you earn it. What do you think about the proposal, John?"

"Well, it will take a very long time to pay that much money - 150 gold sovereigns would be better," said John.

In a rather disturbed and stern voice, Mary remarked, "John, you are in no position to bargain. This is a fair price ... That is my only offer. Do you want to work and turn all the money to me? How long do you think you can keep that up? Don't be stupid, John, and take my offer."

Meekly, John said, "I'll take your offer."

John thought, Mary is a tough woman, and drives a very hard bargain - 200 gold sovereigns. How will I ever make that much money?

"We will go to Doctor Sitz Clinic and have him write up the papers. Then we can both sign our mark," said Mary.

"I can write," boasted John. "I can write it up right now."

"How will I know what you write?" asked Mary.

"I'll read it to you," said John.

"No, I'll have Doctor Sitz do it, and you can read it," said Mary.

"As you wish," sighed John.

# EIGHT

## *John's Shop*

On October 21, 1777, an agreement was drawn up between Mary Miller Bender and John Fetterholft to purchase the blacksmith shop of Mary Bender with the sum of 200 gold sovereigns to be paid as earned but not to be less than one gold sovereign a month; payable the first of every month.

This being agreed by both parties was signed by Mary's mark and John's signature.

Well, thought John, on his first day as the new owner of the only blacksmith shop in the valley except for the debt. How will I ever pay for it?

The first thing John did was to change the name on the sign. Now it read:

Blacksmith
Owner, John Fetterholft

The first month was very good. John's anvil could be heard late into the evening. On November 1st, John paid four gold sovereigns to Mary, and he still had some in his pocket. He was quite comfortable with his business and his little house down by the creek. Life was good to him.

One dreary day, Mrs. Meinhart came by the shop with a heavy fireplace pot. "Good morning, John," she said.

"Good morning, Mrs. Meinhart. What can I do for you?"

Holding up the heavy pot, she asked, "Could you fix this handle so I can hang this pot over my fireplace?"

After looking at it, John remarked, "Sure I'll be able to put a good heavy handle on your pot. It sure is a nice heavy pot."

"How much would it cost me, John? I have little money. I only get money from folks that buy my quilts and table scarfs."

"Um," said John. "It won't be much, ma'am. Let me look it over good, and I'll let you know."

The next afternoon, John had a nice stout handle on Mrs. Meinhart's cooking pot. John had planned to take it to her house after he closed the shop. As he was pounding out a plow sheer, he felt someone watching him. He looked over his shoulder and saw a very pretty girl waiting for his attention. John laid down his hammer and asked, "May I help you, ma'am?"

John had a habit of stripping to his waist while working iron even in the almost cold weather. The girl looked away with a blush. John realized he was not dressed to speak with a female. He made a grab for his shirt past this girl, and she blushed even more.

"I'm sorry," stammered John. "I wasn't expecting a lady."

"I came to pick up Mrs. Meinhart's cooking pot if it's ready."

"Yes, yes, it is. I hope she likes it." Again John passed by this girl to get the pot. She blushed again. "It's very heavy," said John. I'll be glad to take it to Mrs. Meinhart's house for you."

With a bit of flash in her eyes, she answered, "I'm Mrs. Meinhart's niece. I'm a strong girl. I can easily carry this pot." With that, she took the handle out of John's hand

and almost stumbled forward. She quickly regained her balance although it wasn't easy.

"How much is it?" she asked.

"I'll settle with Mrs. Meinhart later," said John.

"Fine," and she turned and walked both hands holding the pot. It was a heavy pot, she realized lugging it down the street.

The next morning when John rode up to his shop, Mrs. Meinhart was waiting for him. As he swung off his horse, Mrs. Meinhart said, "How much?"

"Is the pot as you wished?" asked John.

"Yes, how much?"

"What is the first thing you'll make in this pot?" asked John.

Surprised, Mrs. Meinhart said," I guess a venison haunch. I have one coming today from that Indian half-breed. Yes, a venison haunch."

"I'll buy the haunch if you'll cook me a meal, and we'll call it even," said John.

Mrs. Meinhart could hardly believe her ears. "Just cook a haunch for you, and you'll buy the haunch?"

"Yes, but I want potatoes and fresh bread with my meal. Is it a deal?" asked John.

"Of course it is a deal," said Mrs. Meinhart. "Tonight for supper then."

"Tonight," said John.

"One hour after dark. Is that too early for you?" asked Mrs. Meinhart.

"Fine."

"You're a good boy, John," Mrs. Meinhart said as she hustled down the street.

I need a good meal, John thought. I can't charge that poor old lady to fix her pot. It took no time at all.

That evening about one hour after dark, John rode up to Mrs. Meinhart's cottage. It was a pleasant little home nestled among some tall oaks. The remnants of a little vegetable garden was on the south side of the yard. It looked like a tea rose bush climbing up the north wall of her house. As John tethered his horse to a small tree, he noticed the smoke curl from the chimney. Also, there were smells of something good.

Softly, he knocked on the front door. He heard shuffling. "Good evening," stammered John. "I must have the wrong house."

"Come in, John," shouted Ms. Meinhart from the kitchen.

The girl stepped aside opening the door wide for John to enter. "Good evening," repeated John in the direction of the kitchen. As he made his way to the kitchen, he said, "Am I too early?"

"No, no, John. Please come in," said Mrs. Meinhart.

"You have a cozy little house and a wonderful kitchen, Mrs. Meinhart." John was almost overwhelmed at the sight of the table set with fruit, fresh bread, a pile of pit-baked potatoes and a huge haunch of venison steaming in the center.

"John, I want you to formally meet my niece, Betty. This is John. John, this is Betty from Rifetown. She is visiting her old aunt for awhile."

John extended his hand. She extended hers. John bowed very low lightly kissing the top of her hand.

"I'm pleased to meet you, Betty," said John.

"I'm pleased to meet you, John," as she looked up to him with a little smile.

"Such a gentleman. I told you, Betty. Now lets sit and have a good meal. John, you sit there and Betty here. Betty will give us a prayer of thanks."

The meal was delicious and John couldn't eat another bite when Mrs. Meinhart brought out a deep-dish apple pie. "How will I ever find room for a piece of that?" remarked John.

Betty laughed, "I think somehow you will."

John noticed this lively girl had a sense of humor that was refreshing. She was very pretty, too. John sensed she was also strong willed and proud, like her aunt.

"Betty is 17 years now. How old are you, John?" asked Mrs. Meinhart.

"Twenty-one, almost twenty-two."

"So young to own a business. Betty, John bought the blacksmith shop from Mrs. Bender for 200 sovereigns and already paid four. Mrs. Bender said she was too old for him, and she was right. A good-looking young man should find a girl of his choice."

"Aunt Lizzy, you always did know all the gossip," quipped Betty.

"Its a small town. Everyone knows everything before sundown," said Mrs. Meinhart.

"How long will you be visiting?" asked John.

"Till my father comes for me. You shoed his mules and a horse when he brought me up to Aunt Lizzy.

Remember, you asked about his pistol."

"Oh yes, I remember about a week ago. Was he happy with my work?"

"Yes, he was. When he comes to pick me up he'll have more work for you."

"When will that be?" asked John.

"When the fields are clean, and the bins full. Probably after the butchering so he can bring smoked meat to Aunt Lizzy."

"Why don't you two sit in the other room by the fire and chat? I'll clean up the kitchen," said Mrs. Meinhart.

"I'll help, too," said Betty.

"Shoo, you two get out of here - in the parlor with you."

Like obedient children, they went into the parlor and took chairs opposite the fireplace.

"It's nice you came to visit your aunt," said John.

"I had a problem, and my mother and father thought Aunt Lizzy would be a nice change."

"A problem?"

"Yes. I had a beau this summer. He and some boys went down to the river to net fish. He got caught in the rapids and was drowned. That was in August," Betty said wistfully.

"I'm sorry. Were you going to marry?"

"We didn't talk about it. He was a year younger than me. He was nice, and I liked him. I guess we would have married, but not for a few years yet."

"Do you miss him?" asked John.

"It's better since I came to Aunt Lizzy's. She keeps me so busy I don't have time to think."

"Busy with work hasn't hurt anyone," said Mrs. Meinhart as she came in the room.

John stood up as she entered as any gentleman would.

"Sit, John!" as Mrs. Meinhart sat on the deacons bench between them. "Enjoy your dinner, John?"

"Very much, and the company was delightful," said John as he looked at Betty.

"I was hoping so," said Mrs. Meinhart.

"Oh, Aunt Lizzy," Betty said, with her eyes looking at her shoes in embarrassment.

John decided to change the subject to help Betty recover from Mrs. Meinhart' attempts at match-making.

"I promised to buy the haunch. How much do I owe you?" asked John.

"I paid two and a half pennies."

John handed Mrs. Meinhart three pennies. "This will cover supper I suppose."

"Very good, John. You can come every night for three pennies a meal."

"I wouldn't bother you that much, but maybe once a week?" asked John.

"Splendid," said Mrs. Meinhart. "Let's say every Sunday night."

"Good," remarked John.

"Have your butcher come by my shop after delivering your meat on Saturday, and I'll pay him. That way you wouldn't need to use your money," said John.

"So thoughtful." Mrs. Meinhart nodded to Betty.

"Betty, take a lamp and show John to his horse. Don't forget to put your shawl on. It's cold outside."

Betty put her shawl over her shoulders as John lit an oil lamp. After thank you's and goodbyes, John and Betty walked out the path to the road where John had his horse tethered to a tree. They walked in silence not knowing what to say to each other.

Finally, Betty asked, "Did you enjoy your dinner, John?"

"Yes, yes I did," stammered John. In the moonlight, Betty looked the fine lady she was, and he didn't know what to say for fear of saying something stupid.

"I'm glad you did. I hope I can be there when you come again. It was so nice being with you, John."

By this time, they had approached the horse. As John and Betty came along side, John's horse gave a nicker and turned toward the couple. Betty stroked the horse's muzzle and asked, "What's your horse's name?"

"Willie."

"Hello, Willie," said Betty softly. Willie nickered again.

"I believe he likes you, Betty. He doesn't make up with many folks."

"That's nice if Willie likes me. I'd rather if his owner liked me as well," Betty said as she petted Willie's neck.

"Uh, oh, uh. I guess I like you, Betty," stammered John. Thank God its dark, he thought or she could see how stupid I am.

"Do you, John!" Betty exclaimed. In an instant, she flung her arms around John and kissed him full on the mouth; then again and again. Then she put her arms around his waist and hugged him tight burying her face in his chest. John stood frozen with his arms at his sides. Finally, he put his arms around her; snugly and warmly. They stood there for a little while comfortable and warm. John could feel his emotions rise. She smelled so good!

"I'd better get back in the house, John," said Betty.

"I guess so," said John; very reluctant to release her.

They kissed a soft kiss again, and Betty turned and started toward the house.

"Good night, John."

"Good night, Betty."

John's head was swimming as he rode home. When he put Willie in the stall, he started for the house until he heard Willie nicker again. Oops, he forgot to give Willie his oats. He always gave Willie a bucket of oats when they got home.

All night John did not sleep. Betty was on his mind. He went over their conversation time and time again. She sure is pretty. Near dawn he finally drifted off.

The next day wasn't much better. John had a hard time keeping his mind on his business. Toward evening, he was scolding himself. He thought he had better get over this, and tried again to put Betty out of his mind.

Riding home that night, John could smell snow in the air. It was deep and cold, and the breeze was fresh. The clouds hung heavy across the valley.

John gave Willie an extra measure of oats when he put him in his stall. Then he brought extra wood up to the back door. It was getting colder, and John went back to the barn to put a blanket on Willie.

"That should keep you warm, old friend," John said as Willie nuzzled John. It's a lucky man who has a good horse as a friend, he thought. A friend you can depend on - not like a girl that makes your head go so crazy that you can't think of anything but her. John stayed with his horse for awhile just thinking and talking to Willie. Willie kept chomping away at his treat of oats. John began to realize the cold creeping in and decided to head for the house. He opened the door to the barn and was surprised to see the ground white with snow. It was coming down fine and light. Maybe it won't amount to much. He made his meager supper of smoked meat and potatoes. When it was ready, John didn't have much appetite. Soon, he turned in looking forward to a restless night. John was worn out and was soon in a deep sleep.

The next morning, John woke up cold but refreshed. He stepped outside for wood for the fireplace and realized the snow was about six inches deep and still falling. Soon, he had a cheerful fire going. He got busy making fried biscuits and smoked meat. John ate hungrily. He thought, I must be getting over this sickness for Betty. I feel good today.

By dawn, John was merely hammering out a piece of flat iron to shoe a mule Jack brought in. Jack was a farmer at the edge of town, and John and Jack had become good friends.

"Glad you can fix up old Nellie here. She's a holy terror when she throws a shoe - stumps and kicks around. So be careful with her, John."

"You hold her head, and I'll get her shoe on," said John.

128

In a bit, the mule was fitted with a nice new shoe, and Nellie was gentle as only one could expect.

"You have a way with animals, John. Old Bender always had a fit with Nellie. She's a good mule and will work hard if you treat her right. This Spring if you want to plow a patch, I'll bring her over when you're ready."

"That will be nice. I haven't even thought that far into Spring. I guess I could make a garden patch and some corn for Willie," said John.

"Settled," said Jack. "How much I owe you for the shoe?"

"The plow in the spring, and we'll call it even," said John.

"Oh no you don't. I'll pay you for the shoe. I offered the plow as a friend. Nope. I'll pay for the shoe. Bender always charged me three pennies because she was so difficult."

Jack was dipping in his pants for the money when John said, "Two pennies is what I charge anyone so two pennies it is."

Jack said, "Good and done," as he put the two pennies in John's hand.

"Mrs. Mitchell's coffee is cooking across the street," John said as he whiffed the air.

"Smells mighty good," returned Jack.

John said, "I'm buying. Let's see if Mrs. Mitchell has enough for us."

As John and Jack trumped through the snow across the street, Mrs. Mitchell saw them coming. She had started making coffee and breakfast for those who would come to her house. She converted her front room into tables and chairs. In the Fall, she started to make a good soup and bread to serve her patrons from midday until dark. Actually, this was the first restaurant in Benderstettle.

"Sweep the snow off your boots before you come in," ordered Mrs. Mitchell in a gruff voice as she met them at the front door.

Like obedient children, they swept off their boots and came into the front room. They sat at the table by the window. That way, John could see his shop if someone came. It didn't look like there would be much business with this snow.

"Coffee?" shouted Mrs. Mitchell from the kitchen.

"Yes, please," shouted John.

Mrs. Mitchell came in with two steaming cups of black coffee and put them on the table.

"How about some eggs, ham, and biscuits?" said Mrs. Mitchell.

John was hungry again so he said, "Good, we'll both have some." John and Jack sat by the window enjoying the hot coffee, watching the snow come down.

"Flakes are getting bigger," said Jack.

"It will soon stop then," John said from his experience with winter when he was looking for Deutsch country.

"Hot breakfast coming up," shouted Mrs. Mitchell as she came in the room. It looked good - four eggs, a slab of ham covered with fried potatoes with onions. To top it off, there were two huge biscuits on top of the platters. "Think you can put that away, boys?" she asked as she headed back to the kitchen. "Forgot the honey," she said as she disappeared into the back.

"Sure is good," said Jack.

"Um - huh," mumbled John with his mouth full.

"Here's the honey for your biscuits, boys. Good, ain't it? Mind if I sit with you with my coffee?" Mrs. Mitchell sat down without either looking up.

"John, how are you and Miss Betty getting on?"

John almost choked, "Miss Betty?"

"Now John, you know! Miss Betty, the gal you were with out by the road night before last. Everyone knows she is sweet on you."

"Well, how about that!" exclaimed Jack. "John's got a gal."

"No, I haven't. I haven't seen her since night before last and maybe won't until I go to supper on Sunday night."

"Oh, oh, supper Sunday night. Well, it's better than I thought," said Mrs. Mitchell.

"No, it isn't," said John. "I made a deal with Mrs. Meinhart for dinner on Sunday nights, and it has nothing to do with Betty. Besides she lost a beau last summer in the river and is not ready for a fellow yet."

"That's not the way I heard it, John," said Mrs. Mitchell.

"John, look over the pasture before you pick the cow," said Jack.

"Jack! You could have put it a little nicer than that!" returned Mrs. Mitchell.

"Looks like Neal over at the shop," said John.

"I'm ready to go, too," said Jack.

"Put this on my bill, Mrs. Mitchell, and I'll pay up again on Friday evening."

"You're a good boy, John. Can't say as much for you, Jack. I wonder how your wife puts up with you?"

The snow did stop, and the sun came out in the late afternoon. Business was slow so John worked odd jobs around the shop.

"Hello, John."

John turned around, and there stood Betty. She was wearing a blue bonnet with a black knitted shawl over a colorful dress. "Hello," said John standing their awkwardly not knowing what to say.

"A rider came by this afternoon from Reiftown and told Aunt Lizy my father will come tomorrow. He said he will have some things for you to fix. Then he will take me back to Reiftown to my family. Aunt Lizzy said you should expect my father about midday."

Betty looked sad as she was saying this and not at all anxious to go home.

"That means you won't be there on Sunday night?" asked John.

"That's right, and I don't know when I'll be back," said Betty, "unless - unless someone sends for me. You will keep in touch with Aunt Lizzy, won't you John?"

John just stood there like a bump on a log.

"John, John, oh, oh." Betty turned and ran down the street towards her aunt's house. She was obviously crying as she ran along.

John thought, why do girls do that? Why don't they just say what they want instead of making a man guess. This could drive a fellow crazy. I'm glad Willie didn't do that.

The next day, Betty's father stopped by with some things to be fixed. John could fix all of them except one on the spot. Betty's father said he could leave it with Mrs. Meinhart, and he would pick it up the next time he was in the valley. Not a word about him and Betty came up. Maybe he didn't know ......

# NINE

### *Morning Flower*

It was Friday about mid-afternoon. Bill Heimbough was in the shop when Bill said, "Looks like an Indian coming here."

John looked around from his fire and saw a dark-skinned, black-haired, black-eyed girl. She was dressed in tanned skins, deer hide jacket and pants. Her moccasins were made of fine rabbit hide. She said something to John. He couldn't understand her. She said something else. Again John couldn't understand.

"What is it you want?" John asked.

She couldn't understand him.

Bill said, "John you are talking Deutsch, and she's talking French and English."

"Do you know what she said, Bill?"

"In English, she said you owe her one penny for meat."

"Oh, that's right for Mrs. Meinhart!"

The girl nodded and said something again.

John didn't know what it was but when he reached in his pocket and pulled out a penny, she beamed with a bright smile and nodded.

"Thank you," said John.

Quickly, the girl turned and walked hastily up the road.

"Bill, who was that?"

"She brings meat to town to trade. Her father is a French Canadian and her mother is a Abanacki Indian. They came south a few years ago with their brood. I guess they got tired of the long winter's up north. He's a trapper, and they sell meat and hides to get along. They must have ten or so kids but they keep to themselves up on the mountain. It's good that they do. Not many folks are interested in making friends with them or any other Indian."

"Sounds like they have a hard life," said John. "Seems they are good people, too."

"Not the same, John," said Bill. "They'll cut your throat as soon as look at you. You can't trust them. They're really savages."

"She didn't seem like a savage. She seemed to be scared." John could relate to that. It was time get to work.

Sunday dinner was great, and Mrs. Meinhart kept talking on and on about how great Betty was and how sad she was to have to go home. John was glad to be on his way home when the time came.

On Tuesday afternoon, John noticed this same Indian girl going down the street with a heavy bundle on her shoulder. It must have been heavy the way she was carrying it. She went around to the back door of Mrs. Mitchell's house and soon came around empty handed. As she passed by the shop, she gave John a half-way smile. This is a savage, he thought? Never!

On Friday in mid-afternoon, John sensed someone was looking at him. He turned to look around the shop and was surprised to see the Indian girl standing at the street observing him. When she saw John had noticed her, she stepped into the shop.

134

"Hello," said John.

She said something to John but he couldn't understand again, and there was no one there to translate. He assumed she wanted money for meat for Mrs. Meinhart. John held up one finger meaning one cent. She held up two fingers, and with a very serious look on her face took another finger of her right hand and motioned as if to cut one finger in half. One and a half cents, John thought. He dug in his pocket and pulled one cent and counted out five pents. John handed it to her as she held out her hand palm up. As John dropped the coins into her hand, he couldn't help notice her calloused and strong hands. This girl is used to hard work, he thought. She said something as she put the coins into a pouch hanging from her belt. Not knowing what she said, John just stood there and looked at her. She looked up at him with those deep, dark eyes and said something very softly. She smiled a gentle smile that seemed just for him only. Then she said something very short, turned, and started up the street toward the mountain. A little way up the street, she half turned and looked back. John was still standing there. She gave him a little wave of her hand. He smiled and waved back. Strange girl, he thought. She was not a frilly little thing like Deutsch girls. She is a hard-working girl only asking what is due to her. Oh well, back to work.

Later that day, John had a customer from Lykens Town. He too couldn't speak Deutsch; only English. It was hard for John to understand what the man wanted.

As John was closing up the shop, he noticed Margaret Siefert, the Schoolteacher across the street, coming out of the General Store. She knows English. I wonder if she could teach me? Before John could think again about it, he was across the street.

"Mrs. Siefert, ma'am. I'm John Fetterholft, the blacksmith."

"I know who you are," said Margaret.

"I was wondering, could you help me?" asked John.

Margaret looked puzzled. "How could I help you, John?"

"Teach me the English!"

"You want to know how to read and write English?"

"No, talk English," said John.

"I could teach you all three if you want."

"Good? When do we start?"

"Well, come to my cottage after supper tomorrow night, and we'll get started," said Margaret.

It was a crisp cold night as John rode up to Margaret and Whity Siefert's cottage. He could see in the house through the window as he tied up Willie. It was a cheerful house with a rosy glow from the fireplace.

Margaret and Whity were in their 40's and childless. Whity worked at the grainery and Margaret taught school in one room with all students. Just like in Bot Weiser the children would leave school between 12 and 14 years having mastered reading, writing, and numbers. John knew his numbers. It was the reading, writing, and speaking English he didn't know.

"Good evening," Margaret said in English as she opened the door. The lessons began.

It was late February when John could carry on a conversation in English. It was not very good English and mixed with many German words but he could make himself understood. He was anxious to do better with English so he kept going back to Margaret's house two nights a week. He was getting the knack of writing too.

Soon he could write a letter to his parents, Casper, and even order merchandise from other cities.

Ed Lauer came in the shop with his daughter, Christina. She was about ten years old; a bright and pretty little girl.

John spoke to her in English. "School you're are not today?"

Christina laughed merrily. "He talks funny?" she said to her father.

"Christina!" ordered her father. "You must not make fun of someone trying to learn English. It is not polite."

John could see Christina was hurt at displeasing her father. "Christina," John said in Deutsch. "Could you make my words right? I would like to talk good like you."

"You are not in school today?"

John repeated, "You are not in school today?"

"No, I wasn't feeling well this morning," Christina said in English. John could understand English much better than speak it.

"I'm sorry," said John.

"Perfect," cried Christina. "You said that perfect."

"See how fast I learn from you," said John in Deutsch. He could see Christina swell with pride.

"Looks like I have a little teacher here," said Ed.

"Hello in there," came a voice from the street. John, Ed, and Christina went to the door.

"Are you John Fetterholft?"

"Yes."

"I'm John Adam Messner." Motioning to the young lad next to him, "This is John Adam, Jr. You stayed with my brother and his family last summer."

"Yes, Casper. How are they. Did they survive the winter well?" asked John.

"Oh, yes," said Adam. "Everyone is fine and sends their best wishes; especially Rose!"

John, Adam, and Ed all smiled and chuckled. John was lost in thought for a minute.

"How is Rose?" John asked.

"Getting prettier everyday," There was a louder chuckle, and John came to his senses.

"This is Ed Lauer, and his daughter, Christina," said John.

"Nice to meet you."

"Likewise."

John Adam noticed his boy was mesmerized by this cute pretty ten year old Christina. She seemed to have absolutely no interest in John Adam, Jr.

Her father knew his daughter. She was putting on her act of aloofness. He had seen her glancing at the boy when she didn't think anyone was looking.

"What brings you all the way from Armstrong Valley?" asked John. Must be very important."

John Adam said, "I sold my farm to my younger brother, Philip. Do you remember him, John? He got married last summer and moved in with my father. Philip's new wife and mother didn't get along and it got pretty bad. Philip and my father proposed I sell my farm to Philip since my wife's parents passed away and their farm is abandoned west of Bendustettle. My wife is the only heir so we own the farm. It's three times the size of my farm in Armstrong Valley, but the livestock needs to be built up as well as repairs on the house, barn, pens, and chicken houses. I'll need to do a lot to make it good again."

"Are you living in it now?" asked Ed.

"Yes, and that's why I'm here, John. I need some hinges, nails, a good axe, a hand saw, and a pry bar."

"No problem. I've got them all. Go back into the shop and pick out what you need," said John.

John Adam and Ed Lauer disappeared into the back of the shop. John Adam, Jr. and Christina stayed with John watching him hammer out a hot piece of iron. They both enjoyed the sparks flying as John's hammer hit the red hot iron on the anvil. Then there was a quick thrust into the cold tub of water with hissing and steam so the metal tempered; then again in the fire.

John noticed the coy glances between the children although they didn't talk or look directly at each other.

"Looks like you two will be neighbors," quipped John. "Don't you live west of town, Christina?"

"Yes, sir," adding nothing else. Christina was being very proper and not unnoticed by John Adam, Jr.

Nodding to John Adam, "Is that where your new farm will be?" said John.

"Yes, sir," answered John Adam, Jr. pleased at being very proper, too.

"Looks like we got what we need," said John Adam as he and Ed came from the back of the shop.

John noticed Ed and John Adam became quick friends. He could hear their quiet conversation. It seemed Ed was going to get some friends together to help John Adam get his farm in order. It was not unusual for Deutsch folks to get together helping each other, raising barns and chicken pens, mending fences and even building houses when one burned down.

After some hand shaking and goodbyes, Ed and John Adam went their separate ways. John went back to work. It was good to hear Casper and family were doing well. He wondered about how Rose looked or if she had grown? Someday, I'll ride over the mountain to see her, but not for awhile yet. Maybe he would go next year.

The week rolled by, and it was a good week. He had met John Adam and John Adam, Jr. with news that Casper and his family were doing well. He paid Mrs. Bender six gold sovereigns on the shop. He paid four last week which made ten in two weeks. He'll soon have the shop paid off if business kept on being good.

Mrs. Siefert told him on Thursday night that he was doing well with his English. So on this Saturday morning, John was feeling pretty good with himself. He was hard at work on a wagon axle when he noticed someone approaching the shop. He looked up and there stood the Indian girl. She had her hair pulled back and tied with rawhide. Her hair was black as a raven. She wore an old dilapidated felt hat, buckskin shirt and skirt with a beaded band around her waist. She stood looking at John with those deep dark eyes that seemed to stop John in his tracks.

They looked at each other for a minute. Then she spoke, "Hello," in English.

"Good afternoon, and how are you?" John said proudly.

A look of surprise came over her face. He spoke English, she thought. "Good," was her reply. Do you speak English now?"

"Yes, I am learning English from Mrs. Siefert. I'm not very good at the English yet but I try."

"You speak not so good but you will get better as you learn. You will pay me two pennies for meat for Mrs. Meinhart?"

"Yes, yes," stuttered John. "What is your name?"

As he handed two pennies to the Indian girl their fingers touched for an instant. John felt a reaction but couldn't identify it. The touch of this strange girl mystified him.

"Morning Flower is my name. What is your name?"

"John Fetterholft."

She tried to repeat it and it came out "Gawn Fiterhuft."

John broke into a smile. Then so did Morning Flower. John started to chuckle and she followed him.

He broke into a hearty laugh. Soon they both were laughing together. Then they both snickered and looked at each other and then snickered again. Finally, they settled down and were quiet.

"I must go now," said Morning Flower.

"Where do you go?" asked John.

"Up to Berry Mountain, and I must go before it gets dark."

Just then, John could see Morning Flower stiffen up as she glanced down the street. The Hess brothers were hanging around the General Store. Morning Flower's mood changed to that of a frightened rabbit.

"What's the matter?" asked John.

"I must go quick," said Morning Flower as she turned and started down the street toward the path she would take to Berry Mountain.

John noticed the boys stopped horsing around and started down the same street Morning Flower took. John didn't like the looks of this. As the three boys passed by the shop, John stepped out into the street. "Where are you going boys?" asked John.

"None of your business, dumb Dutchman," said the older one. The Hess brothers were about 17, 16, and 15 years old. They were being raised by their mother. She lost her husband five years ago or so. He was down by the river gambling with the tradesman along the river. It seems as though he was a cheat at cards and got caught at it. He was stabbed and died on the river bank. He left his wife and children nothing but debts. Mrs. Hess took in laundry and cleaned for people to support herself and her three sons. Since their daddy died, they had gotten into a lot of mischief around town and had quite a reputation as a rowdy bunch. Since the boys had gotten older, their mother hadn't been able to control them.

John watched the boys going down the street laughing and pushing at each other as they went along. He thought he heard a reference to red skin. John didn't like it at all. He decided to untie Willie and ride down the street after the boys.

John and Willie were about 50 yards behind the boys. They were moving along a little faster now. He could see Morning Flower walking very fast down the hill out of town and the boys 30 or 40 yards behind her. He could hear them calling to her.

Just then, Morning Flower broke into a run, and immediately the boys started running after her. John gave Willie his heels in the ribs and growled, "Come on Willie!" Down the hill John rode past the boys and caught up to Morning Flower just over the hill. He pulled Willie to a stop.

"Get up behind me," John ordered. "Hurry, take my arm!" Without a word, Morning Flower grabbed John's arm, put her foot in the stirrup and swung up behind John. Willie started down the road at a slow walk not being used to two riders. John urged Willie along in a soft voice. The boys stopped at the top of the little hill watching the couple ride further down the road.

Morning Flower was exhausted and still breathing heavy. John could feel her arms around his waist. Her body was tight against his back. He could hear her breath slowing down. She thought, he came after me to keep the bad boys away from me, and he's a white man. She could feel his strong waist and the muscle ripple of his strong back. She sensed his aroma, his warmth, and caring. As they rode along, she became aware the path up the mountain would be only a short way. She laid her head on his shoulder, and was thinking, this man has the strength to protect his woman.

John liked the feel of this woman and her arms around him as she laid her head on his shoulder. He could ride like this on and on, he thought.

"You must let me off now," said Morning Flower. "This is the path up the mountain."

"I'll take you up," said John.

"No, you mustn't, my father would not like that. He would very angry if he knew as a man is not for me till my father says so. Please let me off. I know the way."

"But it's almost dark," protested John.

"Don't worry, John. I will be all right," she said as she slid off Willie.

She walked around to the front of Willie and stroked the horse's muzzle. He softly nickered. "Thank you, Willie," she said as she gave Willie a kiss on the muzzle. She looked up to John and said, "Thank you, too," with a smile. She turned and started up the path. He's a good man, she thought. He's smart; learned the English in a very short time. He's so strong. She loved to watch him with his heavy hammer on the hot iron glistening with sweat and looking wonderful. He is kind and would not beat his woman like her father does. The climb up the mountain didn't seem so steep to her tonight. As she climbed to a rock ridge, she stopped and looked over the valley. She could see in the almost darkness a dark spot on the road near the town. That must be John and Willie, moving along very slowly. She sighed and started up the steepest part of the path to the top of the mountain.

John and Willie watched Morning Flower disappear up the wooded curvy path going up the mountain. When she disappeared from sight, John urged Willie around and they slowly plodded back to town. Those boys sure had Morning Flower afraid. Wonder what they did to her, he thought. Too bad; she's a nice girl. Very strong and independent. John liked that.

The next morning, Bill Heinbaugh came into the shop. "Heard you were riding down the road with an Indian girl," said Bill.

"The Hess boys were chasing her so I gave her a ride to the base of the mountain," said John.

"They were just having a little fun," said Bill. "You know, Indians are fair game anytime. They are nothing but savages. About 10 years ago, they burned out a family up the valley at Short Mountain just for meanness. About 15 years ago, a boy from up the valley got tangled up with an Indian gal from up Wiconisco Creek. When he tried to leave with her, they chased both of them up the valley to the South and up to a rock ledge on top. There they jumped rather than be butchered by the young bucks. I tell you, John, they're savages. The least you have to do with them the better."

The next three days John got a lot of lectures on making friends with Indians from almost everyone he met. He wondered why one little Indian girl could make so much fuss.

Saturday came and went and Morning Flower didn't come by to be paid. When he stopped by Mrs. Meinhart's house for his Saturday night supper, he found out why. Mrs. Meinhart explained a traveler brought smoked meat from her relations in Reiftown. She had heard John and the Indian girl rode out of town together and asked John to explain.

John told Mrs. Meinhart the story, and when he was finished, she sat there very quiet pondering what to say. "Those Hess boys are a bad bunch that's for sure," Mrs. Meinhart began. "It's not right they chase and scare anyone, not even Indian girls. That was good of you to get her out of that trouble, but John I must warn you, don't get involved with Indians. That always spells trouble. They think different than we do, and they are people who will turn on you in a whip stitch. Why don't you ride down to see Betty in Reiftown tomorrow? She would be ever so glad to see you again. If you leave at daybreak, you'll be able to see her for a good little while before heading back."

"I don't know where she lives," said John.

"Well you follow the west road out of town across the flat. Then you go down the hill to the creek. Cross the creek and follow the road up the hill and out on the flat to the next hill. When you come to the top of the next hill, you take the wagon path to the left. They are the second farm along the creek. It's easy to find. Go on, John. Go see her."

"I think I will. I'd better get home and get some sleep if I'm going to start at daybreak."

Daybreak came cool and bright. It looked like a very good day weather wise. As the sun lifted off the East mountain, John and Willie were past the last house in town and soon to be up on the first flat. By the time they got to the crossing at the creek, the sun was full up. Across the second flat and up the last hill and the sun was bearing down from the cloudless sky. He turned on the wagon path and was soon past the first farm. The wagon path curved down a slope to the creek. It was quite a size down here. The farm was to the right spiralling along the little valley with fields up the slope.

John and Willie rode up to the barn where two boys were eyeing them. He pulled Willie to a stop.

"Hello boys. I came to see Betty."

"We'll fetch her," said one of the boys. They turned and ran to the house. John could hear a commotion in the house as Willie walked lazily to the fence around the house. John swung off Willie and tied him to the fence. When the door opened, Betty, her mother, and father and two boys came to meet him.

John took off his hat and said, "Hello."

"Hello, John, come in," said Betty's father.

John opened the gate and stepped in the yard.

"Hello, John," said Betty in a very soft voice.

"You must be thirsty," said Betty's mother. "Come in, and have a drink. Boys take John's horse down to the creek for a drink, and then give him some oats." The boys took off like a shot as the rest of them went in to the kitchen. They sat around the kitchen table while Betty and her mother poured coffee.

"So you came to visit with Betty," said Betty's father looking over his coffee cup. "You plan to court her?"

"We didn't talk about that yet," said John.

"She's at the right age, and soon will be finding a man," said her mother.

An embarrassed Betty could only say, "Oh, mama!"

"Almost have Mrs. Bender paid off. One or two good months, and the shop will be paid for," said John a bit proud of himself.

"Can you raise a family on that?" asked Betty's mother.

"Yes, I'm sure," replied John.

"If you're done with your coffee, John, maybe we should go for a walk," broke in Betty.

Relieved to find a way out from the questioning, John agreed. In a few minutes, they were walking down to the creek. They were not talking, just walking.

When they got to the creek, John said, "Maybe I shouldn't have come."

"I'm glad you did. I think about you everyday but I'm sorry Mother and Father were pushing you for answers."

"That's all right. They just want to know what's going on with their daughter."

"What's going on, John?" she said looking up to him.

"Do you have anyone interested in you?" asked John.

"I was hoping you would. John Manis, a widower from out in the valley asked to court me but I'm not interested. He's 36 years old already and has three young ones. I want my own children in time - not some other woman's."

"I can understand that," said John.

Do you want to court me, John?" Betty asked in a low purring voice.

"I thought about it," said John with mixed feelings. "We'll have to think on it?"

I don't have to think on it, thought Betty. Better not push him or I'll scare him off. Sure would like to have a good-looking strong man like John for a husband. "You'll stay for dinner, won't you?" asked Betty.

"If I'm invited?" said John.

"You're invited! We had better start up to the house so I can help Mama." In a flash, Betty threw her arms around John's neck and kissed him full on the mouth. He put his arms around her waist and kissed her back. Rather breathlessly, they started up to the house.

It was past mid-afternoon when John swung up on Willie's saddle. After goodbyes and come again, John rode up the wagon path to the road to Benderstettle.

On the ride back, John's head was in a muddle again. Did he want Betty for a wife? She's so headstrong and could take over a situation. John didn't know if he liked these qualities. She sure is pretty though and really could kiss a fellow.

John was making rivets for a wagon wheel when he heard from the street, "Injun lover." He turned around and there they were - the three Hess brothers. John started for them, and they ran down the street and ducked between two houses. Those boys were bound to make trouble.

That night, John went to Mrs. Siefert's for his English lesson. Margaret and her husband expressed their concern about John's friendship with the half-breed Indian girl.

"Why is everyone so concerned about this?" John asked the couple.

"Because anyone who befriends the Indians always live to regret it," said Margaret. "We like you John, and we don't want to see you make a mistake. There are a lot of nice girls who would love your company."

"Like Betty?" said John.

"Like Betty!" said Margaret.

After his lesson, John started home. He wondered why everyone was throwing Betty at him and condemned Morning Flower. Morning Flower had twice the will power, and the strength to deal with what's dealt to her as any one of them. It was starting to get to him. People should mind their own business.

It was warm this evening but not too warm for late June. John had spoken with Morning Flower when she came to pick up her money for the last four Saturdays. John had to admire her ability to cover long distances on foot. She would have to leave before light to get to town, do her business, and get back home before it got very late. She also had a fetching beauty. Not the flashy kind but a subtle warm presence.

# TEN

## *The Shame*

**J**ohn was happy. He paid off Mrs. Bender this afternoon. She said she was surprised he was able to pay her off so soon. Jokingly she said if she thought it was so easy to pay 200 gold sovereigns she would have charged him more. She didn't know John did without many things to get out of debt.

As he was closing up shop, he noticed the Hess boys going down Main Street towards the west. Wonder what they are up to, he thought as he saddled up Willie. Something's wrong he felt as he started home. The further he went, the more he felt this dread. Suddenly, he pulled Willie to a stop. He sat there for a minute. Willie nickered and pawed the ground. John relaxed his reigns and Willie turned around and started going the opposite way and went down Main Street. It was near dusk now as Willie went on walking along a little faster.

As they crested the hill outside of town, Willie stopped in his tracks. John sat there listening to evening sounds.

There was rustling in the bushes along the road with low whispered voices. There was a whimpered and muffled cry - a girl's voice. Then someone ordered, "Shut her up."

John got down from Willie and peered into the bushes. What he saw horrified and angered him to the bottom of his soul.

The Hess brothers had Morning Flower on the ground. She was gagged and tied. They had her arms pulled over her head and tied by the wrists to a tree. Another rope was tied at the ankle to a stump. One boy was holding down her other leg. Another boy was holding down her shoulders. The other boy had her skirt pulled up and was on top of her, humping away.

John flew into a rage and piled into the boys kicking, punching, and physically throwing them down on to the ground. One by one, they ran for their lives.

John knelt down and cut the ropes from Morning Flower's wrists and leg. He helped her up as she clung to him crying. He held her for a minute. Then suddenly she broke loose and ran into the woods. John tried to follow her but she was swift as a deer. Finally, he gave up and went back to Willie along the road. He had almost killed the boys. He would have if they hadn't run.

John didn't see hide nor hair of the Hess boys that next week. Someone said they got hurt somehow and were home healing up. Bunch of animals, John thought.

It was Saturday again. John was looking forward to seeing Morning Flower. He wondered if she was hurt badly by the Hess boys. Poor girl, the thought. She must have been scared beyond her wits.

Mid-afternoon went by, and Morning Flower was late. I hope she is all right, John thought as he worked. Then he saw her coming up the street. He stopped his work and walked to the front of the shop to meet her. She was walking swiftly toward him with her eyes down avoiding John's gaze. She came up to him still avoiding his eyes.

"Two pennies please," she said.

"Are you all right?" asked John.

"Two pennies, please," she repeated.

"Morning Flower, are you feeling all right?" insisted John.

Morning Flower looked directly up into John's eyes with a black, stern look. With a very strong voice, she repeated, "Two pennies, please!"

John dug into his pocket and handed her two pennies.

"Thank you," said Morning Flower as she abruptly turned and trotted down the street.

"Morning Flower, Morning Flower," shouted John after her.

She ignored him and kept running. Why didn't she want to talk to me, he thought. He noticed bruises on her forehead and cheeks and also a cut on her legs. He also noticed rope bruises on her wrists when he handed her the money. By this time, she was out of sight.

Then another sight caught his attention. Betty was walking toward him from the side street. She was smiling brightly as she hurried along looking at John all the time. As she drew near, she called, "Hello, John, surprise, surprise."

"Sure is," John called back.

"I just got to Aunt Lizzy's and had to come see you. Daddy brought Aunt Lizzy some flour and lard, and I just had to come along. I'll be staying with Aunt Lizzy until next week. Isn't that wonderful? We can see each other every evening. I'm so happy."

"Wonderful," remarked John not quite so enthusiastic.

"Oh John." She threw her arms around his neck and gave him a quick kiss.

Embarrassed, all John could say was, "Come in the shop. I still have work to do."

She followed him in and John got to work bellowing the fire hot to heat a piece of iron.

"You're coming to dinner tonight, aren't you?" asked Betty.

"Yes, I'll be there," said John as he continued his work.

Just then Jack Smink came in. He saw Betty and smiled. "You're Lizzy's niece, aren't you?" "Yes, I'm Betty," she remarked. "I live in Reiftown and came up to visit Aunt Lizzy."

"And just happened to stop by to visit John, too."

"Well, yes," said Betty a little embarrassed at being so transparent. "John, I must go now to help Aunt Lizzy with dinner. Don't be late."

When Betty left, Jack said to John, "It must be wonderful to court a girl so pretty."

"I wouldn't know. We're not courting, just friends," returned John.

"Oh come on, John. I see how she looks at you. If you're not courting now you soon will be."

"Maybe, maybe not. Only time will tell," replied John.

It was almost dark when John tied Willie to the old tree in front of Mrs. Meinhart' cottage. Willie enjoyed the sweet grass around this old tree. John stepped up to the door, raised his hand to knock, and the door opened. Betty stepped out and threw herself in John's arms and kissed him passionately full on the mouth. He pushed her back a bit and took a step backward.

"Betty, your aunt will see."

"I don't care," she said as she came forward again.

John held her off with his hands on her shoulders.

"We'd better go in," said John.

"All right!" Betty said in her best pouting voice.

"Come, come," urged Mrs. Meinhart when she heard John and Betty come in from outside. "Come sit down before everything gets cold."

"Looks good and smells good," said John as he sat down.

They ate in silence for awhile, when Mrs. Meinhart said, You two gonna be courting?"

"Hope so," piped up Betty.

"We'll need to get a little more acquainted," said John.

"Seems you know each other long enough," Aunt Lizy said in a thinking manner.

"I think so, too," said Betty in her pouty voice.

John could see he was hemmed in by these two women. Not much he could say they wouldn't agree with except getting him to say they were courting. He was not enjoying his dinner very much. He knew they were waiting for an answer. Finally, John thought of a way out for the time being. "Mrs. Meinhart, isn't it proper that I go ask Betty's parents for their permission to count?"

Mrs. Meinhart sat back on her chair. After thinking a bit, she said, "You're right, John. It is proper but I know what their answer will be."

"It's still the right thing to do. It's only courtesy and respect for her parents if a boy wants to court a girl in Hesson. Even if everyone knows the answer. It's only right!"

"Yes, John. You're a good boy, and I'm proud that you would only want to do what is right and proper. Don't make such a face, Betty! You should be glad John is an honorable man and not some clod you can't trust or respect."

"I just don't see why we have to go through all that fuss. We even kissed already, Aunt Lizzy!" said Betty with a disgusted voice.

Mrs. Meinhart smiled and winked at John. "Kissing is just fine. It's what it leads to if you're not careful, and I'm glad John has morals." It seems John had won over Betty's Aunt Lizzy, and Betty was not very happy about that.

After a little light conversation and a miffed Betty, supper was over. John was pleased to be out of that jam for the moment. "When will you come to Rieftown and talk to my parents?"

"I'll have to see how busy the shop is," evading the question as best he could.

"Monday? Tuesday? Next week?" continued Betty.

"Betty!" exclaimed Mrs. Meinhart. "Stop badgering the man. He has a business to run and don't be so impatient. You're just like my sister. Now you two get out of the kitchen while I clean up."

"I should be on my way," said John. "I've got much to do tomorrow. Thank you for a wonderful supper, Mrs. Meinhart."

"I'll go out with you, John," said Betty as she grabbed her shawl off the peg at the door.

The fresh air felt good as the couple walked slowly away from the house. A soft breeze was coming up the valley and gave Betty a bit of a chill. She took John's hand and pushed her body up against him as they walked along. He didn't make an effort to pull away and soon realized her breasts were moving about his arm as they walked along. He also realized her nipples were hard. He felt himself getting a bit excited.

"John."

"Yes?"

"Do you like me?"

"Uh, uh, well I guess."

"Do you like me a lot?" she said as she tried to get closer as they walked along.

"You're a very nice girl," murmured John.

154

"Nice girl!" she exclaimed pulling away in a mock surprise. "Huh, wouldn't you rather have a naughty woman?" tightly holding on to John.

Willie nickered as they stopped beside John's horse. John turned to face her and she threw her arms around John's neck.

"Oh, John. Take me to your place tonight. My father will come for me tomorrow afternoon. We'll have a great night together," she said through hugs and kisses handing on to his neck.

"Betty," John said in the most commanding voice he could muster at the moment. "It would not be proper, and what would your Aunt Lizzy think?"

"Pooh, I don't give a snit what Aunt Lizzy thinks or anyone else. I want to be with you tonight, John."

This is very tempting, thought John. She's very pretty as he could see in the moonlight. He almost told her to swing up behind him on Willie when he thought, the whole town will know by noon tomorrow. Lizzy would be furious; not to forget her parents. Supposed she got pregnant. He thought nope, this would not do.

"Betty," John said as soft as he could. "You better go back into the house."

"No, John, no. Then let's go behind the big tree and, and ..."

"No, Betty, it's not right," erupted John. "Now go back to the house and that's final!"

Betty stood back and put her hands on her hips. Standing like stone and staring into John's eyes with frustration and again she spat, "You are a fool. We could have a great time until dawn but you're too stupid to realize that. I hate you, John," and in an instant, she turned and ran to the house.

John stood there stunned. How could a person be so sweet and inviting one minute and so damning the next, he thought. Just then he heard the front door slam and the latch drop.

On the way home, John kept thinking it would have been nice to have her come home with him. She sure did arouse his manhood. Even taking her behind the big tree, there would have been hell to pay if she got pregnant, and everyone would know. John thought he did the right thing! She would have his head messed up from now on, and he had a business to run. He didn't need someone pulling him around by the nose.

It was Tuesday morning, and John was having his breakfast at the house restaurant across the street.

Soaking up the last bit of coffee from his cup, he looked across the street to his shop. Morning Flower was trudging by with a sack over her shoulder and glancing toward the shop. John got to his feet and out the door in nothing flat. "Morning Flower," he called to her in English.

She stopped and looked in his direction. Then she turned and trotted clumsily down the street. John took after her and soon caught up. "Morning Flower, stop," he shouted.

"No, you mustn't," she replied as she trotted on under the heavy load.

"It's too heavy for you!"

"No, no. I can do it. You mustn't look at me."

John stopped in his tracks. He was dumbfounded. Morning Flower disappeared around a corner. What did I do to her? What did she do to me? Why can't I look at her? Well, John, he thought if that's the way she wants it that's the way it will be!

The days went by and the winter was cold and snowy when Morning Flower asked for her money looking at the ground. John paid her with very little conversation.

As the winter began to relax its grip on the land, John noticed little glances from Morning Flower when she thought he wasn't looking.

Aunt Lizzy was trying very hard at match making until early in March. This Sunday night is different, John thought as she was putting the dishes in the dry sink. She hadn't mentioned Betty ever since.

They were sipping some grape wine by the fire when Aunt Lizzy spoke up. "I've got some news for you, John. You may not like it."

"Is there a problem?"

"No, not a problem. Betty's getting married in April."

"That was quick," uttered John.

"She's been seeing this old farmer near her, and she found herself pregnant this winter about December I think. So it couldn't be yours. I'm sure of that."

John turned his head with a jerk, "Mine? We didn't ever, ever."

"I know John. I know but she tried her damndest that last night she was here in September. I was watching by the window, you know."

"I didn't know," muttered John.

"I was so proud of you that night," said Lizy. "You are an honorable man, and that's rare around here. I hope you don't take it too badly about Betty. She was just ready, and you weren't. I guess you'll find a nice lady one day. John, I'm very sure of that."

John felt a little relieved riding home that evening. He wouldn't have to deal with Betty anymore and felt no loss.

The first day in April of 1778 was cold and windy with gray clouds spilling a chilling mist over the land.

John was feeling pretty good in spite of the weather. He had Mrs. Bender paid off long ago. Last month, he had made a deal on a solid wagon. He had bought another horse; a brown chestnut mare. She seemed to be a gentle animal, and Willie seemed to like her. His house served him well during the winter. All in all, things were pretty good for a big not great-looking blacksmith.

His love life was a little frustrating. A few ladies had let him know they would like his company this winter. There was the grass widow with four children in the center of the Valley. Her husband ran off with a river woman. Then there was Bill Himbaugh's niece from up the valley. She was too young - 15 years old and looked like 25. There was also Mrs. Mitchell who ran the restaurant across the street. John was having his breakfast while he was going over this in his mind. Mrs. Mitchell walked up to his table, bent over, and filled John's cup with fresh coffee. She always did this in order to give John a view of her massive cleavage. He had a feeling she would pull down her blouse a bit before pouring coffee for him.

She put down a cup across the table from John, filled it, sat down the pot, and plunked into the chair.

"This weather isn't good for business,"she said almost to herself.

"No one came to the shop yet either," agreed John.

"Maybe we should take a holiday, John. We could close up and go upstairs and make whoopee!" Mrs. Mitchell said behind her cup, peering over the top with devilish eyes.

"If I'd say yes you would run like a scared rabbit," flipped John.

She folded her arms under her breasts as she leaned on the table and said in a straight-forward manner.

"Try me!"

"Got too much work to do today. Make it some other time," said John as he stood up and dropped two cents on the table. As John went through the door into the cold drizzle, he felt a relief to be going back to the shop. Mrs. Mitchell was half his height, twice his width, and twice his age. She was always pleasant with an easy smile. What a story for the gossips if he and Mrs. Mitchell got together.

Later that day, the weather turned into a dark steady rain. It was cold enough to see your breath while speaking. Few customers came in so John got a lot of back log work done. He brought Willie and Girlie into the shop to keep them dry when he noticed Morning Flower trudging down the muddy street soaked to the skin. Mud was splattered on her boots and on her skirt.

John called to her but she didn't hear him or just ignored him. He grabbed a blanket and ran after her and called again.

"Morning Flower," he breathed as he caught up with her holding the blanket over his head. She stopped as he stepped in front of her. She was looking down.

"Come into the shop and dry off. You're soaked," begged John as he tried to shelter her with his blanket.

"I'll be all right. I'm going home now."

"Please come by the fire and dry off. I can see you are shivering." John gently took her arm and guided her to the shop. She came along without a word of protest.

The first thing he needed to do was fire up the hearth. Then he needed to close the shop. He turned to see Morning Flower warming her hands by the flame. She was shivering uncontrollably in her wet clothes. He took down a dry horse blanket.

"Take this back to a stall and bring me your wet clothes," he demanded.

To his surprise, she obeyed like a little child. When she came from the stall wrapped in the blanket. She handed John her clothes. John was surprised how heavy they were in their sodden state. He spread out the deer hide skirt, her under jacket and her over jacket. Her boots were a mess. He brushed off as much mud as he could and hung them upside down to try to dry them on the inside.

All this time neither of them spoke. Morning Flower stopped shivering while sitting on a stump John used for a stool by the fire.

"Are you hungry?" asked John.

"I'll be all right."

"That's not what I asked you. Are you hungry?" snapped John.

She nodded her head. John had made some tea earlier. He checked the pot. There was still a little bit left. He put it on the side of the fire. He pulled from his saddle bags a stock of venison jerky and a chunk of bread he had bought earlier. He walked up to Morning Flower and handed it to her, and then poured her a cup of tea.

She ate the bread greedily and chewed venison and washed it down with the tea. John got her another cup of tea and sat on a stump next to her.

"Feel better?"

She nodded again.

"Getting warm?"

She nodded again.

"Why don't you talk to me or look at me anymore?"

She slowly looked up to John. Her eyes were dark and pleading. She was like a fawn in the forest, John thought. She was afraid of every move. Finally, she spoke, "I am ashamed."

"You're ashamed?"

"Yes."

"Of what?" John demanded.

"You saw what those boys did."

"You couldn't help that. They forced you and hurt you. You needn't be ashamed of that!"

"I am now spoiled for a good man," she said as she looked into John's eyes. "So now I cannot offer myself anymore."

All John could feel for this dark and mischievous girl was a genuine affection. She actually thought she was not a worthy woman. She had more integrity, more strength, and more ability than any woman he knew.

"Morning Flower," John whispered. "You are not spoiled in my eyes. You are beautiful like, uh like, a Morning Flower."

"You make me feel warm," she said with a blush.

John reached out and took her hand very gently in his own. For a long moment, John sat there holding her hand and looking at this lovely girl. She kept her head down looking at her toes peaking out from under the blanket.

Finally, she turned and looked at John. "You make my heart jump!"

"You make my heart jump too," said John.

"I must go now," she said.

"It's still raining, and your clothes are not quite dry I think," protested John.

"It's getting dark, and I must go John," she said with pleading eyes. She got up and collected her clothes. She then went into the back stall to change.

John went up to the loft to retrieve a calf hide he had used a time or two in the rain. Soon Morning Flower came out of the stall and handed John the horse blanket. "Thank you, John," she whispered.

"Here, I want you to cover yourself with this. It will keep the rain off you."

She hesitated. "Take it," ordered John. "I don't want you to get sick. Now come," John took her by the hand and led her over to the horses.

"Climb up on Girlie and Willie and I will take you to the mountain." John opened the doors to the shop.

"Get up on Girlie," he ordered.

In a hop, Morning Flower was on top of Girlie and covered with the calf hide. They rode in silence through the town. In a short while, they were on the road out of town. The rain eased up by the time they reached the path up the mountain. "Will you be careful going up the mountain? The rocks can be slippery. I will worry about you."

"You are a good man, John. I would like to be the one by your fire if you would want me."

Her directness completely took John by surprise so in order to gain some time he said, "I would have to talk to your father, wouldn't I?"

"Yes, if you didn't he would beat me."

Morning Flower slipped off Girlie with little effort. "Thank you John," she said as she turned and climbed up the path.

John sat on Willie and watched her until she was out of sight. Then he turned the horses and headed back to town. The rain had all but stopped but the road was ankle deep with mud. It made it slow going for Willie.

Morning Flower is very direct, John thought. She said right out she would want to be by my fire. I guess its the Indian way of saying she would be my woman if I wanted her. She's so humble and appreciates every jester of affection. Much different from the others always demanding. She mentioned her father would beat her if he knew she was with me without seeing him first. He wondered if he would beat her for other things?

# ELEVEN

## *The Decision*

Tuesday morning  John was making a brace for the wagon of Jack Shink when Morning Flower appeared at the shop.

"Thank you for the calf skin," she said handing it up into his arms. He looked into her eyes.  They both smiled and John said, "You're welcome."

She turned and walked across the street and rounded Mrs. Mitchell's house. A small sack was strapped on her back. John thought it was probably some meat for Mrs. Mitchell.

Jack was sitting on a stump smoking his pipe as John climbed the ladder and put the calf skin away.

When he came down and got back to work, John noticed Jack in deep thought. Finally Jack asked, "You doing that Injun girl, John?"

"No, we're just friends."

"Hell! It ain't no crime to get a little red meat once in awhile. Did it myself when I was younger. You can get what you want from them and walk away. They never complain or hound you. Use to enjoy the Injun gals pretty good. Then Bessie came along and that put an end to that!"

Jack sat there deep in thought while John finished the brace and nailed it to the wagon.

"That's it! All done," exclaimed John. His remark startled Jack out of his deep thoughts.

As Jack was paying John, Jack was saying, "Have your fun with that Injun gal but don't get involved and don't let the gossips know. They will have a field day if they catch you with that gal. You know there is a few around here have their bonnets set for you so have your fun before you get hitched. Your fun is over then, that's for sure."

"Thanks Jack."

"Member what I told you. Bye John."

Folks don't have much regard for the Indian thought John. They did a lot of damage up the valley from what I hear. Maybe it was because the white man did something first. Casper was raised up with an Indian friend. They can't be all bad. The rest of the afternoon John was pondering on this problem.

Close to the end of the day, a weary traveler pulled in with a broken axle on his wagon. His wagon was loaded with pots, pans, tools, blankets, and whiskey. John watched him as he got down from the wagon and came into the shop. John noticed he was dressed different than the local folks. He wore leather boots, black pants, buckskin shirt, and a leather hat with a hawk feather sticking out of the band.

"Welcome," John said in English.

"Good evening," returned the man with a definite French accent. "I have a broken axle. Can you fix it?"

"Yes," replied John.

"Can you do it now?"

"It will take an hour or so," replied John.

"Do it! I must get up the valley before morning," retorted the man.

John got to work jacking up the wagon, pulling the axle, and getting it in the fire. "Where can I get something to eat?" asked the man.

"Across the street at Mrs. Mitchell's restaurant. She puts out a great meal. I think you'll enjoy it."

John heard what sounded like a "thank you" in French as he watched the man cross the street and enter the restaurant.

John was working away at the axle when he heard a commotion across the street. Mrs. Mitchell was smacking the man with a long handled spoon and yelling at him to get out and not to come back. The fellow came across the street to the shop with a smurky smile on his face.

"Ze lady is not so happy right now," he said to John.

"What happened?" asked John.

"Everything was fine. The meal was very good and the lady was bountiful so as she stopped by my table I ran my hand up under her skirt. She hit me! She did not like it and she hit me! Crazy woman. I'm anxious to get up the valley. The Indian women like it and giggle not like that crazy woman."

"You're lucky she didn't shoot you. She's not an easy woman to get next to," said John as he tightened the lug nut to the wheel. "All set," said John as he dropped the wagon off the jack.

The man went around the back of the wagon and started to move things about. He pulled out a pint bottle of whiskey and handed to John. "This should pay for the axle," he said.

John looked at the bottle with surprise. "I don't drink whiskey," said John.

"Keep it for winter consumption," said the man as he climbed up on his wagon., snapped the reigns and was off.

John just stood there looking after the wagon going up the road. Mrs. Mitchell was coming across the road with her jaws tight.

"Who was that bastard?" she yelled.

"Some peddler going up the valley to trade with the Indians, I guess."

"You owe me for his supper. Do you know what he did? He reached up my skirt and I threw him out. He did it just to get out of paying up. You sent him over so you owe me, John!"

John chuckled and said, "Can I reach up your skirt too?"

Mrs. Mitchell put her fists on her hips and said, "There is a time and place for everything. Right now you owe me three pennies. Then we'll talk about the other."

John reached into his pocket and handed Mrs. Mitchell her three pennies.

"What you got there, John?" she said spying the bottle.

"Whiskey."

"Yes, whiskey. He paid me off with this pint of whiskey," said John in a disappointed voice.

"What are you going to do with it, John. I actually would not drink it. That stuff can kill you."

"I'll just keep it and trade if for something. Who knows, someone might want it."

In the first week of May, the weather turned mild with everything green again. Flowers were everywhere and John was feeling his need for a woman. He thought about going up the valley as some other bachelors were doing. He even thought of taking Mrs. Mitchell up on her offer then thought he'd better not.

It was late in the afternoon when Morning Flower stopped by his shop. "Good to see you John," she said as she came into the shop.

John turned around knowing that voice anywhere. "Good to see you too," John said a little tongue tied.

She is beautiful John thought. She was like a fawn in spring. John just stood there and gazed into her eyes.

"Are you all right John?" she asked.

John snapped out of it and stuttered, "Uh yes, uh yes, I'm all right."

"Would you like me to take Willie and Girlie down to the stream for a fresh drink and some new grass?"

"I don't know if Willie would go. He is a one-man horse," said John.

"We'll see," said Morning Flower as she went to the horses by the watering trough. John continued his work and watched her go between the horses. She was talking to them and nuzzling them in a very feminine way. After a bit she was riding Willie and leading Girlie past the shop.

"We won't be long John," she called as they proceeded down the street to the stream and meadow.

After a while, Bill Smirk stopped by.

"That Indian girl has your horses down by the creek!"

"She offered to get them some fresh water and some new grass," said John.

"Getting pretty thick with that Indian, John. Folks won't like that," said Bill.

"That's too bad. I like her. I like her a lot, and if she wants to water and feed my horses, I'm grateful" snapped John!

"I'm telling you John. Folks are talking. She's an Indian, and ain't good for nothing. Wouldn't surprise me if she runs off with your horses." At that they both looked down the street at the sound of clippety clop. She was riding Willie up the street. She had tucked wild flowers around his bridle and Girlie's too. She also had wild flowers in her hair, and she looked wonderful.

John turned to Bill and said, "If she's stealing my horses she's going the wrong way."

Bill swung up on his horse and looked down at John.

"Better be careful John. She could ruin you," said Bill as he turned his horse and rode off.

Morning Flower tethered the horses and came around to the front of the shop. "They really liked their trip to the spring. Willie was very grateful. I guess he likes me," said Morning Flower with a sparkle in her eye.

"We both like you," said John.

"I like you too John," whispered Morning Flower.

"Would you mind if I talked to your father?" asked John.

"It's a hard climb to our cabin."

"Would you mind?" repeated John.

"I would be honored," said Morning Flower looking longingly at John.

"I'll come Sunday morning to talk with your father. Will he be there about sun up?"

"Don't come then," pleaded Morning Flower. "He will not be in a good mood if you wake him. He likes berry juice at night and sometimes drinks too much. Then he is mean until about midday. Yes, midday would be better."

"Good! Midday Sunday. Will your mother be there too?"

"I don't know but my father will." Looking around Morning Flower said, "I must go now."

Before John could protest she was walking briskly down the street. Midday Sunday, John thought. I'll be there.

Sunday morning arrived. A breezy, cloudy, gray day. The weather was warm with a promise of cooling in the air. John had a breakfast of smoked ham and six eggs, fried in a pan with plenty of lard. Feeling satisfied with a good meal for breakfast, he could last until supper to eat, then went on to the barn. Taking Girlie out of the stall, Willie wanted to come too. "Stay here Willie. We'll be making a long trip today," said John as he led Girlie out of the barn and into the pasture. Then he let Girlie go to grass and frolic for the day. Then he came back to the barn and began to saddle Willie. Willie wasn't used to being without Girlie and kept wanting to go to Girlie in the pasture. Finally, John got Willie ready and swung up into the saddle and headed for town in a slow walk. John thought he would save Willie's strength for the climb up the mountain. The sun was peaking through the clouds when he proceeded down Main Street. Lots of people were out and about in their Sunday finest. Ladies with children and families were all going to church. John nodded and waved to the folks as he rode by.

Finally, The weather felt colder as John passed the last house in Benderstettle heading west. There were wagons and buggies going to town that passed John and Willie at regular intervals. He realized he knew most all the men and had done work for them. The women looked stern holding their Bibles looking forward to stormy sermons the preachers taught about drinking, gambling, and carousing sinners. The children weren't anxious to get to church. It's a long day for them and very hard to sit still and behave for hours on end.

Finally, John got to the path up the mountain. At the lower levels the path was well traveled and a very gentle slope down to the small creek. John crossed the creek and immediately the path led up a steep climb zigzagging between the rocks and trees. The path leveled out after the first hard climb. Willie was breathing heavy so John got off and gave Willie a time to rest. The pristine forest was quiet and beautiful. From his rock ledge, John could see the small stream below twisting and turning on its way to meet the larger, Wiconisco Creek on its way to the great Susquehanna River. He figured he was now about one fourth the way up the mountain. Willie is a good old horse. He can't carry me all the way, he thought. I'll just lead him and it won't be so hard on Willie to climb.

The path became steeper and rockier as they plodded up the mountain. They came to an outcrop of huge boulders. There the path leveled off and John and Willie slowed as they made their way through the big boulders. There was evidence of fire pits here and there among the big stones. Looks like this path had been used for centuries and the outcrop had been used as an overnight stop and a resting stop as well. John stopped and looked down into the valley. It reminded him of his first sight of Armstrong Valley so long ago.

As they were climbing the last 100 yards to the summit John couldn't help thinking of Morning Flower climbing up this steep and dangerous path in total darkness. She's not only brave but tough like my iron. John could not help but admire her ability to cope with what she had to do.

When John and Willie came to the summit, the path split four ways. One went down into Armstrong Valley, the other two, less traveled went along to the top of the mountain. Now, what way do I want to go, East or West? He thought he saw a faint wisp of smoke to the East along the gentle rise on the spine of the mountain.

Willie was rested from his climb so John swung into the saddle and started up the path, heading East. As they crested the gentle rise, John saw a rough cabin not 20 yards ahead. Smoke was coming from the mud and stick chimney. There were drying racks with deer, rabbit, fox, raccoon, and beaver pelts facing the South. This man is quite a hunter, John thought. Four children were working at something at the edge of the woods as John and Willie rode up.

A short, stocky, salt and pepper-haired man stepped out of the house followed by a round, brown, black-eyed, black-haired Indian woman.

"Hello," said John in English.

"You are John the blacksmith?" the man said in a French accent.

"Yes."

"Get down off your horse," said the man, "and come. We can talk."

John got down, loosely tied Willie to a sapling on the path. Then he followed the man to a tree where he and his squaw sat down on a blanket.

When John walked up to them, the man motioned to sit on a deer skin placed opposite them. John sat down.

"You are John the blacksmith, and I am Pierre Dupree. This is Running Water."

"I am John Fetterholft," returned John.

"John Fetterholft," repeated Pierre.

"I have come to talk about your daughter, Morning Flower," said John.

"You want her for your woman?"

"Yes, oh, yes, I guess," stuttered John.

Pierre turned and spoke French to his squaw. She returned with some comments and turned to smile at John.

"What did she say?" asked John.

With a smile, Pierre said, "At least you didn't steal her."

"Where is Morning Flower?" asked John.

"She will not be here when we talk business," grunted Pierre.

"Business?" asked John.

"Yes, business," said Pierre.

"I came to ask your permission to see your daughter, not business," remarked John.

"You said you want my daughter for your woman. You can buy her. That's business," said Pierre as he sat up straight with his arms folded.

With an astonished look, John blurted, "Buy her?"

"Yes, what do you offer?" remarked Pierre with a definite attitude.

"What do you want?" asked John.

Pierre smiled a wary smile. "Iron hoops to dry pelts, a bolt and hammer for my rifle, two skinning knives, a long knife, an axe and hatchet with a handle. Also two iron kettles, four large forks for holding meat, ten hooks for hanging meat, two big dippers, ten small spoons, forks, and knives, and ...

"Whoa," said John, "we'll have to talk about this - that's a lot of things."

"You want Morning Flower for your woman. You will have to pay." Dupree knew John and his limit so he asked, "What will you pay?"

"Four iron hoops, a bolt and hammer for your gun, one skinning knife, one large knife, one axe head, no handle, one hatchet head, no handle, one small kettle, one large fork, and five hooks for meat. That's enough," said John.

"Two skinning knives, a big pot, and a little pot and ..."

"No, said John, "I told you what I will give, and that's it!"

Pierre looked at his wife and told her what John offered in French. She smiled and nodded to John.

Pierre asked, "When do you have these things?"

"One week," replied John.

"Good," said Pierre as he rose from his blanket. John stood up also. As the men stood facing each other, Pierre thrust out his hand. John reached out with his hand, and they shook hands.

"It is done," said Pierre.

"Done," said John. "Where is Morning Flower?"

"You get Morning Flower when you bring our agreement."

A surprised John said, "I only want to talk with her."

"You don't see her until our business is done!" snarled Pierre.

John was taken aback by Pierre's stern remark. He tried to think of a response but thought it would be better to remain silent and agree. Surely this man could be violent in an instant. John smiled and nodded his head, turned and walked slowly to Willie. As he swung up into the saddle, he turned and waved to the couple still standing where he left them. They both waved back without any emotion.

Tough people, John thought as he rode along the spine of the mountain. When he got to the path down the mountain, he dismounted and walked ahead of Willie. The path was steep and rocky but Willie was sure-footed. Going down was much easier than climbing this old mountain. They rested among the big boulders. The sun was well into the afternoon. Two more hours, and it will be dark. I'd better keep moving, he thought.

Today had held more surprises than John expected.

Monday was gloomy and chilly. Business was good at the very start and had him busy until early afternoon. It was quite late in the afternoon when John got to making the items for Morning Flower's Father.

While he was putting the finishing touches to the second stretching rack, Ludwig came into the shop.

"What's that thing," asked Ludwig.

"Stretching rack for pelts!" replied John.

"Who would order that?" asked Ludwig.

"Morning Flower's Father," replied John.

Ludwig gave John a curious look as he was placing the last rivet. Wham! With one strike of the hammer, the rivet was in place. Quite impressive, thought Ludwig. John took the rack over to the wall and roped it up.

"How is he going to pay you, John? You know he only trades," said Ludwig with a curious look. John was considering how to answer this when Ludwig asked, "He going to let you borrow his daughter now and then, John?" He had a smirk on his face, and he knew he had hit on it. John's hammer stopped in mid-air. He put the hammer down gently on the anvil and turned to face Ludwig. "That's it, ain't it," laughed Ludwig.

"Well, hell why not. That's a sweet deal, John. You can have your fun for a couple pieces of iron."

Temper drained from John quickly before he answered Ludwig. "How I'm being paid has never bothered you before. Why would you be interested now?" asked John as calmly as he could knowing Ludwig knew he hit a nerve. John picked up the iron he was about to work and put it back into the fire.

Ludwig knew he'd better not push John any further. John is big, strong, and slow to anger. No one had seen John angry except the Hess boys, and they are a tough lot. Still they took a terrible beating. Nope, better not, thought Ludwig!

"Well John, your business is your business," rumbled Ludwig as sort of an apology.

Just then, Mrs. Mitchell came in with a broken skillet. "The handle broke off. John, can you fix this right away? I need it to cook, and I should be getting started now."

"How did you break the handle?" asked John.

"I hit that young Moffet fella. He grabbed me from behind when I was at the stove," Mrs. Mitchell replied.

"What was he doing in your kitchen?" asked Ludwig.

"Just came in while I was cooking," she said with a smile. "Guess he thought he'd get a little dessert.

Probably would too if he asked nice but I hate to be grabbed especially on my tits. Makes me mad as the devil. John, come on. Can you fix this?" shaking the old handle toward John.

"Set it on my anvil. I'll put on a new handle. I'll bring it over in a little while."

"You're sweet, John. I'll see you get something special," she teased as she left the shop to cross the street to her restaurant.

"They are all after you, John," quipped Ludwig. "You lucky dog."

"Naah, we're just friends," said John smiling.

"You bet, John, and my cow flies too," said Ludwig as he was leaving.

John was busy putting on the handle for Mrs. Mitchell when he decided to call it a day when he finished this. He made her a stronger handle than before just in case she decided to use it as a weapon again. When it was finished, John closed the shop and crossed the street to Mrs. Mitchell's restaurant.

"Here is your pan," said John as he stuck his head through the doorway to the kitchen. She was at the stove checking and stirring a thick stew.

"Don't dare come in," teased John. "Might get my head bashed in."

Mrs. Mitchell turned around with her hands on her hips and smiled, "John, you can come in my kitchen, my parlor, and my bedroom anytime you want. Besides, I would have to stand on the table to smack you on the head, you big ox. Now what's that I hear you're making things for the French trapper up on the mountain? You know he only trades, don't you? What does he have you would trade for? John, you're not sweet on his daughter, are you? I see her over at the shop now and then, and I know you gave her a ride on Girlie to the foot of the mountain. Even gave her a deer skin to keep her dry. Saw her bring it back a couple of days later. I know you got a big heart, John, but you sure can be stubborn," she said as she turned back to her stew and started stirring. "I can give you what that Indian girl can and more, John." This she said with a giggle. "There's more of me."

"Who else knows about this?" asked John.

"The whole town I guess by now. You know how gossip travels in Benderstettle. "Ha! They'll have you married with kids by breakfast. You know how they talk about me."

"I never heard anything," said John.

"You're not a gossip, John. The old biddies don't gossip with you because you're all business and can't add fuel to the fire. How much do I owe you for the handle?"

"Oh nothing. You're my friend," said John.

"Thanks, John until I can pay you better. Going to stay for supper, John?"

"No, but thanks. I have to get home. I have Girlie out in the pasture, and it's time I bring her in. Willie gets anxious too about this time of day, so I better get along. Bye."

"See you for breakfast, John."

Mrs. Mitchell doesn't dance around with words thought John as he rode home. She's twice my age.

Wouldn't the gossips have a heyday if Mrs. Mitchell and I got together. He had an amused look on his face as he pondered this.

The rest of the week rolled by rather quickly. Friday afternoon, John had everything ready for Morning Flower's Father. He was beginning to wonder if this is really what he wanted to do. The way people carry on about Indians gives a fellow doubts, John thought. People would not be kind to her even if he did marry her. They might not be nice to him either.

176

Just then, he noticed Morning Flower coming around the building from the back door of Mrs.

Mitchell's restaurant. She saw him, broke out in a big smile, and John's heart melted. She is so beautiful, John thought, as she glided across the street. "Good afternoon, John," she breathed as she came up to John looking up with those dark eyes.

"I didn't expect to see you until Sunday," croaked John.

"I had to bring a haunch to Mrs. Mitchell. I don't think she likes me much."

"What makes you think that?" asked John.

"Oh, she is very bossy and told me not to talk to you; that all you want is to use my body and nothing more."

"Do you believe her?" asked John.

"I didn't think about it before but I guess that is the way men are. Do you use her body, John?"

"Heavens no!" exclaimed John. "She's twice my age, one-half my height, and twice my width. Besides I can't stand that sharp tongue. No, Mrs. Mitchell and I haven't anything together. I haven't had any women yet. I expect you will be my first."

Morning Flower, half impressed, half ashamed for asking the questions stood looking solemnly at her feet. She remembered her rape by the Hess brothers. John reached out and crooked his finger under her chin to tilt her head up. Looking straight into her eyes, John said, "We can have a wonderful life together. We must always tell each other the truth, and ask each other what we don't understand. We must not let our temper spoil our days. Together if we do this, we will always be happy."

Morning Flower looked relieved and started to smile. "Yes John, I want us to be happy," she said with hope in her voice.

"I have everything done for your Father. I'll bring it up Sunday afternoon," said John.

"I'd better go now," said Morning Flower. "I'll look for you after midday. Bye, John."

"Bye. See you Sunday," said John.

John watched Morning Flower walk down the street and out of sight before he went to work back in the shop.

No sooner was Morning Flower out of sight when Mrs. Mitchell came storming across the street. "John! You messing with that Injun gal?" bellowed Mrs. Mitchell. "What the hell you a good-looking boy playing around with that Indian bunch for?"

John turned his back and went into the shop with Mrs. Mitchell raving behind him as they went. John turned around with a dark look about him stopping her in mid sentence. "If you don't mind, what I do with my time is my business!" said John through clenched teeth.

"Swell!" Mrs. Mitchell shouted over her shoulder as she stalked across the road, stomped up her steps, and slammed the door.

# TWELVE

## *The Trade*

**S**unday morning was bright and sunny with not a cloud in the sky. John decided to take both horses.

He thought he would load Girlie with the items for Morning Flower's Father and ride Willie to the foot of the mountain. There he would tie Willie and walk with Girlie up to the cabin. The load on Girlie would be enough for the climb.

When John got to the rocks, he noticed Girlie took the climb better than Willie. She didn't seem the least bit winded. He felt confident she could make the climb without any trouble.

By the time John and Girlie crested the top of the mountain, the weather turned cloudy with a threat of rain in the air. As they approached the cabin, it seemed deserted. He stopped Girlie and started unloading the merchandise.

"I see you have come," called Pierre as he came through the door of the cabin.

"Yes, I brought the merchandise," said John pointing to the neat pile in front of him.

"Humm," uttered Pierre as he walked up and started inspecting what John had brought.

"You're short two knives and one pot," barked Pierre.

"Take it or leave it!" spat John.

"You're short two knives," repeated Pierre.

John started picking up the merchandise to place on Girlie's pack when Pierre said, "Good, good. This will do."

John put the merchandise back on the pile. He was about to tell Pierre he would come for Morning Flower next week when Pierre called to the cabin. "Morning Flower, get out here! Right now!"

The door opened and Morning Flower came to her Father. He grabbed her by the shoulder of her rawhide jacket and pushed her into John. "She yours now! Take her with you"

Stunned, John put his hand on Morning Flower's shoulders while she just looked up at him. He could see Pierre going through the pile sorting and checking out everything.

Without a word, John took Morning Flower's hand and took Girlie's reins. Together they proceeded up the path. They walked in silence along the spine of the mountain. When they came to the path that would lead down the mountain, John stopped. He looked at Morning Flower. She had been walking with her head down which John took as a sad feeling she might have. He lifted her head up with his crooked finger under her chin until he could look into her eyes. "Are you all right?"

Looking up into his eyes, Morning Flower whispered, "I am happy...to be your woman."

Gently, John leaned forward and kissed her on the lips. He drew back, smiled and said, "Let's go home."

When they got to the bottom of the mountain, it was almost dark with a hint of rain in the air. Willie snorted and nickered to Girlie, and she nickered again. The couple mounted and started down the road towards town.

As they were entering town, John noticed Morning Flower lagging behind. He slowed Willie until they were riding side by side. Soon Morning Flower and Girlie were trailing behind again. He slowed Willie again and still Morning Flower trailed behind. It was dark now and a little rain was falling so John decided to press on.

When they entered the barn, it was raining steadily. They dismounted silently, and John lit a lantern. Morning Flower got to work taking the gear off Girlie and started to rub her down. John was amazed. She didn't have to be told what to do - just went right to it. A few minutes later, she had climbed up in the hay and pitched enough down for Willie and Girlie while John put oats in the troughs for the horses. He couldn't help thinking it was great having someone help with the chores.

The horses were settled for the night in their stalls when John picked up the lamp. "We're done here. Let's go to the house, and I'll find some supper," said John.

Without a word, they ducked between the rain drops as they scurried to the house. Once inside, Morning Flower was busy making a fire in the fireplace while John lifted the trap door to the root cellar and disappeared into the darkness of the cellar. When John came up, he had some potatoes, a few turnips, and a chunk of pork out of the salt brine barrel. Before John could put them on the table, Morning Flower had pots in the fire ready for the food. She pulled her knife from her belt, pointed it at John, and said, "Sit, I will make your supper."

John watched as she sliced, pealed and chopped. He was again amazed how well she handled her knife. In a few moments, the meat and vegetables were boiling away, and she was tidying up.

"You are very good with the cooking," remarked John.

"I hope I please you, and your supper is good." John's supper was good, and he ate with vigor when he noticed Morning Flower not getting a platter ready for herself . "Morning Flower, get a platter, and eat your supper."

"I must wait until you are finished. If anything is left, I will eat. That is our custom, John."

"It's not my custom. You will get a platter, fill it, sit down in this chair, and eat with me."

Morning Flower filled a platter and sat down opposite John at the table. "Now let's eat together," John said softly. They ate quietly for a few minutes when John noticed Morning Flower not looking up but ate with her head bowed. "Morning Flower?" said John. She looked across the table to John. "Is something wrong?" he asked.

"You are not pleased with me!" she said as she put her eyes down again as if ashamed.

"I am pleased with you. I am happy you are here, having supper with me. Why do you think I am not pleased?"

"I am not used to your ways," she said raising her eyes with hope. "I was raised that the men ate the best and first. After that the women and girl children would eat what was left and never at the table, especially when men were in the cabin."

"Our ways will be different," said John. "We will eat together always. The best food will be divided equal between us." There was a quiet pause, then John went on. "If we have children, they, too, will eat when we eat whether they are boys or girls. They, too, will have their portion of the best food." John noticed Morning Flower smiling. "What makes you smile?" asked John.

"We will have children?" asked Morning Flower.

"If it happens, I'll be happy. It will be nice to have a family," mused John. He sat back in his chair and looked at Morning Flower. He was wondering what their children would look like. He had blue eyes with blond hair and was tall and white. She had black eyes and black hair. She was not tall and had copper-brown skin.

While he sat there staring off in space, smiling, Morning Flower wondered what John was thinking. He seemed to be happy because he was smiling. She had never known anyone that smiled so much. He is a good man, she thought. She felt very lucky she was his woman. She knew she would do everything possible to please him.

John stood up breaking the silence. "I will fetch a bucket of water from the well," said John as he picked up the water bucket. Morning Flower was on her feet. I'll get it, John. You can rest now."

"It's dark, Morning Flower. I'd rather get the water because we don't know what animals are out there. Stay in the house, and I'll be right back." He turned and went out the door and into the darkness.

When John came back in, Morning Flower had the table cleared and the kettle ready for water to clean the dishes. Without a word, Morning Flower dipped water into the kettle and swung the kettle on the davit, over the fire. Again, John marveled at her efficiency in the house. Again he thought it was nice to have someone help with the chores.

The evening drifted away. The dishes were done, and the fire built up giving the house a warm, comfortable glow. John and Morning Flower were sitting on a deer-skin rug near the hearth. He was watching Morning Flower staring at the fire. "Do you miss your home?" asked John.

Morning Flower slowly turned her eyes toward John. "I don't know how I feel. I miss the children and Mother but not where I lived or my Father. He was very mean to all of us, and I was very afraid of him. Yes, I am very happy to be here."

"Did your Father ever hit you?" asked John.

"He hit, punched, slapped, pinched, and pushed all of us," she said through her teeth. "He even tried to, to ugh, do what the Hess boys did but I was able to get away from him. He was only one man. I hope I never see him again."

John could see real hatred for her Father in her face - a hard, determined look. He thought that he had better go real easy with her. He felt she would make a great help mate but shouldn't abuse her or treat her badly. He was remembering his Mother. She was like that, too. She would take a lot before she would go into action. Then you'd better watch out! Yes, John thought, Morning Flower would be just like his Mother - hard working, smart, and faithful.

The fire crackled on as the couple sat facing it. The warmth and companionship was felt strongly by John. It was a pleasant feeling to be with someone in the evening, he was thinking. "I am glad you are here," said John.

"I am glad to be here."

"This house was very lonely when I was here alone in the evenings," said John.

"I felt alone, too, even with the children and my Mother there. I felt lonely to be with someone."

"Do you feel lonely now?" asked John.

"No, now I feel that hunger no more. I am your woman now. I know I can take care of you and your cabin. You make me feel bright inside," said Morning Flower as she turned toward John.

He could see her eyes were a bit misty. He didn't know what to say. This woman is such a mystery he thought.

The fire was settling down, so John went out the back door and brought in an arm load of wood. Morning Flower jumped up and started to unload the wood from his arm. As she took the logs one by one and stacked them by the fireplace, she would glance up to John with a faint smile. His heart flip flopped. He went out again and came back w ith another huge arm load. This time, she met him at the door and took four logs on her own arm to the wood stack. John put the last two logs on the fire.

They just stood there for a moment while the new wood caught and flamed up. "Are you sleepy yet?" asked John.

"Yes, I am tired," she said. "That blanket on the box. I may use it tonight?"

"Yes, if you want," said John.

Morning Flower walked over to the corner of the room and picked up the old horse blanket. Then she came back to John and said, "Have a good sleep." Then she proceeded to the door, opened it, and started out the door.

Puzzled, John called to her, "Morning Flower, where are you going?"

"To the barn," was her reply. "I always sleep with the animals at my Father's cabin."

"Come in here!" demanded John.

She turned to face John, her head down, biting her lower lip. She felt like she had angered him. As she stood there just outside of the open door, she waited for his next outburst. John stepped outside and reached for her hand. She instinctively flinched expecting to be cuffed about. Instead, John took her hand gently, and in a quiet tender manner said, "Come. Come in the house. I want you to sleep in the warm house."

Obediently, she followed John through the doorway clinging to his hand. Once inside, he closed the door to the cold outside. He turned to Morning Flower and tenderly put his arms around her. As he held her close, he could feel her nervous shiver. They stood holding each other for a minute or so until he could feel her relax. He tilted her chin up and looked into her eyes. Surprised, John could see fear and uneasiness.

"Did I make you angry?" she asked in a whisper-like whimper.

"No," John said gently. "You make me happy," as he tenderly kissed her lips.

She put her arms around his neck, stood on tip toes and hungrily kissed him back. "It's time to put you to bed," said John in a low husky voice. Taking her hand, he led her to the middle room where he had his bed. From a peg on the wall, he took an old shirt he sleeps in and handed it to Morning Flower. Pulling back the blankets John said, "This is where you will sleep tonight."

She stood riveted to the floor. "I have never slept in a bed," she said.

"You will tonight. Now take off your buckskins and put on this shirt. Then get into bed and cover up. I'll be right back."

John went outside to get an arm load of logs for the fireplace. When he came back in, he fired up the fireplace. When the wood caught into a warm fire, John went into the bedroom. Morning Flower was in bed, fast asleep. He stood and looked at her for a moment then turned down the oil lamp and went back to the fireplace. Rather than disturb her, John thought it would be better if he curled up in the old horse blanket by the fire. As he was dosing off, his mind was going over the days events. His last thoughts were of holding Morning Flower close.

John woke to soft pattering in the kitchen and good smells coming from the little kitchen fireplace. He sat up stiffly and watched Morning Flower busy in the next room. She turned and saw him awaken. She came to him with a hot cup of tea and a little flat piece of tanned rawhide. Placed neatly on the rawhide were three pointed little sticks hardly bigger than a wood splinter. She sat squarely across from him, cross legged on the floor as she placed the cup of

186

tea and the rawhide in front of him. "What are these little sticks for?" he asked.

"To clean your teeth," she said.

"What?" exclaimed John.

"They make your mouth feel good. I'll show you." She began to show John how to clean between his teeth and gums. He picked up a little stick and started.

"This tastes good. What is it?" asked John.

"Birch wood," she said.

"Umm," was his reply as he picked up and sipped on his tea.

She went to the kitchen and poured hot water in a pan, placed a bar of foul-smelling yellow soap on a cotton cloth by the pan. She looked in at John, and said pointing to the pan, "Wash, you will feel better."

Like a good boy, he got up and splashed and lathered. His breakfast consisted of hot biscuits, bacon, and honey. Morning Flower watched while he was busy cleaning up his plate. John leaned back in his chair and let out a long, "AAAH, that was good."

"I'm glad you liked it," she said as she started to clean up the table.

"Shall I saddle Willie?" she asked.

"I'll do it," said John getting up and putting on his coat and hat. Without a word, he opened the door and went to the barn. As he entered the stalls to the horses, he stopped in surprise. The horses had been fed, fresh straw put down, and the water buckets were full. Plus they looked as though they had been curried and brushed. Willie and Girlie nickered as John was looking around. She must have done all this while I slept thought John. What a help mate, he thought, as he saddled Willie.

John had Willie out of the barn when he noticed Morning Flower standing by the back door. "I will take

Girlie for a run in the pasture if it pleases you," she said as John swung up on Willie.

"That will be fine," said John. "I appreciate your taking care of the horses too. I will be back shortly after nightfall." He slowly tipped his hat like a gentleman would. Willie and John went down the lane to the road leading to town.

Morning Flower watched them until they were out of sight thinking of all the things she wanted to do before John came back. She felt excited to be a woman to a man that didn't find fault with everything she did. She did so want to please John.

Instead of going over to Mrs. Mitchell's restaurant for breakfast as he usually did, John put up Willie and got to work in the shop. About mid-morning, he turned around to face Mrs. Mitchell with a start. "Where were you this morning John? I had a nice piece of ham saved for you but you didn't come for your breakfast!"

"I had breakfast at home," said John as he got back to work.

"Since when are you having breakfast at home?" said Mrs. Mitchell crossly. "Isn't my cooking good enough for you anymore?"

"Your cooking is just fine," John assured her. "I'll be over at midday for some of that rabbit stew I can smell clean over here." He leaned down and gave her a peck on the forehead. "Smells good too," said John.

Mrs. Mitchell blushed red and a little befuddled said, "I'll see in you in a little while then."

Jack Shink walked up and said, "Looks like you'll have two men to feed, won't she John?"

"Looks that way," said John as he shook Jack's hand. Mrs. Mitchell, with a little smile, started across the street as the men talked about their business.

The day went on and before he knew it, the sun was low in the West. John found himself looking for the first time of going home. A bit earlier than usual, he closed the shop and headed home. It was just dark as he and Willie came up the lane. The house looked so cheery with the oil lamps lit inside. An oil lamp was lit on the post just outside of the barn. He swung off Willie and turned up the wick for more light. That was thoughtful of her. She must have known how it is to fumble around in the dark until you get a lamp lit. He unsaddled Willie and led him into his stall. You might know, thought John. Girlie was happily chomping on oats, fresh hay, and the water buckets were full. Willie nickered to Girlie as he started to chomp on his trough of oats.

John walked to the back door of the cabin when Morning Flower opened the door. "Good evening, John. Was it a good day for you?"

"Yes it was. What smells good?" said John.

"Squirrels - I caught six today. They are roasting and almost done," she said as she got a pan of hot water for John to wash up.

"You caught squirrels?" asked John.

"Yes, six and four rabbits."

"How?" asked John.

"I set snares this morning and by midday, I had these. The rabbits are in the salt brine in the root cellar."

"After John washed up, they sat down to a fine supper of biscuits, roasted squirrel with wild onions. John was hungry and ate four squirrels. Morning Flower smiled as he dug into his supper.

John put an armful of smaller logs on the fire in the sitting room and sat down to enjoy the evening. Morning Flower came in from the kitchen with some small cakes and two cups of hot tea. John took a sip of the hot brew. "Ummm. This is good. What kind is it?"

"Penneroyal and Wild Spearmint," she said.

"Where did you find this?" asked John.

"Down by the creek, there are many kinds of teas, seeds, berries and barks along the creek. It seems no one uses what nature has for us. So many things to collect. I hope you like the tea."

John watched her as she opened up to him for the first time. Her eyes shone with excitement talking about her discoveries and her ability to gather these things to make their home interesting. John decided to take a nibble of the little cake she had made. This was another surprise - tangy and sweet.

"These are great. What are these little red things?"

"Dried teaberries. They grow on a tiny plant on the floor of the forest hiding under a leaf of a plant. Sometimes the animals don't find them, and they dry up. I found a handful this morning. Do you like them, John?" She was smiling as he reached for a second one.

"Good, good," mumbled John as he sipped and nibbled on the cakes.

They sat in silence for awhile, enjoying the warmth of the fire, the cakes, the tea, and being together. Morning Flower was thinking how pleasant it is here with John. No more being pushed and batted around when her Father felt like it or having to go to the stables to sleep. This wasn't bad in the Summer but miserable in the Winter especially when it rained. That old stable roof always did leak. Here with John she felt safe and warm.

She was concerned about taking John's wonderful bed last night. She slept so sound and woke up very rested.

Tonight, she was thinking, she would sleep by the fire, and he could sleep in his bed. She did feel a little guilty this morning when he woke up stiff and sore from sleeping on the floor. Even the hay would be softer.

John was thinking too. This is nice. He would glance now and then at Morning Flower. Her eyes danced and her black hair glistened from the light of the fire. She seemed so dainty and frail yet he knew how strong she could be. When she would look at him, his heart would melt. She always dropped her eyes when she realized John was looking at her. She did so much today. He just realized she had swept and washed the floor in the sitting room. Also, everything was dusted and wiped clean. Even a feed bag curtain was tacked up at the kitchen window. "I noticed you put a curtain up in the kitchen," said John.

"Do you like it? I found it under the hay this morning. I'll look for more tomorrow. I can make many things if I can find more."

John could see again her quick enthusiasm when she would see things she could do to make their existence more pleasant.

"I'm pleased you like doing things like that," said John.

"Doing for you and your house and animals makes me feel I am earning my way. I enjoy being busy. I always had much to do at my Father's but I didn't feel as much joy as I do with you, John." John wasn't sure how to respond to this when Morning Flower said, "I washed your other shirt and pants. The shirt is not good anymore. It has holes and burned parts from your work. If you bring cloth, I'll make you another shirt unless you would want a deer hide shirt. I could do that."

John thought for a minute and then said, "I'll bring material tomorrow. I'm surprised you can make shirts. You surprise me a lot, Morning Flower."

She sat there smiling pleased that John was happy. She hoped John was going to be pleased enough to start to thinking of her as a woman. So far, he was nice but he had not made a move toward her as a woman. She was worried he thought of her as spoiled since he found her with the Hess Brothers. Maybe he would keep her for a while until he would find a pure woman and cast her out. She didn't know what she could do about this except make him happy in anyway she could.

"Tired?" asked John.

"A little," she replied.

"Well, I guess it's time to sleep. I'm pretty tired, and I have a lot of work tomorrow," said John.

Morning Flower got up and put the dishes into the kitchen. Coming back to the sitting room she had the horse blanket over her arm. "John, tonight you sleep in the bed, and I'll sleep by the fire."

"No," said John. "You will sleep in the bed, and I'll sleep at the fire."

"But, John."

"No buts. You will sleep in the bed. Now give me the blanket."

She handed him the blanket, and John drew her to him in a brotherly hug. "Now get a good nights sleep," he said in a low husky voice. "You will need it with all the projects you are planning."

She looked up with a mischievous smile and said, "Thank you, John." She kissed him full on the mouth, and then turned and went to the bedroom. John was still standing there as she disappeared into the room.

The next day while John was working, he was also thinking about Morning Flower and their evening conversation. He needed to go over to the General Store and buy some material. He was almost caught up with the work promised today so he decided to go over to Mrs. Mitchell for his midday meal. When he opened the door, he could hear her in the kitchen. "Hello," he called.

Mrs. Mitchell looked around the corner and said, "Well, John. You must be hungry. You didn't come to see me, now did you? Sit anywhere, John. Most of my customers were in already." John sat down at a table where he could see the shop through the window. Mrs. Mitchell came out with a plate of stew, chunk of bread, and a cup of hot tea. "Bout all I got left, John. Business was good today."

No sooner had she said this when someone knocked on the back door. Mrs. Mitchell went to the back door. A boy with a dark complexion, black hair, and black hair was standing there. He was about 15 or 16 years old, short, with a  stocky build. He spoke to Mrs. Mitchell in French. John heard her buying deer meat and rabbits. The door closed and she came back to John's table and sat down with a grunt and a sigh.

"Wonder what happened to the girl that used to bring the meat. The boy came yesterday to ask me what I wanted, and now today he brought it. Good-looking little devil for a half-breed. You seen the girl, John?"

"Yup," said John as he got up to leave. "Good-looking little devil you say," teased John as he handed Mrs. Mitchell a two-bit piece.

No one was at the blacksmith shop so John crossed the street to the General Store. As he entered, he made his way to the back of the store where the bolts of cloth were stacked on a table. Three ladies were chatting as they were looking and fondling different pieces of cloth and trim. When John approached, they went silent. John started to inspect the different yardage trying to look like he knew what he was doing. Amy, Mrs. Bender's daughter spoke up, "Hello, John."

"Oh, hello." John turned and looked at her as if he first recognized her. "How have you been?" John was surprised at how much she had grown since he had since her last.

"Fine. Are you looking for a special material?" she asked.

"I'm looking for a good cloth to make a shirt," mumbled John.

In an instant, the three women broke into a chatter pulling out this material and that. They were showing John different patterns and strengths. Finally, a bewildered John agreed on a dark gray.

"Who is going to make the shirt for you, John?" asked Amy with a coy smile as she stood very close and cozy.

"Morning Flower," replied John not looking up.

"An Indian!" screeched Amy. "No, John. I can make you a nice shirt. Those Indians don't know nothing and besides, I can't see you mixed with a lousy half-breed. She'll want something from you and probably steal it too. I'm surprised at you, John!"

"I don't think she'll steal from me, and she's very handy, too," said John. "I think I'll take a pretty print cloth for her to make something for herself, too."

"Oh my God!" exclaimed one of the women. "Come on ladies," said another. They started towards the front of the store. "Leave this Indian lover to fend for himself. What he gets is what he deserves. Imagine that! A good-looking boy like that ruining his life." They went chattering and bustling along.

Quietly, John selected a bright blue and white polka dot cloth. He took the bolts to the front to Edwin who was a Co-owner.

"Cut enough here to make me a shirt and enough of this to make a dress or something."

Without a word, Edwin started to lay out the material to measure and cut. With mischief in his eyes, Edwin said, "Sure gave those gossips plenty to talk about. Be all over town by sundown."

"What will be all over town?" asked John.

"You being sweet on that half-breed up on the mountain. Can't say I blame you, John. Ain't bad lookin' for an Indian. I often thought I might ask her to come in the back room a couple of times for a little pushy ."

"Think she would have gone," rumbled John.

"Sure!" boasted Edwin. "She had a roll in the weeds with the Hess boys and who knows who else.

Yep, don't blame you for getting a little of that though I'd keep it quiet around the women folks around here.

They are pretty uneasy about Indian girls. Especially those whose husbands and sons find excuses to go up the valley to the Indian camp North of Lykens Town."

John's temper was starting to rise hearing Edwin's remarks and the attitude of the women. Some may be bad and steal but so do white folks. Some of them are bad too. John paid for the material and got back to his shop. People were waiting so John got to work and soon his fuming settled down.

As the day drew to a close, John started for home with his bundle of material. Entering the lane, he saw the familiar sight of light in the cabin, smoke rolling out of the chimney, and the lantern lit on the post waiting for his arrival. He was anxious to see Morning Flower. Savage? Steal from me? Loose with men? Never! John thought as he put Willie into his stall ready with fresh hay, oats and water. Even Girlie nickered a welcome as they arrived.

When John opened the door, Morning Flower stood wide eyed at the material John laid on the table.

"Oh John! This is beautiful. This will make nice shirts for you," she exclaimed.

"The blue material with white dots is for you. Maybe you can make something nice for yourself," said John as he hung up his jacket.

All of a sudden, John felt strong feminine arms around his waist, and Morning Flower squeaking with joy hugging him from behind. "For me John! For me?" John pulled her arms free and turned around, bent down, and looked into her face.

"Yes for you," said John.

She was so overcome with joy, she jumped up and threw her arms around his neck. She hung on while John straightened up pulling her feet clear off the floor. "That is the most wonderful surprise; a present. I never had a surprise present like that," she said as she hugged his neck. John could feel her body; strong and lean. He could smell her female aroma and her warmth. John felt excitement rising so he let her down to the floor very gently. Both were flushed and suddenly shy of each other. She went directly to her pots to check on their progress as John went out for extra wood. It was a chilly night. They might need more wood for the fireplace.

Besides he needed to get away from her and settle down as she might see and laugh at him.

When he came back in, supper was ready and Morning Flower was sitting in her chair at the table inspecting the material. "This is wonderful material, John. I will make you a handsome shirt, and I'll start after supper."

And so she did while they were sitting by a roaring fire in the sitting room. Morning Flower and John sat peacefully. She was cutting and sewing. Once in awhile, she would measure John's arms or back to make sure her calculations were correct. They made small talk throughout the evening, and John started to think again of the ladies at the store and Edwin's remarks. When John grew silent from time to time, Morning Flower would look up from her work to ask if he would like this or that or a snack. She was trying her best to keep him content.

John was becoming disturbed about the attitude of the folks towards Indians. Women thought they were dirty, lazy, and couldn't be trusted. The men had the same attitude except they didn't mind using them for sex.

Some of the young fellows made regular trips to the camps up the Valley. Maybe some couldn't be trusted and were dirty savages he thought. While watching Morning Flower happy and busy at her task, it was hard to think of her that way.

"I'm about ready to go to sleep," said John.

Morning Flower put down her sewing, rubbed her eyes, and yawned in agreement. "I will sleep by the fire, John. It's not fair that I take your wonderful bed from you."

"No, I'll sleep by the fire," said John.

Morning Flower stood up with her fists on her hips. "Then we'll both sleep in the bed!" she said in a very firm manner. She then disappeared into the bedroom. In a few minutes, she came back to the sitting room combing out her black shiny hair. She was wearing one of John's old shirts which served as a nightgown. "Your bed is ready," she announced. "Take off your boots and pants. You'll sleep better."

Like a good boy, he listened to her and went into the bedroom and climbed into bed. A few minutes later, Morning Flower slipped under the blankets. They both laid there on their backs with their eyes closed but very wide awake. John's hand touched her hand ever so lightly under the cover. They laid like this for awhile.

Then John took her hand in his. Morning Flower smiled as she pretended to be asleep. Soon they were in a contented sleep.

Before dawn, Morning Flower was up and going. By the time the sun came up, she had the horses fed and watered. Breakfast was ready and John's pants and shirt were brushed and aired. He needs a new pair of pants too, she thought. A tanned apron wouldn't be bad either. This was another project for her. She was working on his new shirt when John stumbled out of the bedroom. He went straight for the wash bowl which he was now accustomed to. Warm water, soap, and a drying rag were always there waiting for him as he woke up with his little sticks for his teeth. He was settling into a comfortable routine and was enjoying it very much. He liked being waited on and fussed over.

"Morning," uttered John as he was drying off.

Morning Flower just nodded, smiled, and started to make his breakfast plate ready with fresh biscuits and smoked fish she had caught in the stream yesterday and hot tea.

"What kind of fish is this?" asked John.

"Shad. They are coming from the sea to spawn. I will catch more and smoke them if you like them."

"They're good," munched John.

Morning Flower smiled. "John, we need some things from the store.

"What?" asked John busily eating.

"Flour, salt, sugar, beans, bacon..."

John broke in. "Why don't you come down to the shop with Girlie. I'll give you money, and you buy what you want."

"Do you think it will be all right?" she asked.

"Of course it will be all right!" retorted John.

"Just the same. I'd better go in the back door," said Morning Flower.

"Oh no you don't! You will go in the front door! It's time the people know you are my woman."

Morning Flower sat in the chair with her hands in her lap. Her head was down with her heart racing.

She looked up with a broad smile. "I liked it when you said my woman. I will be a good woman for you John. I like being your woman."

John realized this was the first time he committed to her that she was his woman. Not knowing what to say next, he got up and announced. "I'm going to the shop now."

She stood up to him on her tiptoes and kissed him lightly. "I hope it's a good day for you," she whispered.

A little after midday, Morning Flower came to the shop. It was a warm day, and John took an anvil out to the open roof end of the shop. Three loafers from town were sitting around watching John work. These old men would sit and talk, spit tobacco and watch the ladies bustle about town. John was working on a buggy wheel for Ed Miller out in the Valley.

Morning Flower tethered Girlie by Willie. The horses liked each other. They nickered and nuzzled each other. As she approached John smiling brightly, he put down the hoop for the wheel he was making. "Do you know what you want?" asked John.

She nodded. "I still think I should go to the back door," said Morning Flower.

"I told you the front door!" said John as he handed her a gold coin.

Smiling , she started across the street to the General Store.

"Ain't that your horse that half-breed was riding?" asked one of the loafers.

Another one asked," She workin' for you John?"

John was back to work making the sparks fly. He turned to the loafers and rumbled, "She's my woman!"

A long stunned silence followed. The men looked at each other with a shrug here and a nod there while John attacked a cross bar fresh out of the fire - red hot!

"Looks like rain," one said trying to change the subject. "Yep," said another. "My knee is telling me so." And so the small talk went on.

In a little while, Morning Flower came back to the shop with a large feed bag full of things. John met her halfway across the street relieving her of the heavy sack. John asked, "Have any trouble?"

"No, Mr. Edwin was very nice. So was Lizzy Meinhart. She said she missed me and hoped you were well and happy."

Soon Morning Flower was headed home with the sack securely tied to Girlie's rump. The loafers started to split up to spread the gossip.

Later that afternoon, Edwin came over from the store. "John, I think you should know. The ladies and some of the men don't like your choice for a woman. They are talking their heads off."

"Do you think they'll settle down in a little while?" asked John.

"I suppose," said Edwin. "I'd tell Morning Flower to be careful and not come to town unless she has to."

"Thanks Edwin," said John as he got back to work.

Edwin stood there for a minute and then he said, "John, it don't make a difference what you do. It's none of my business. If you want a woman, you should have any woman that will take you and don't you worry about what those old biddies are saying."

John stopped working for a second, turned and said in a low voice, "I won't Edwin." He then turned and got back to work. Edwin got the hint and left.

That evening as John was riding home, he saw the Hess boys running along a fence between two houses. They were carrying something as they were running along and laughing. When they saw John, they stopped and glared at him. They turned and ran for all they were worth in the opposite direction.

Wonder what that was all about John thought to himself. No good likely.

After supper, Morning Flower came to him with his new shirt. "Try this on John and see if it will fit," said Morning Flower. John could see in her eyes how excited she was. He slipped off his worn-out shirt and slipped into the new one.

"Perfect fit," he said smiling down at her.

"Do you like it? Does it feel good? Are the sleeves long enough?"

"Yes, yes, yes. It's perfect. Now what have you done on your dress so far?" asked John.

"Well, I started but I don't want you to see it until I'm finished."

"Why?" asked John.

"I want to surprise you," she said coyly.

"You are full of surprises, woman!" exclaimed John.

"Say that again," whispered Morning Flower.

"Say what again?" asked John.

"Woman," she said.

"Woman?" John said.

"Oh, you mean, my woman," she answered.

He took her in his arms, and they kissed and cuddled and kissed some more. Again, John was aware of the sweet scent of her. His desire for her was becoming obvious. She clung to him and whispered, "I want to be your woman John to make you happy."

John knew he had better do something or he would be very embarrassed. Then John had a real surprise. Morning Flower whispered, "I'm ready for bed John." She turned and walked into the bedroom.

John stood there stunned for a moment, and then finally came to his senses. He stoked the fire, blew out the lamps, and made his way into the darkness of the bedroom. He sat on the bed and took off his boots.

He then stood up and took off his pants and shirt. In the silence of the darkness, he could hear her soft breathing. Pulling back the covers, he slid into bed laying on his back. It wasn't long before his hand was slowly wandering around for hers under the covers. Suddenly, he touched her bare hip. As if it were electricity, he recoiled his hand to his side.

In a bit, he felt her hand touch his and then her fingers close over his hand. John lay there, heart pounding, wide awake. Then she rolled over toward him taking his right hand over her head and over her bare shoulder. Lying there tight beside him her hand exploring around on his chest.

"You would be more comfortable if you took off this shirt," she whispered.

John sat up and pulled off his shirt hardly believing his ears. As he lay down, she came to him again.

He could feel her naked body next to his; her breasts very firm against his side. John's manhood was in full bloom as her exploring hand moved below his undershorts. John gasped as she found her target. She pulled the string of his undershorts, pushed them down to his knees, and then slowly slid over him eagerly kissing him as he pulled her to him, kissing her back.

A short time later, she lay cuddled up close sound asleep. John still lay on his back wide awake realizing he had the most wonderful experience of his whole life. This wonderful girl. I'll never let her go.

The next day, John was happily back at work. It promised to be a real nice spring-like day. John Adam came into the shop and asked, "Do you know anything about four chickens stolen from my chicken pen last night?"

This took John completely by surprise. Why was he asking me, he thought. John thought for a minute and then answered, "No, Mister Adam. I have no idea."

Jack Smink walked into the shop just then. John and Mr. Adam greeted him. "Someone stole my axe last night," said Jack. "I went out to chop some wood for the stove, and it was just gone. Who would do such a thing?"

Mr. Adam said, "I lost four chickens last night"

"We never have things stolen around here," said Jack. "Beats me who would steal chickens. Must have been mighty hungry. Maybe that's why they needed my axe."

The two men were talking as they made their way across the street to Mrs. Mitchell's restaurant.

That afternoon, Morning Flower was down by the creek tending to her fish traps. She had set the traps the day before, and so far, they were yielding two to three fish per trap. These traps were an ingenious invention. They were made the old Northern Indian way. A basket of wild grape vines were woven in such a way water would pass through easily yet too small for a decent size fish. The back side had a removable flap. The front had a funnel-shaped hole for the fish to enter. In each trap, she tied down a few minnows as bait. These traps worked well enough to produce enough fish for a good meal.

She was crossing over a quiet part of the stream when she heard voices. Instinctively, she settled low in the brush and peered in the direction of the voices. She could hear them along the road along the stream.

They soon became visible from her vantage point. As soon as she saw the three unkempt young men, she recognized them - the Hess boys. She felt the cold chill of fear and anger as they came ambling along going towards town. She could hear parts of their conversation as they drew near her hiding place. It seems they had been up the Valley to the Indian camps vising the Indian girls.

Soon they passed and moved out of sight. Morning Flower realized she needed to hurry with the traps and get home. She wanted to have a good fish dinner for John.

As the days passed and the weather grew warmer, more and more reports of theft in and around town.

The townsfolk were becoming more and more concerned about the thefts. Chickens, eggs, a small pig, pots, axes, ropes, and buckets were reported stolen. Soon they were putting together that the thefts started about the time John brought his half-breed Indian down from the mountain to live with him. The men, urged by their wives, were being pushed into talking to John about the situation. Very reluctantly, the men met one evening and formed a committee of three to talk to him. They were Jack Smink, Bill Heimbough, and Ludwig Wolfgang.

Jack was to head up the committee and ask the questions. Bill and Ludwig were the witnesses.

The very next morning, the three men met at the general store across the street from the blacksmith shop. Edwin knew what was going on and felt very badly about what these men were planning to do. He felt so strongly about it he felt he needed to say something to the three men. The men were in a huddle around the store when Edwin walked up to them.

"Gonna do it, ain't you?" questioned Edwin.

"Guess so," answered Jack.

"How you goin' to do it?" asked Edwin.

Bill said, "Just ask him, I guess?"

"Just like that!" said Edwin. "You gonna ask John if his woman is stealing chickens, eggs, and other things. Huh! You think he won't knock you all on your ass? Stop and think! John makes enough that this woman has all she needs. John nor she needs to steal anything from anybody. I'll tell you what you're going to do.

You're going to cause us to lose the best blacksmith we ever had. That's what you're going to do." Edwin turned and stormed away rather than say more and say something he would be sorry for.

"Boy, is he mad," said Bill.

"Sure gave us a mouthful," muttered Ludwig.

Jack said, "Maybe we better soft paddle it with John. Let me do the talking fellows. I know John pretty well. I think I can get the point across without getting him upset."

The three men wandered across the street and into the blacksmith shop. John was working a hot piece of iron on the anvil. John nodded a welcome to the men as they entered and continued working the iron. When he go it to the right shape, he grabbed the iron with tongs and doused it into the tub of water.

"Good morning," John greeted the men.

Very uncomfortable mumbling's came from the three men avoiding John's eyes.

"We need to talk," said Jack.

"We do?" questioned John.

"We think so," said Jack.

"What about?" asked John.

"Well, a lot of things have been stolen around here lately. We have been wondering if you knew anything about it?"

"Why should I?" asked John fishing the cooled iron out of the tub to examine it. Then he turned around and asked in a surprised tone, "You think I stole these things?"

"No, no, no John. We were just wondering if you knew anything about it," said Jack.

"You're not making much sense, Jack. I don't need to steal what I hear was stolen. If you are accusing me of stealing, you can get the hell out of my shop!"

Jack could see John was insulted and a little mad at their questions so Jack thought he had better soothe his feelings a bit. "We've been looking everywhere for an answer to this problem. Since you being in the center of town, we naturally thought you might have heard something. Now John, don't get your dander up. We need your help."

John settled down and went back to work. "Didn't hear a thing fellows," said John rather darkly.

"Some talk has been its been Indians," volunteered Ludwig.

"Ever heard of Indians doing that sort of thing?" asked John. "Besides no one has seen Indians around town lately. They go to Lykens Town but mostly they stay in their village north of the town. You fellows should know that. Some of the young boys and even some men go up there once in awhile to be with the Indian girls.

Nope! I don't think it's Indians."

"Well," said Ludwig. "Most of the town does think it's Indians. Everyone knows they steal, cheat, and lie."

Just then Morning Flower rode up on Girlie. She looked beautiful. Her silk black hair was pulled back in a braid with her dark complexion and dark black smiling eyes. She was dressed in her light tan buckskins with moccasins on her feet. She always rode Girlie bare back and was quite at home with the Girlie. The horse and the girl had become good friends. She slipped off Girlie with ease hefting a string of 12 or 15 squirrels straddled on Girlie's back. She turned toward the men and her husband.

"You have quite a string of squirrels there," said Ludwig.

"I caught them in my snares this morning. John, I kept five for the pan tonight so I thought I might sell these in town."

"That's a good idea," said John. "Who do you thing will want them?"

"Maybe, Mrs. Siefert or Mrs. Gunderman or even Mrs. Mitchell. I think I'll try her first," she said as she started across the street.

"She's livin' with you?" mumbled Ludwig.

"Yup," said John.

"People in town here sayin' so," added Jack.

John smacked the hot iron hard so hard that the sparks flew from the anvil - five powerful strokes!

"It's my business," spoke up John over the hiss of the hot iron as he stuck it into the tub of water.

Behind Mrs. Mitchell's restaurant, the men could hear a commotion. In that instant, Morning Flower came running around the corner of the house and out into the street toward the blacksmith shop.

Shouting and cursing just behind Morning Flower, Mrs. Mitchell appeared round the same corner, waving her fist. "You stay away from here you thieving Indian bitch. Then she shouted across the street to John, "You keep your Indian whore where she belongs. You better keep her out of town or there will be trouble." Still shouting and raving, Mrs. Mitchell turned and disappeared into the back of the building.

Morning Flower trotted to a stop in front of John and the men. A little breathless, she asked, "What did I do John?"

"I don't know," said John. "What happened over there?"

"I just asked her if she wanted any squirrels today. Then she just started screaming at me. I tried to ask her what was wrong but she wouldn't listen so I ran away."

The other men were in a huddle talking quietly. Ludwig came over to John and Morning Flower.

"Maybe Mrs. Mitchell is right John. With all the thieving around, maybe its best if Morning Flower stays out of town. People are suspicious about her already. You know how we feel about Indians."

John stood for a moment reading Morning Flower's fear in her eyes. His temper was rising like a pot of water soon ready to boil. He turned to face Ludwig trying to hold back. He said, "My wife will go anywhere she pleases. She is honest, hard-working, and good. Continuing in a low and purposeful voice, John continued, "If anyone hurts or abuses her, they will have to answer fully to me."

The men looked at each other, rather embarrassed. They said goodbye to John and Morning Flower and left the shop.

Morning Flower asked, "What is this talk about thievery?"

"Some people have been missing things. Someone is stealing, and they don't know who. They blame the Indians."

"What kind of things?" asked Morning Flower.

"An axe, chickens, pots, and other things."

"Indians wouldn't steal such things. Food if they were hungry, a knife if they needed it to survive, but not those things. It sounds more like boys just having fun."

"The folks around here are quick to suspect the Indians," said John.

"And now they suspect me, don't they John? And now they want me to stay out of town!" she said with black eyes flashing. "I was good enough to bring meat and furs to town since I was a little girl, hardly able to carry the load. They looked for me then! Now! I'm not to come to town?"

John could see a spirit in this girl that was not to be denied. Smiling he said to her, "I told the men how we felt.

You do and go anywhere you want in this town. You can hold your head high. We give to this town more than they give us." Morning Flower's attitude changed back to her old self as John spoke.

"I'll go sell the squirrels now," she said.

John turned her around and kissed her full on the mouth. Surprised at first, she then kissed him back.

From across the street, Edwin was sweeping out his shop. He looked across the street and broke into a smile. Those two will make it yet, he thought.

The next week went by uneventful as the weather warmed. Then Sunday Morning at the Deutsch Reformed Church came news of more thievery Saturday evening around town. After church, the men stayed to have a meeting and tried to determine who was responsible. The items stolen were a piglet, six chickens, a bag of flour out of Edwin's store room, and a jug of whiskey Bill Heinbough had hidden from his wife in the barn. It was indicated again to be the Indians.

The women held a meeting outside the church in small groups. Some groups weren't even interested thinking it was the men's duties. Another group thought the Indians probably did these things. The other group, the gossips, were arguing strongly. Three women were convinced the problem lay with Morning Flower. It all started when she came to town. Mrs. Meinhart and Edwin's wife were the only ones that stood in her defense.

Mrs. Meinhart was heard to say, "How could she do such things? She's a sweet girl, and besides, she's half white - French I think."

Another snorted, "The half Indian is like all Indian. She's Indian through and through."

"And a thief too," added another.

Still another spoke up, "John is as bad as she is for taking her in. He better not try to make me accept her in this town because I certainly won't!"

Edwin's wife broke in. "She was good enough to bring you wild meat for your table. All of you bought from her, and she always gave you good measure. Now she's not good enough to come to town? I think you are wrong to blame John and her for this thievery. It may be Indians but not John and his wife. What do you say, Lizzy?"

Mrs. Meinhart spoke right up, "I know John to be a very honorable man, and I've always liked Morning Flower."

The door of the church opened, and the men poured out and mingled with the children and women.

# THIRTEEN

## *The Accused*

**M**orning Flower and John decided on Saturday afternoon, they needed some venison for the salt barrel so they saddled up the horses and headed up to Short Mountain where the deer population was reported to be most plentiful. John had hopes of bagging a large stag with heavy haunches. By nightfall, they camped by a natural spring near the flat top of the mountain. By daybreak, John downed a magnificent buck. Soon Morning Flower had it skinned and rolled tight while John was at work cutting out the choice pieces. Morning Flower made rump baskets for the horses and was busy packing. By midday, they were starting down the mountain leaving the rest to scavengers. They were slowly plodding down the road toward town by mid-afternoon when Luke Hassinger and his family came up the road with his family. As they passed Morning Flower and John on their way to their farm, Luke tipped his hat as did John. Luke's wife and children looked down from the wagon as they passed. They couldn't help but see the mass of meat in the rump baskets.

The next morning, John was at work in the shop when Luke and four other men rode to an abrupt stop in front of John as he worked iron at the anvil.

"You!" roared Luke, "and your Indian bitch are a thief."

John stood there dumbfounded. "What are you talking about?" asked John.

"You known damn well what I'm talking about," shouted Luke. "And you're going to pay for that calf you butchered!"

John still couldn't believe his ears. "What calf are you talking about?" asked John.

"Don't stand there and barefaced lie, John. Me and my family saw you and your thieving woman with rump baskets full of meat on the road coming down from my farm.

A crowd was beginning to collect as the two men argued. "That was deer meat!" retorted John. "We killed a buck on Short Mountain Sunday morning and butchered it there. We were bringing the meat back when we passed you and your family."

"Another lie! You can't get up to Short Mountain, shoot a deer, butcher it, and be all the way down the Valley to where you passed us. John, why lie? We got you red handed!"

The crowd was murmuring that's right and nodding their heads.

"Morning Flower and I went up Saturday afternoon and camped up there!" shouted John. "I shot the buck at first light, and we had plenty of time to butcher it and be down in the Valley. Luke, you better check the tracks around your butchered calf. You won't find this hoof mark." John turned and went around the building. In a moment, he came back with Willie. He lifted Willie's left back hoof to display a heavy horseshoe.

Boldly displayed on the horseshoe just ahead of the heel was an extra piece of iron with the letters J. F. John pointed to the hoof and at the clear imprint in the dust.

"Look, you won't find this imprint anywhere around your farm. Both Willie and Girlie wear these shoes. Now get out of here and look somewhere else for your butcher!"

As they left the shop, Luke turned and said, "You'll hear from me John. I'll check the hoof prints, and I'll bet I'll find yours right there!" Luke mounted and started back up the road with his friends following.

The crowd started to break up murmuring and glancing back to the shop as John got busy at his anvil.

Although his explanation seemed to make sense, the seed of doubt was planted. They would never accept Morning Flower  as an equal in their town, he thought. What are we to do? She needed to know also but he needed to break it to her gently even though she had been the target of "Indian" since she was born. She's so beautiful. Her skin was like dark silk; warm and inviting. John's thoughts now turned to making love, and how he wanted her right now.

John closed up the shop and went home. When he got there he knew Morning Flower was gone.

Girlie was still in the meadow so he unsaddled Willie and let him run down to Girlie. He watched them as they frolicked in the afternoon sun. They seemed to enjoy being together - nickering, running, and nuzzling.

The house seemed so empty without Morning Flower. He was home early. She hadn't even started supper yet. John went out to the barn to make the horses stalls ready for the evening. His thoughts ran from needing Morning Flower to how to tell her about the day's events and back to his aching need for her.

"You're home early?" John turned and saw Morning Flower standing,  framed by the afternoon light and the barn doorway. She was wearing one of John's old shirts with a short buckskin skirt. Her black hair was pulled back in a plat that hung down and over her shoulder. She put down the basket of berries and walked over to him with a puzzled look in her eyes. "You're home early."

"Yes," he said as he approached. He could smell her womanness and her sweat on this warm afternoon. Her shirt was open to below her breasts so that the roundness showed a bit in the opening. John pulled her to him and kissed her with a long and passionate embrace.

"Climb up the ladder to the hay," John instructed her. Without a question, she turned to the ladder and started up. John followed looking up. He could see she was wearing nothing under the buckskin skirt. The fire of desire burst into full bloom as he pulled her down into the hay. She smiled when she realized John's manhood was not to be denied. As he kissed her neck and breasts, her desire was a perfect match to his.

They lay there in the fading light and the prickly straw. John was leaning on his arm looking at her beautiful body. He noticed the sweat drops on her flat stomach and her wet black hair below. He could see the evidence of being there oozing from her soft folds. This excited him all over again. She opened her eyes in surprise as he mounted her again.

"You needed me," she teased as she met his thrusts lifting to meet him.

"I needed you," he said as he moaned to another climax.

Willie and Girlie were put away a little late that evening and supper was even later. It turned chilly so after supper a warm fire in the fireplace felt really good.

John slowly started to unravel to Morning Flower what had happened that day. She sat quietly and listened while she worked on her sewing. Finally, John said it all and fell quiet.

"What can we do John?" she asked.

"I'm not sure."

"I could go away. They would forget, and you could get a white woman and ..."

"Never!" grunted John as he stood up and walked over to the fireplace. "Never," he repeated. "You are my woman. We'll work this out somehow. If not, we'll both go somewhere else."

Morning Flower put aside her sewing and came to him. They stood holding each other by the fire for a long time. He was considering just what to do. Her heart was soaring because he had stood up for her and again stated she was his woman no matter what!

The next few days at the shop were very quiet. Only two people came to the shop. One came from way over near Berries Mountain, a half days ride. The other came from Lykens Town. Finally, Edwin ambled across the street and came into the shop. "Been quiet for you John?" asked Edwin.

"Very!" answered John.

"Well, folks around here don't know what to think. Some are ashamed and others are mad as hell."

"Mad about what?" asked John knowing what might be the answer.

"You taking up with a half breed. There was a lot of bonnets shaken when they heard that. You know John, I like Morning Flower. She's always showed more grit than all the girls in this town put together but they still look on her as an Indian."

John was pondering Edwin's remarks while he was working Edwin continued, "By the way John, they couldn't find any horse prints around that calf up at Luke's. Only bare feet tracks, and they lead up the Valley. Must have been three of them."

"They weren't Indians," spoke up John.

"How you figure that?" asked Edwin.

215

"Bare feet! Indians wear moccasins. They never travel in bare feet. Only white men would be foolish enough to do that."

"Well, that seems right. Anyway, you and Morning Flower are off the hook. You won't get an apology from Luke though. He made such an ass of himself, he'll not come to town for a long time. That goes for some of the folks in town too."

Just then, Morning Flower rode up on Girlie. She swung down in a hurry. John could see she was troubled. "What's wrong?" asked John.

"Some boys smashed my fish traps. They were smashing them when I went to check them."

"What boys?" asked Edwin.

"Little boys, maybe 8 or 10 years old. There were about six or seven of them. I recognized two of them from town. They ran when they saw me. My traps are gone John. Why did they do that John?"

"Just mischievous I guess," answered John.

"Maybe not John," added Edwin. "They probably heard their parents discussing the problems around here and just assumed they could do what they wanted to you two. If that's so, you can look for more trouble before things die down."

"Well, that does it!" shouted John placing his fists on his hips standing tall holding his temper as best he could. "Morning Flower, we're going to leave this place. We'll look for another town to do our blacksmithing!"

Edwin could see John was determined. "John, don't give up yet. Things will die down. Besides, we need you here. Good blacksmiths are hard to find," begged Edwin.

"Edwin, I can't live like this. I won't have people saying and doing things to my woman. It won't stop Edwin! We'll just have to start over somewhere else."

"Now John, this will blow over and folks will come to accept your woman too. I'm sure of it. Don't do anything you'll be sorry for."

"John," said Morning Flower, "I'm beginning to feel afraid around here. Look at those ladies across the street at your store Edwin. They have hate in their eyes when they look over here."

One of the ladies shouted to Edwin as he was half-way there, "Edwin, you been visiting with that Indian lover? Maybe you are a dirty Indian lover too! Your wife will hear about this." The other ladies were nodding.

Edwin didn't say a word and just went into his store. Certainly they will tell his wife before he got home that evening. Then he knew he was in for a rough time.

That evening, John and Morning Flower started to make plans to relocate. They considered moving further up William's Valley, but there were few settlers up there who would need his services. There were lots of people down by the river - maybe too many, though John.

"There is a small village down Armstrong Valley," said Morning Flower reading John's thoughts.

John looked over to her as she sat in her chair, sewing busily. Again he was taken by her quiet beauty in the glow of the fire light. She even knows my thoughts.

"How do you know of the village?" asked John.

"I took meat and pelts down there when we had extra. It was much further than Benderstettle but my Father made me do it rather than have meat spoil. Sometimes I wouldn't get back much before the sun came up. It was a hard trip."

"Are the people nice?" asked John.

"Yes, they are very nice - mostly Scotch, Irish, and German. Not many live in the village though. They are spread out on farms. I could take you there so you could see."

217

"Hmm, that sound like a good idea. We could go tomorrow. There is no business anyway. Everyone is staying away. If they keep staying away from the shop, we'll have to go somewhere else," mused John.

That night when John slipped into bed, he moved his arm under Morning Flower's shoulders. She had her back toward him. He slowly rolled her around and wrapped his arms around her. He was surprised and pleased as they kissed, and he fondled her. She was ready for him, and they made love a long time.

Later, as they lay together, sweaty and exhausted, Morning Flower whispered, "You are a wonderful man, John. You make our loving last and last." Smiling while laying her head on John's chest, she said, "I'm glad to be your woman."

The next morning they were up early, and were on their way before the sun came up over the rim of the East Mountain. They had packed travel rolls in case they would be gone longer than one day.

At the foot of the South Mountain as they were about to start their climb, John noticed Morning Flower stiffen. He looked to where she was staring. Down the path along the creek were the three Hess brothers. It looked like one was carrying a freshly killed piglet. When they saw John and Morning Flower, they stopped, glanced at each other, and then jumped into the bushes along the creek.

As John and Morning Flower were climbing the mountain, John said, "Wonder what that was all about?"

The climb was getting steeper and Morning Flower swung down to walk and give Girlie a lighter load.

John did the same. They led the horses up the primitive road, huffing and puffing. They came around the last bend toward the top of the mountain. The next hundred yards would be even steeper. On this curve was a natural spring of cold and sweet water. They stopped there and took long drinks and watered the horses.

Morning Flower was standing on the road looking up to the summit. "I think we know who the thieves are!" she said in a quiet way still gazing up the road.

"Who?" asked John.

"The Hess boys. You saw the piglet they had."

"Yes," said John as they started up the road.

"It was a black and white," said Morning Flower.

"Only black and whites I know of is what the Adams have. They must have caught it and stolen it.

Now what do you think they'll do with it?" asked John.

"I think I know," she said. "I've seen those boys go back and forth up the Valley for quite sometime now. They go up to see those Indian girls."

"Well, the mystery is solved," puffed John.

The last ten yards to the top was tough but they were finally on the small plateau on the spine of the mountain. They stopped for another rest and looked at the view of William's Valley. To the east, a mountain pushed its way down the middle of the valley and abruptly stopped. This was where John had shot the buck.

This would form two small valleys further east. William's Valley was in front of them and to the west spread to about 20 miles wide when it ended at the mighty Susquehanna. This was a beautiful sight on this pretty sunny day.

They crossed the small flat of the top of the mountain. At the edge before starting down , they mounted their horses. Looking west, the beautiful broad valley spread before them. The dense woodland was broken only by isolated farms here and there. The valley floor was a succession of rolling hills to the river.

They descended the mountain on the rutty road heading west. They came to a stream at the base of the mountain. As they came near the stream, three young Indian boys appeared from the bushes. John and Morning Flower stopped on the road. The boys spread out on the road on the other side of the stream as though to block their way. They were a fierce bunch and were talking excitedly back and forth.

"Do you understand them?" asked John.

"Some of the words are familiar," said Morning Flower. They are from up North somewhere; not from around here. Sounds like they want our horses and me."

The Indian boys were carrying lances and axes. John could not see any firearms or bows. They looked a bit beat up too. One had a large bruise on his side and another was cut on his left arm. They were getting very noisy now. They could charge through them at risk of hurting Morning Flower or the horses, or they could dash back up the mountain. They would probably follow. There is only one way out of this, John thought. John cocked his pistol and pulled the long sword he had made from its sheath along his saddle. He eased himself off the horse and handed the reins to Morning Flower. "You stay here. If something happens to me, run like the wind."

"No John," she said. "There are three of them. They could hurt you."

John ignored her pleas and walked cautiously toward the boys. They really started to yip and whoop then. John stopped by the stream facing them. All of a sudden, the one in the middle broke into a run through the stream with his lance pointed at John. John raised his pistol and shot him full in the face. He fell in the water at John's feet. The other two started for John - one with a lance and the other with an axe. All John had was his sword and his knife. The one with the lance came straight for John. With a two-handed swing, John cut the lance in two. Stunned, the Indian turned and ran down the stream screaming his lungs out. The other Indian ran right passed John toward Morning Flower flailing his axe. John stood transfixed as Morning Flower pulled up John's musket from the saddle holster, aimed, and fired. The Indian took the shot in the chest. He doubled forward, turned, and ran into the woods. They looked at each other, staring into each others eyes as if not to believe what happened.

John walked back to Morning Flower. She got down still holding the musket. John took the musket from her shaking hands and put it back in its holster. He turned and put his arms around her and held her until her shaking stopped.

Finally, she said, "I was afraid for you."

"I was afraid for you too," he said.

The body of the Indian shot in the water floated downstream and out of sight. John thought to look after him but decided they needed to move on. After reloading the musket and pistol and watering the horses, they were again on their way. After the scrimmage, the countryside seemed so peaceful.

It was mid-afternoon when they broke through the trees to a wide cleared field along the road. Ahead they could see a cabin by the road with stock pens and sheds. As they got near the cabin, a farmer came riding up to meet them. He was a stocky fellow wearing the kind of pants and shirts he remembered from his home in Bot Weiser. As he drew near, John noticed his musket cradled in his arm. John and Morning Flower stopped as the man rode up. John held up his hand in peace. The man stopped about twenty paces away. He sat quite still looking the couple over. Willie and Girlie were sniffing and nickering to the scraggly brown horse in front of them - a tired old animal in his late years.

"Ver you come from?" called the man.

"Benderstettle," called John.

"Ju haff a farm dar," asked the man as he moved a bit closer.

John noticed his dialect and answered in German, "Nine. I'm a blacksmith."

The man's eyes lit up. "You are Deutsch?" he questioned in German.

"Ya, I am Deutsch." said John.

"Where are you going?" he asked.

"We are looking for a place to settle down near the river," said John.

"This is your woman?" asked the man.

"This is my woman!" spoke John in English. He did this to bring Morning Flower into the conversation.

"Indian!" grunted the man.

"French!" snapped John.

The man looked surprisingly at Morning Flower and then carefully pronounced in French, "Good day, Mademoiselle ."

Morning Flower responded in perfect French. "I am fine monsieur and I hope you and your family are well."

Still in French the man said, "You and your husband are dressed in Indian fashion. Are you Indian as well?"

Morning Flower looked to John who was completely out of the conversation before she spoke, "My husband told you French," she said with pride, "and he is German!"

"Why are you dressed in Indian fashion?" repeated the man in English.

"It's the most comfortable way to travel. Their clothes are great for warmth, coolness, rain or snow.

As you sit there in your horse, your shirt is wet with sweat and feels bad. My buckskins are cool. Also you can see your shirt a mile off. These buckskins are like the earth and not easily seen in the distance. This is a good thing these days with the Indian problems up and down the frontier." John seemed to have all the answers to satisfy the man.

"So you are passing through, ugh, blacksmith?"

John nodded and the farmer let them pass. As they proceeded down the road, the farmer came along behind about twenty paces, still holding his musket in the crook of his arm.

When they were well past the farmer's cabin and over a little hill the farmer called, "Blacksmith? What are you called?"

"Fetterholft, John Fetterholft," answered John.

"Fritz Muller," returned the farmer. "Go in good health."

After a mile or so, John said, "He was not very friendly."

"Maybe it's because the road goes right through his land and by his cabin," said Morning Flower.

"Some travelers may have been bad to him so he is bad first."

Makes sense thought John. She always makes sense. John looked over to Morning Flower to say something and noticed a sly smile. "What makes you smile? What are you thinking?"

"With a teasing smile, Morning Flower asked," What part do you like best? The French part or the Indian part? John rode silent for a bit thinking, what does she mean? "Well John! Tell me what part do you like best?" She asked him again with a sly teasing look in her eye and a happy grin. In an instant, she yanked off her shirt, bearing her upper body. John turned and stared. Her firm breasts were bouncing with each step of the horse.

"I like them both," blundered John as he pulled up Willie and took the reins of Girlie to a stop. John slipped off Willie and took a giggling Morning Flower by the waist and pulled her off Girlie.

She pulled back and pushed out her breasts and again asked, "Which one is French and which one is Indian?" she asked smiling and giggling.

John grabbed her and lifted her in his arms and walked to the edge of the road. As he laid her in the tall grass, he said, "Neither French or Indian. You're my woman."

They made love until the sun was well in the West. When they finally were on their way again, John realized they had quite a way to go to get to the river. He now hoped to make it to the village by dark.

The village wasn't much of a village John thought as they passed a cabin here and there scattered among the trees with small garden patches near them. It was a warm evening and folks were out and about. As they rode through the area, folks would wave and some called out greetings.

As they were approaching a cabin near the edge of the little village, a man with his family was standing by the road. He stepped in front of the horses and held up his hand. He looked like a poor dirt farmer with little means. "Good evening," said the man.

John and Morning Flower stopped but stayed seated in the saddle. John looked with some suspicion at the man. Morning Flower looked to the woman and the children. She was short and round, dressed in a plain dress, a cloth apron, and a funny little cap on her head. Her hair showed streaks of gray as it was pulled back into a bun under her little cap. The children were in steps -all twelve of them. It looked like number thirteen was on the way. The oldest was a boy about 13 or 14 years old. The children were simply dressed. All three boys wore black work pants with shoulder straps, baggy white shirts, and black brim hats like their Father. The girls were dressed like their Mother including the funny little hats except for the baby. One of the girls who looked to be about seven years old, seemed to be in charge of the baby - not yet a year old. They all stood in a row in their place as if ordered to line up. Morning Flower smiled down at this poor bunch and received bashful smiles back.

Finally, John said, "Good evening."

"We would like to invite thee and thou to our humble table this evening," said the man.

John and Morning Flower looked at each other in surprise. This poor farmer with all these mouths to feed was inviting them to his table.

Dumbfounded, John asked, "Did I hear you right? You have invited us to your evening meal?"

"Yes, we would be honored, friend," said the farmer.

John swung down off his horse and walked up to the farmer. John reached out his hand. "I'm John Fetterholft from Benderstettle, and this is Morning Flower." John motioned to her as she slid off Girlie.

"I am William Battarf, Edna my wife, and my children."

The two men shook hands as the women engaged in conversation.

"After our meal, thou may rest in our barn before going on," William said as the group started to go toward the house.

John took Girlie's reins from Morning Flower as the two men started toward the barn with the horses.

John was not quite comfortable with this big farmer. Why was he so friendly? And they dressed funny too. As they stabled the horses, John noticed everything was neat and in its place. All the tools were neatly hung in a convenient manner. The floor of the barn was swept clean. Even the hay was stacked in bundles. John had never seen such a well-organized barn. This farmer wasn't much of a talker either.

On the way to the house, John could see up the hill to his garden patch - the same thing. All was very neat and straight. Nothing was wasted.

As they came to the back of the house, John got a homesick pang. Sitting on a high bench were two wooden buckets of water with a huge chunk of yellow soap on the side. Two drying clothes hung neatly on pegs on the side of the building. This was just like home.

"Thee will wash as my wife will not allow us to her table until we do," said William.

John gave a little chuckle and said, "My mother was that way too."

"Was she also Amish?" asked William.

"Amish?" asked John.

"The plain people," said William.

"No, she was German. I am from Germany."

"I have met some from Germany. Some are not nice to us and think we are strange. We are friends even with our enemies," said William.

John was ready to make a comment and then thought better of it. These Amish make friends even with their enemies. These are strange people.

After they cleaned up, the men went into the house. Again, John was amazed. Everyone was busy doing something; even Morning Flower. Very few words were spoken and again everything was spotless and in order. The table was set very precisely. William motioned to John to sit at the foot of the table and William sat at the head. The children moved to their places quietly and orderly. Morning Flower was placed to John's right.

As the last of the simple meal was placed on the table, Mrs. Battarf sat down.

"Thee will pray with us?" asked William.

"Yes, we will," returned John.

After the meal, John and William went outside for a stroll. As they were walking along, William spoke, "I will ask thee a favor."

"I will do what I can for you," said John.

"My first son is now 14 years old. He does not have God in his heart and is very unruly. I have worked with him and punished him to mend his ways yet he insists on unholy ways."

"What kind of unholy ways?" asked John.

"He molested the girls down the road on the next farm. One is 13 years old and the other is 15 years.

They are not of our faith so when I talked to their parents they saw nothing wrong with Nathanial sneaking off with their daughter into the woods and swimming in the creek without clothing on."

It was good it was dark as they walked along because John had a smile on his face. "How can I help you?" asked John.

"Because the boy has no will to obey God's wishes and insists on being cruel to his sisters, disrespectful to his Mother and defies me, we must cast him out! God speaks of bad seed among the good seed and must be cast out."

John was thinking, what does he want me to do? Take the boy away?

William continued, "My wife's brother floats rafts of goods down the Susquehanna River to the mighty Chesapeake Bay. He also is not of our faith but a good man though I don't approve of his ways. He stops at Port Halifax on his way down river."

"You want me to take Nathanial to Port Halifax?" asked John.

"If thee would," said William.

"What is Edna's brothers name?"

"Wilber Stoner. He stays at Catherine's Place when going and coming," said William.

"How do I find Catherine's Place?" asked John.

"Thee will know it. Many men visit her place of business for sin. All thee need to do is ask."

"We can take him as far as the Port," said John.

"We thank thee," said William. Then he grew silent until the men approached the house. Morning Flower and Edna were waiting as the men walked up. William spoke up with, "Thee may take your rest in our barn. Good night to thee."

Edna and William simply walked into the house and closed the door. John and Morning Flower made themselves comfortable in the hay and were getting drowsy. "Funny people!" whispered John.

"They are kind John and very strict with themselves and their children. Although the oldest, Nathanial is different some how."

John then told Morning Flower of William's request. The quiet of the night soon had both in a sound sleep.

Before light, they awoke to the chores of the morning. William and the children were working the livestock, milking the cows, and feeding the animals. By the time Morning Flower and John had the horses ready, the East was bright with life. Edna came out to them with wheat cakes and cheese to start their travel.

William brought Nathanial.

They decided Nathanial would ride behind Morning Flower on Girlie. With goodbyes, they were off in the fresh early morning light. The air was cool and moist, and the ride was easy. The hills were steep but short rippling toward the river. Little streams were usually between the little hills.

About midday, just after cresting one of the hills, Nathanial gave a yell clutching his right ribs with pain.

John spun around on Willie with surprise. "What's wrong?" he asked.

"My elbow hit his ribs," said Morning Flower.

"Your elbow?" asked John.

"His hands would not behave, and my elbow got angry and hit him."

With half a smile, John asked Nathanial, "Will your hands behave or must we force you to walk the rest of the way?"

Eagerly and still in pain, Nathanial was nodding fast in compliance, and so he did behave. Morning Flower had a powerful elbow.

Very soon they came to the river, and found Port Halifax. William was right. Catherine's Place by the water was easy to find. They rode up the muddy street and stopped in front of the establishment. Three men were sitting on the front porch; a tough-looking lot. As John stepped up on the porch, a loudly dressed heavy-set woman came to the door. She had a broad nose and heavy chin with small beady eyes that looked John up and down. Her hair was stringy and dirty piled on top of her head.

"I'm looking for Wilber Stoner," said John.

"Ain't here!" said the woman.

"When will he be here?" asked John.

"Don't know. Maybe never. Can't tell bout the rafters. They get kilt sometimes. He stops going up and down river."

"When did you see him last?" asked John.

"Last month, I think. Yup, it was last month goin' up stream. He goes up to Endless Mountain to build his raft and trades down river. Be coming by next month, I guess."

Nathanial walked up to John on the porch. "This is Nathanial, Wilber's nephew on his mother's side.

They sent him down here to wait for Wilber. I guess Wilber will put him to work on the raft," said John.

The woman took a long look at the boy, and then said, "Who pays for his keep. I ain't going to be his Mama!"

"Wilber will, and the boy works good. He'll be real handy around here until Wilber comes," said John.

"Huh! Don't know about that. What can you do, boy?" asked the woman.

"I can feed stock, work in the garden, fetch things, put up and down hay, carry wood, and ..."

The men on the porch broke out in laughter and howls embarrassing Nathanial. The woman turned toward the men and shouted, "Shut your damn mouths," but they still laughed and poked each other. Finally, they settled down.

"Now boy, can you carry out slops, wash dishes, scrub floor, wash out cloths, carry water, and carry meals?" asked the woman.

"Yes, ma'am," said the boy in a very reserved way.

"You got your things with you?" asked the woman.

"What I'm wearing," said Nathanial.

"Hmph, they don't believe in spoiling the boy," growled the woman.

There was a long silence with everyone eyeing each other. Finally she said, "All right. Guess we can put up with you that long as long as I get paid. You goin' to pay me?"

"Wilber will pay you when he comes by," said John.

"If he comes by. Never know about Wilber," rumbled one of the men on the porch.

Another broke in and said, "Kat, why don't you get this Indian gal for awhile?"

"Want to make some money, boy?" said Catherine. "Your woman could line your pockets in lets say about a week. Just leave her here and come back next week. She'll have a sack of money for you."

"She's not for sale," barked John. He turned and stepped off the porch, mounted Willie, and spun around. "NOT FOR SALE!" again John shouted as they rode off.

As they rode out of town, John's temper settled down. Soon they came to a fork at the edge of town, and they stopped to rest the horses. "This road must lead up river," said John. "The other takes us back the way we came."

"What road do you want to take?" asked Morning Flower.

"Don't know," said John. "What do you think?"

"Let's go back the way we came. There is a stream of fresh spring water that comes down between two hills. Looks like a great place to settle. I like the looks of the land there, and it's about half way between the village and Port Halifax. We could get smithing from both, and I could sell game and furs too."

It was late in the day when John and Morning Flower stopped by the stream of spring water. In the late afternoon, it looked much better than John remembered it. The stream spread out as it moved south to a flat meadow on its way to meet another stream on its way to the great Susquehanna to the north upstream into dense woods higher up. The stream was fed by a series of deep water springs. This would ensure a steady flow of cold water even in dry weather. John and Morning Flower explored the area until dusk. Then they settled down by one of the springs for the evening. John was pleased by Morning Flower's sharp eye for a good settlement place. This looks ideal he thought.

After dark by the fire, Morning Flower said, "This is a good place to settle, John. Plenty of woods for timber. Good water and close enough to settlements."

"We will build our home here!" said John.

Morning Flower smiled as she cuddled up to John under the blanket and soon both were fast asleep.

# FOURTEEN

## *The Flight*

The next morning they were up early and on the way up the Valley. The morning gave way to the afternoon. The trip to the top of the mountain was hard and uneventful. Then they stopped in the late afternoon to enjoy the view over the Valley.

The sun was low in the west as they rode down the Main Street into town. John noticed a surprised look on people's faces as they rode along. Coming to the other side of town about a mile from their home, John turned to Morning Flower and asked, "Do the townsfolk seem strange this evening?"

"Yes, I thought so too," she said. "It's like they just saw a ghost. Some even looked frightened."

"Wonder what that's all about?" mused John.

They rode along in silence as they got closer to their cabin. "I smell smoke," said Morning Flower.

They could see a wisp of smoke coming from the other side of the trees, near their cabin. "I smell it now too," said John as they rounded the last bend in the road. What they saw slowly sunk in. The horses came to a halt. John and Morning Flower looked at the burned-out home, then to each other, then to the ruins again.

All that was left were burning ambers that was their cozy cabin. The bed frame and fireplace stood above the rubble. "At least the barn didn't burn," said John as though in a disbelieving shock. "Wonder when it happened," continued John.

"Maybe two to three days ago," she said. "It's down to smoldering like a lightning fire in the mountains." They put the horses in the barn and walked around the rubble until it was quite dark.

The next morning they picked and pulled all the iron they could find and put it in the wagon. Some was still a little hot to handle."

"Well, that does it," said John. "We'll take the wagon to the shop and load our tools and stock. Then we'll head out for our spot down the next valley. I'll be glad to get out of this godforsaken town."

"We will do better on our own John," said Morning Flower. "I will make you happy," she promised.

While they were in town at the shop loading the wagon, Edwin came across the street. "Thank God you two are alive," shouted Edwin as he hurried up to John throwing his arms around John in a bear hug. Then he went to Morning Flower and gave her a hug. "We all thought you perished in the fire," he said.

"How did it start?" asked John.

"I don't know because a lot of people aren't talking. It started three nights ago, and we naturally thought you two were in it. I went down with a few men from town but there was nothing we could do. It was engulfed in flames so we let it burn itself out."

"Do you think someone set it off?" asked John.

"Well John, I can't say but a lot of folks refuse to talk about it. I don't see how it could have started by itself. You must have left early that morning, and I'm sure you put out your fire."

"I'm sure our fires were out," mumbled John. Morning Flower nodded in agreement.

"Well John," said Edwin. "I'm glad you weren't in it but you would have been if you would have been there. The way that cabin burned looks like they piled brush around because the whole thing went up together.

Looks like someone is after you."

"Looks that way," said John.

"Don't blame you two for pulling out," said Edwin. "I know I'll miss you and so will a lot of folks but they don't realize it yet."

It was midday when they had the wagon loaded with their meager possessions, the blacksmith tools, and the scrap metal from the house. As they were pulling out, Edwin came running out with a sack of food supplies and threw it up to John on the buggy seat. "Where are you going, John?" asked Edwin in a choked-up voice. "I won't tell anyone."

"Down the next Valley, near the river," said John.

Edwin reached up to shake John's hand. As they shook, Edwin said, "Good luck to you two, and God bless you."

The pull up the mountain was difficult for the horses. John and Morning Flower pushed, pulled, and puffed along with the horses. It was late in the day when they finally got to the top of the mountain. They decided to camp here and continue on tomorrow. As the sun settled in the west, they made themselves comfortable under the wagon. The horses were grazing nearby in the quiet of the evening.

"It's so beautiful looking down the Valley to the sunset," said Morning Flower.

She was sitting on a flat rock above John. Her knees were pulled up under her chin with her arms around her legs. The last rays of the sun reflected on her face causing blue highlights reflecting off her black hair. Her eyes were shining like diamonds. As John saw her watching the sunset, he saw no defeat in her face; only hope and eagerness to go on with their life. His heart went out to this wisp of a girl that was such a resilient woman. He thought that she was so strong and firm minded. She has brute strength. Her strength was much stronger than his. Her's is from within.

John went over to the rock she was sitting on when she turned to look down at him. "Why do you look so sad John?" she asked.

"We lost so many of our things in that fire, and now I'm dragging you to an uncertain future with hardly any possessions to start over again.

"Yes, John, to start over. I'm so happy that I'm still your woman, and we will have a good life. I'll make you happy, John." She slid off the rock down into John's arms. As they held each other close and kissed, John heard her whisper, "I'll make you very happy tonight, and every night."

The next dawn broke; clear, crisp, and beautiful. Before long, they were on their way down the mountain toward their new home. It was quite late in the afternoon when a bone-tired couple with two exhausted horses pulled to a stop by a pristine creek bordered by tall oaks, chestnut, beech, and fir trees. Still sitting in the wagon seat, John said, "We made it. This is the stream we saw on the way back."

They climbed off the wagon, released the horses to graze along the little meadow, while they made a meager meal of beans and bacon. It was dark by then so they curled up by the fire and soon were fast asleep.

The next morning they woke to another bright and sunny day. They busily surveyed their little corner of the world deciding where to build their blacksmith shop near the road. The house and barn were to be built up on the meadow on a flat spot near the tree line.

Days went into weeks then months. When the first snow fell in the late Fall, the blacksmith shop was well established with a customer or two everyday. The barn, although small, was complete. The house, more like a cabin, was up and under roof. Morning Flower was busy making the inside pleasant and liveable, and loved every minute of it. She needed things - material, buttons, needles, and other things. She mentioned it to John a few times but as men are, he gave her an uh huh and then promptly forgot it.

That evening during supper John said, "I need some iron for the shop. I'll soon need to make a trip to Port Halifax to place an order or find some iron somewhere else."

Morning Flower looked up and smiled. Well, she thought! Now that he needs something, we can go to town!

"When do we go?" asked Morning Flower.

"Do you want to go too?" asked John.

"Yes, I want to go. I need things too! I told you many times John."

"Oh, yes, I remember - needles and cloth and other things. Well, we could go tomorrow if you can be ready."

"I'm ready now but I guess tomorrow morning will be just fine."

Just as dawn was breaking, John and Morning Flower were off to Port Halifax and to the banks of the mighty Susquehanna River. The autumn leaves were bright and pretty along the way; almost at peak color. It was noon when they arrived into town. The day had grown warm in the bright sunshine. They rode down the rutty main street of Port Halifax with their bumpy wagon. Willie and Girlie had no trouble pulling through the ruts. John could tell they were excited seeing and smelling other horses.

"Hi there," came a shout from the side of the street. John pulled to a halt as the young man walked up to the wagon.

"Nathanial?" asked John not quite recognizing him.

"Yes John. It's me. And to Morning Flower, ain't you the pretty one?" She blushed and looked away in embarrassment.

Nathanial just went on. "What are you two in town for; supplies or a little fun?"

"How is it you are still here?" asked John. "I thought your uncle was going to take you on the river."

"He came but I decided to stay with Catherine. She pays me good for steering the gents to her house for some fun. She even lets me sleep with her now and then. Yes, I do right good there."

"I thought you were dressed nicer than in that woodsy cloth when we brought you here," said John.

"What can I help you with John?" asked Nathanial.

"I came to see if I could buy or find any old iron for my shop. Morning Flower needs things from the shops."

"Well," said Nathanial. "I don't know anyone that sells iron. I know the shops, and I can help Morning Flower pick out some things. Where are you going to stay tonight?"

"We'll sleep under the wagon at the edge of town. We'll be just fine, Nathanial." John climbed down from the wagon, and said, "Let's go see about the shops."

The rest of the afternoon was a blur to Morning Flower . Shop after shop had things she wanted but she had just a little money.  She had made this  money by selling game and furs to the village east of their home.

Nathanial started to realize her dilemma and asked, "Do you need some money Morning Flower?" Embarrassed again, she didn't know what to answer.

Nathanial said, "That's it, isn't it? I can give you a loan. I make lots of money, and you can pay me back when you get back to town."

"No, no thanks," said John. "We'll make do with what we have, but thanks anyway."

"It's just a loan, John," continued Nathanial.

John just looked down at Nathanial. The look had a meaning, and Nathanial got the message.

Later they gave Nathanial a ride back to Catherine's. On the way, John asked Nathanial if he knew of any old buildings or anywhere he could get some iron. Nathanial told him of the rafts that were abandoned along the river. Some might have some iron, nails, bolts, or locks.

Early the next morning, John was picking his way along the river bank. Morning Flower was leading the team on the wagon along the rough and rutted river road. She could see John along the bank searching through the tickets.

"I found one," shouted John as he came up the bank towards the wagon. "I'll need a hammer and a pry bar," he said as he got to the tail gate of the wagon.

"I'll come down and help," said Morning Flower.

"No," said John. "Stay with the horses. They are in strange country, and they need someone to keep them settled down."

John made five trips from the bank loaded with iron straps, spikes, tie bars, and an old wood stove. He was back at the river bank when Morning Flower noticed three men riding along the road down river. As they came closer, she could see they looked like a rough lot. One of them looked like a man that had been sitting on Catherine's porch when they delivered Nathanial.

The horses became a bit nervous as the men came closer. "Well, lookie here," said one of the men as they stopped their horses and looked at Morning Flower.

239

"That's the Indian gal I tried to get Kat to take in. Ain't she a beauty."

"Sure is," said the other.

"How bout that now, we can have some fun and not even have to pay for it. Come here, girl," said the one fellow as he swung off his horse.

Morning Flower still holding the nervous horses, pulled a knife from her belt. "She got a knife," warned one still sitting on his horse. Slowly, the grinning fellow with the filthy beard and cracked-yellow teeth moved toward the girl. Girlie gave out a shrill cry and started prancing making it hard for Morning Flower to hold them.

All of a sudden the man made a lunge for her. Numbly, she stepped aside, and he went tumbling into the brush along the road.

When he finally pulled himself up and free of the brush, his two friends dismounted and tried to encircle Morning Flower being very cautious of her flashing knife.

"Come on Injun, we just want a little fun," said one just as the other made a try for her. Quick as a flash, she flicked her knife, and he pulled away with a long gash in his forearm.

"You, bitch!" he shouted as his arm started to gush blood.

The other, coming out of the brush, said, "I'll show her." He went to his horse, pulled a snake whip from his saddle, and uncurled it with a snap. "Now you Injun whore, I'll teach you a lesson you won't forget," he said as he cracked the whip straight at her face. Her reflexes were fast enough to duck the sharp end of the whip. John burst out of the brush in a fury, and the man pulled the whip back. John charged at them with so much surprise and determination that the other two men ran for their horses. The other man looked surprised but not afraid as John reached Morning

Flower. John had his hammer with him, but this wasn't much for a man with a snake whip.

"Want her for all yourself?" shouted the man. "Well, it ain't goin' to happen."

"Better be on your way, mister," growled John.

Again the man raised his whip, and John charged him. Before the man could bring his arm down, John was on him. John hit him hard in the mid-section, and then again as he went sprawling on the ground. One of the other men came off his horse and charged at John. John whipped his hammer just in time to catch him in the ribs. He screamed and doubled up in pain. They both turned and ran to their horses as the one with the cut arm galloped off. The other two were soon gone.

John walked over to Morning Flower who dropped her knife and threw her arms around John's neck.

She started to sob quietly. He could feel her nervous shiver while he held her and soothed her. Finally, she settled down and said to John," I was so afraid - afraid they would force me into the woods. I am so happy you came to stop them."

"Are you all right now?" asked John.

"Yes, I'm just nervous. I'll be fine."

"We have enough iron so we'll go home now. You'll be more comfortable when we get home," said John.

"You always think of me as I think of you, John. You make me so happy to be your woman." Again, they hugged and kissed.

The moon was high when the weary travelers pulled to a stop at the horse shed behind their house. Willie and Girlie were tuckered out, hot, hungry, and thirsty. They stood with their heads down as Morning Flower and John unhitched them. They quietly accepted the praise and petting they were getting for a job well done as they were lead into their stalls. John brought fresh water from the creek while Morning Flower fed them. Soon they were settled in, and John and Morning Flower started for the house.

"Tired?" asked John.

"Yes, very tired."

"It's a warm night," said John. "Let's go down to the creek for a swim."

"Sounds like a good idea, John. I could sure use a bath. Let's take our clothes off here and put them on the porch. That way we don't need to carry them back."

It was a strange sight to see this big man and this petite woman walking buck naked towards the pool in the stream. It was almost full moon in a cloudless sky - almost daylight. They splashed, giggled, and played in the cool; almost cold water. Lying refreshed in a clump of grass by the bank, they made love.

It was the first cool day of the late summer. John was working in his shop when he looked down the road toward the river. A strange-looking character was coming toward him. He was all dressed in black with a top hat, black coat, pants, and boots. Over his shoulder, he carried a feed-bag sack. John noticed he had an ungamely walk probably because he was old and bow-legged. You could hear him before you could see him which was odd. He whistled songs as he walked along. He was still whistling as he walked up to John.

"Morning to you," said the man.

"Good morning," said John.

"What's your name, son?" asked the man.

"John Fetterholft. What's yours?"

"Just call me preacher," said the man.

"Where are you going, preacher?"

"Not very far anymore. Gettin' too old. I'm looking for a place to set up a church and stay put for the rest of my days. Tired of goin' town to town. Folks don't appreciate the word as they should."

"Well sit down, and rest yourself for awhile," said John. The preacher sat on one of John's stumps and watched John work his iron. He liked the way this no-nonsense young man took to his work without any frills just to get the work done. The preacher noticed a wagon coming down the road carrying two men or rather a man and a boy. As they drew near, they looked like farmers rather than travelers. They pulled to a stop in front of the shop. John put down his hammer and came to meet them.

"You the blacksmith?" said the older man.

"Yes, I am."

"Got me a busted axle. Can you fix it?" he asked.

"Let me see what I can do," said John as the young fellow handed John the two pieces of the axle.

"Can you do it now?" asked the older fellow. "Got some haying to get done."

"I'll do my best," said John as he disappeared into the shop.

"Who are you?" asked the man of the preacher.

"I'm a travelin' preacher, spreadin' the word," said the preacher as he got up and walked to the wagon at the road. There he stood looking across the Valley. "Lookin' for a place to settle and build a church. This Valley is as pretty as I've ever seen."

The man and boy got down from the wagon and stood along side of the preacher, looking across the Valley. "Yep, our Valley is a pretty one. We ain't got no church anywhere in the Valley, and I'm sure some would come to hear you preach. The woman folk anyway."

The preacher rubbed his stubbly grin, squinted at the older man, and asked, "You think so?"

"The Germans meet together now and then, and the Amish have their ways, but lots of folks need churchin'."

"You think if I built a church, say, over there, people would come?"

"I'd come," said the boy.

The man said, "You and your Mama and the rest of the kids can come!"

"Well then, it's settled. I'll talk to John, and see what he thinks," said the preacher. "I think I'll go down the creek for a look-see.

A little while later, John came out of the shop with the axle mended as good as new. "Where did the preacher go?" asked John.

"Took a walk down the creek. Crazy guy wants to build a church way out here in the middle of nowhere."

That evening, John told Morning Flower about the preacher. "Where is he sleeping tonight?" she asked.

"I let him bunk in the shop. Seems to be a harmless old man. Must be 50 or so. Guess he's just getting old and wants to settle down."

"I think I'll come down to the shop tomorrow and meet him," said Morning Flower.

It was about midday when Morning Flower entered the shop. John and the preacher were talking while John worked on a buggy spring. Both men stopped talking and turned as she came in. "Preacher, this is my wife, Morning Flower."

"My pleasure to meet you," expressed the preacher with a slight bow from the waist.

Morning Flower, not used to formalities, did not know how to respond. She bowed her head and stood in silence. The preacher stepped forward, reached out, and touched a finger under her chin. He tilted her head up and exclaimed, "Yes, she is a beautiful flower. Hold your head high girl. You needn't bow your head to anyone."

She looked to John, then to the preacher, and then back to John. John chuckled and said, "I told you he was a strange one.

The preacher broke out in a hardy laugh followed by John. Morning Flower broke a smile, then a giggle, and soon all three were laughing.

Later that afternoon, the preacher was down the road along the creek pacing off the land placing a cut-off stick here and there. He was a funny sight squatting on his honches, squinting one eye to line up his sticks.

Meriam Hentzel pulled her team to a stop in front of the blacksmith's shop. The wagon creaked as she climbed down. She was a husky woman with a no-nonsense attitude. Since her husband passed away last year, she and her three children kept the farm going not very far up the road.

"Hi, John."

"Afternoon Meriam. What can I do for you?"

She turned and looked down the creek. "Who's that old man down there walking around sticking itty bitty sticks in the ground?"

"He's the preacher. That's all I know him by. Came by a couple of days ago and wants to build a church and settle down."

"Hmm, don't say," mused Meriam.

Just then, Morning Flower came around the corner of the shop. She had four rabbits and a squirrel on her belt. "Trappin' must have been good today," expressed Meriam.

"Very good," said Morning Flower. "We'll have enough for three mouths to feed tonight."

"You feedin' that old man, too?" asked Meriam.

"He sleeps in the shop. It's only right we give him supper," said John.

"Guess so," said Meriam. "Well, I need some latch hooks. You got any made, John?"

"No, but I can have them ready tomorrow. How many do you need?"

"Five should do it," said Meriam.

The preacher came stumbling up to the shop and around the wagon. He stopped abrupt coming face-to-face with Meriam. It was a funny sight with him standing there in his black clothes and hat and Meriam in all her girth, fists on her hips, and full head taller than the preacher.

"So you're the preacher!" said Meriam with an examining eye.

"At your service, madam."

"My name is Meriam, Meriam Hentzel. Understand you're goin' to build some kind of church here."

"Yes I am," said the preacher. "Across the road and up on the creek by those big oaks there," he said while pointing in their direction. "Goin' to build me a little house down the creek. John told me he'd help me get started."

"Well, how about that?" said Meriam. "Seems you'll need more help than that if you want to get your cabin under roof before cold weather."

"Maybe so," mused the preacher.

"John and I will help," spoke up Morning Flower.

"Still a lot of work," mumbled Meriam.

"John, I'm going up to our cabin and start supper," said Morning Flower. "You're welcome to stay for supper, Meriam."

"Thanks anyway, I got to get home to my kids."

Morning Flower started up the hill to the cabin. The preacher sat on a wooden block John had around for seats for his customers.

Meriam climbed up on her wagon and got settled. Then she turned her team around to head home. She pulled up and stopped again in front of the blacksmith shop.

246

"Preacher," she barked, "you can count on me for some help. I'll bring the kids too. They can fetch water and things. The oldest can help lift too."

"Mighty nice of you," grinned the preacher.

"Congratulations, John," said Meriam.

"For what?" asked John.

"You don't know?" asked Meriam.

"Know what?" asked a puzzled John.

"Your wife is in the family way."

"The what way?" asked John.

"Men!" said a disgusted Meriam. "Your wife is going to have a baby."

"A baby," gasped John as he stood there dumbfounded.

"Yes, a baby, probably April or May," said Meriam in a thoughtful way.

"How do you know?" asked John.

"Women know these things, John. They just know. Be back tomorrow," nodding to the preacher and John as she and her wagon went lumbering up the road.

That evening after supper with the livestock taken care of, John sat on the stoop at the back of the cabin. In a minute or so, Morning Flower came out from the kitchen and sat down beside him. They sat there for awhile watching the sun set beyond the river. The sky turned red with its reflection off the high clouds.

"Pretty," whispered Morning Flower.

"Yes, you are," he said.

"Oh John. I'm not pretty; the sunset is."

"Yes, you are, Morning Flower; more than ever. Meriam told me something that makes me very happy."

"Meriam?" questioned Morning Flower.

"Yes, she told me you are going to have a baby."

Morning Flower bowed her head as if ashamed. "I was not sure until a few days ago. I missed two moon times, and now I'm losing my breakfast in the mornings. I was worried you would not be pleased, and I have been waiting for the right time to tell you."

"Did you think I wouldn't be pleased?" asked John.

"I didn't know. We did not speak of it," she said.

John pulled her close to him, kissed her, and whispered, "I'm very pleased."

Nestled against his shoulder, she smiled and starting crying. Morning Flower was a very happy woman.

Later that evening after the moon came up, John and Morning Flower walked to the top of the hill where they could look up and down the Valley. A cool fresh breeze came up from the river. They stood there on the hill holding hands and enjoying the scenery.

Soon John said, "We are so fortunate. We have a snug cabin, a good business, and plenty to eat. We have our health, and we have each other." Morning Flower moved closer to John and laid her head against his shoulder. John continued, "Now we're going to have a baby... Maybe even more babies. They will grow up and they will have babies... And so will those babies... I wonder what this Valley will be like and how many Fetterholfts will there be in ...200 years..............?